More books from Diana Palmer

Wyoming Men

Long, Tall Texans

The Morcai Battalion

For a complete list of titles available by Diana Palmer, please visit www.dianapalmer.com.

DIANA PALMER

WYOMING TRUE

HQN

MIX
Paper from
responsible sources
FSC
www.fsc.org FSC® C021394

ISBN-13: 978-1-335-08062-2

Recycling programs
for this product may
not exist in your area.

Wyoming True

This edition published by arrangement with Harlequin Books S.A.

For questions and comments about the quality of this book,
please contact us at CustomerService@Harlequin.com.

HQN
22 Adelaide St. West, 40th Floor
Toronto, Ontario M5H 4E3, Canada
www.Harlequin.com

Printed in Lithuania

Dear Reader,

Ida turned up in *Wyoming Heart*, Cort Grier's book, and I had this idea of who she was. She didn't share it. I was more or less drawn into her tragic background, and she changed my mind about her true self. (I am not out of my mind. Most writers go through some weird interactions with their characters. They become quite real during the writing of a novel.)

I loved Jake McGuire from the time he turned up in *Diamond in the Rough*. I was just waiting for a story that would suit him. He and Ida were instant enemies. But a flat tire changed all that. Two damaged people found each other, and this was one story I truly enjoyed telling.

I hope you like the book. As I get older (seventy-four this year, you know), and after writing over two hundred novels, I sometimes repeat myself. And I am certainly not a mainstream person. I live in a very small, wonderful mountain town in North Georgia and I'm mostly confined to my home due to disabilities. Jim, who has far more health issues than I do, and I stay home and play video games for fun and social interaction. We're sort of out of step with society. So I write about what I know—small communities, where all of us know each other and talk over the fence and wave at anybody who walks past the front porch. And walk the dog and brush the cats and weed the herb patch. That's my world.

Thank you for your kindness and your prayers and the love you all give to me so freely. I wish I could do more for you than just give you a couple of new books a year. Take care, love one another, be safe. I am still your biggest fan.

Love and hugs,

Diana Palmer

As much as we love our doctors who take care of us, we also love our veterinarians, vet techs, groomers and staff who look after our precious fur babies. I've been very fortunate to have a great crew take care of my own at Northeast Veterinary Hospital in Cornelia. This book is dedicated to them: Dr. Doug and Dr. Cecily Nieh, Hollis, Debbie, Wynn, Amber, Zach, Rene, Taylor, Emma, Shannon, Jenna, Madi, Diane, Marissa, Mariah and Chris. You guys are just wonderful.

I also must mention with deep gratitude our friends at Cornelia Veterinary Hospital, who have saved so many of our pets in years past.

I love all of you. Thanks for all you do for animal lovers everywhere!

CHAPTER ONE

JAKE MCGUIRE WAS happy for Mina. She'd married a Texan, Cort Grier, who turned out to be a wealthy cattle baron; quite a surprise when she'd known him only as a working cowboy who was helping out on his cousin Bart Riddle's ranch outside Catelow, Wyoming.

It had been an odd love story. Mina was a famous author of romance novels, who actually went on commando missions with a bunch of mercenaries who'd taken her under their wing for research. Cort Grier hadn't known that. But he was wearing a mask, too, pretending to be a poor cowboy. It was only after she'd married him that she knew who he really was. And he found out about her profession in a totally unexpected way, when she went to live on his ranch and her mercenary group helped round up a gang of drug smugglers on the border of his property. Many adjustments had been made, but the two seemed destined for happiness. They had a brand-new son named Jeremiah, and while Mina kept the family ranch in Catelow, which her father was now managing, she lived with Cort and Jeremiah at Cort's enormous family ranch, Latigo, in West Texas.

Jake was glad for her. But he was miserable. He'd had a real case on her, and it had hurt to realize that even his own wealth and status wasn't enough to attract her. It was the first time in his life that he'd ever been truly smitten with a woman, and she turned out to be in love with someone else.

Well, he could go back to the cattle station he shared with Mina's cousin Rogan in Australia, but fires in the outback were seriously impacting their vast herds of cattle. Along with hundreds of wildfires, many set deliberately, there was drought and lack of feed. Rogan had already mentioned that they'd have to sell off a lot of their purebred stock to break even. Jake had come back to the States to help get their finances on target and send assistance to get the fires out on the large property and the surviving livestock shipped to a safer location.

The wildfires had hit Rogan even harder than Jake. Mina's cousin loved the Australian property. He owned a big ranch outside Catelow, as well, but he hated snow, so he only came home in warm months, leaving his manager in charge. Well, unless Jake was there to hold the reins.

Less and less did Jake like being out of the country. He missed Catelow. While he was squiring Mina Michaels around town and to various far-flung five-star restaurants in other states, he'd become accustomed to being back in the States. He was reluctant to leave the country.

Stupid, really, because he'd lost Mina and he had no other female interests here. He sipped coffee in the café and glared into the cup. He felt more alone than he had since the deaths of his parents long ago. He was an only child. There had been an older brother, who'd died tragically, but no other siblings. He missed his mother, although he never spoke of his father. He had no family left.

He'd have loved a child. The thought of it had sustained

him while he was courting Mina, hoping against hope that he could win out over the Texas rancher. But that hadn't happened. He was nursing a broken heart and trying not to let it show. Meanwhile, the social lions of Catelow, especially Pam Simpson, had been pouncing, trying to set him up with widows and divorcées. He had no interest in any of the local women now. He'd had his share of brief affairs, but he felt jaded, used. Women wanted what he had. He could, and did, bestow his favors generously on the women he dated. Diamonds, five-star hotels and restaurants, travels abroad on his own private jet. But more and more, he felt he was buying them. Or, he thought facetiously, renting them.

He made a sound deep in his throat as the thought processed, drawing an interested glance from people at the counter waiting for orders to take out.

One of them was glaring. That local divorcée, Ida Merridan. She was drop-dead gorgeous. Short, thick black hair, blue eyes, impossibly long eyelashes and a killer figure. The problem with her was that she was promiscuous, he thought irritably. Everybody knew she collected men like dolls and tossed them aside when she'd had her fill. She was twice married, gossip said. Her first husband had died, but nobody knew about the second husband, except that she'd divorced him. Cort Grier had dated her before he became entangled with Mina. He'd seen them on a dance floor, glued to each other at a party, and they left together. They'd dated often while he was in town. So presumably the cattle baron had a brief liaison with her. From what people said about her, she wasn't picky about men. Anybody would do.

He didn't like women like that. That was probably hypocritical, he considered, because he'd sown his own wild oats years ago. He averted his eyes from the divorcée's blistering glare with magnificent indifference and sipped coffee.

People talked about the double standard, about men sleeping around while women were chastised for it. But there had been a legitimate reason for it a hundred and fifty years ago, when there was no real method of birth control. A husband wandered and spread his favors around so that he wouldn't have an eternally pregnant wife who would die before reaching the age of forty. He wondered how many modern women even knew that or considered that social mores sometimes had justifiable foundations. Well, he amended, somewhat justifiable.

He glanced at the woman, who was smiling at the clerk and paying for her takeout. He didn't like her. She knew it. He'd made his opinion of her quite clear at a party they'd both attended a week back. Their hostess had been matchmaking and nudged them together onto the dance floor. He could do Latin dances. So could she. But this was a slow two-step and he hated the contact.

"I don't have a fatal contagious disease," Ida had said bitingly when he held her as if he had a stick of dynamite in his reluctant arms. She was hating the contact, too, and hiding it in bad temper.

He lifted an eyebrow, his pale, glittery silver eyes lancing down into her china-blue ones. "Really? Have you had lab work to make sure?" he added, just to irritate her.

The glare grew hotter. "I don't want to dance with you," she said curtly. She was stiff even in the light embrace. Amazing, with her reputation, that she seemed to dislike him.

"They say any man will do, where you're concerned," he drawled. "I don't appeal to you?"

She swallowed, hard, and glanced around as if hoping the music would stop.

"And here I thought you'd come up with something trite, along the lines that you only dated men in your own species," he taunted.

Another couple, spinning around, came a little too close, and Jake pulled Ida abruptly closer and turned her to avoid a collision.

Her reaction was sudden and stark. She jerked away from him, almost shivering, her eyes lowered. "I can't…" she began in a choked tone.

He'd glared at her. "Any man but me, is that how it goes?" he asked in a deep, biting whisper, viciously offended and not even sure why he was offended.

She hadn't even looked at him. She'd turned and walked off the dance floor. Minutes later she'd thanked her hostess for the invitation and driven her car away. Jake, standing by the punch bowl, was confounded by her behavior. She'd actually seemed afraid of him. And that was fanciful thinking when the whole town knew what she was.

He glanced toward the counter, where she was picking up her order and smiling at the female clerk.

Maybe it was an act, he mused. Maybe she pretended to be nervous toward a man when she was stalking him. The problem with that theory was that she hadn't come near Jake since the party. In fact, when she left the café, she went the long way around to the front door, so that she wouldn't have to pass the table where he was sitting.

He finished his coffee and took the cup back to the counter. "You make good coffee, Cindy," he told the employee, who was a married grandmother.

She grinned at him. "Thanks, Mr. McGuire. My husband runs on black coffee. He's a trucker. If I couldn't make it to suit him, I'd be in divorce court in no time," she joked.

"Fat chance. Mack's crazy about you," he chuckled. He glanced toward the door. "The happy divorcée doesn't eat with the common folk?" he added.

"Oh, you mean Ida," she said. She grimaced. "She doesn't go out much. She lives near us, you know. One night I heard her screaming and I called the sheriff's department. I was afraid somebody might have broken in on her. Cody Banks, our sheriff, was working that shift, and he went by to see what had happened."

He frowned, just waiting.

She sighed. "He said she was white as a sheet and looked as if she'd seen a ghost. She told him it was an old nightmare that she had from time to time and she apologized for disturbing the neighbors."

"Nightmares." He shook his head. "Who'd have thought it?"

"I went over to see her the next day, it was Sunday, on my way to church, to apologize for calling the law. She just smiled and said she didn't blame me. She apologized, too, for making a fuss."

"Did she say why she had the nightmare?" he asked.

She shook her head. "She mentioned something about her second husband making a threat. He's involved in some illegal stuff, I gathered, and she's rich."

"Did she get rich by divorcing him?" he asked with a grin.

She shook her head. "Her first husband had the money. The second... Apparently he married her for what she had. Nobody knows much about it."

"Did she move here recently?" Jake asked. "I don't mix

much with local people, even though I have my ranch and I still own the feed supply store here. I'm away on business a lot."

"Her grandparents were from here. So was her mother. In fact, she was born here. But when her father got a good-paying job in Denver, they moved away. She was in fifth grade." She drew in a breath. "It was just after Bess Grady killed herself."

"My best friend's brother had a crush on the Grady girl. He took it hard," he commented, not going into details. Like Cindy, he'd gone through school here. He hadn't always been rich. "What about Ida's parents?"

She shook her head. "Her father had a massive heart attack when he was just thirty-five," she said with a sigh. "Her mother lived on, but not happily. She lived only for Ida. When Ida was eighteen, her mother went on a cruise and fell overboard. They never found the body."

"That would have been hard," he conceded.

"So Ida was working for a graphics firm in Denver, right out of high school, and her boss felt sorry for her, I guess, because he married her shortly afterward. There was gossip, they said, because of the age difference. He was very wealthy and had never been married at all."

"Was it a happy marriage?" He hated asking. He didn't know why he even cared.

"Well…"

"Come on," he teased. "You know I don't gossip."

"Well, my second cousin, who knew the owner of the graphics store, said he was gay."

His eyebrows arched.

"I know, why would he want to marry Ida? But he was kind to her."

"I heard he committed suicide."

She nodded, looking around to make sure nobody was within earshot. "His boyfriend had left him. He'd had other problems, but this had sent him over the edge. He was so distraught that he went to the top floor of his building and jumped off. The boyfriend tried to sue Ida afterward. He thought he deserved something for his time with the older man. Ida took him to court and counter-sued. He had to pay court costs. She had a really mean attorney." She grinned. "Her husband left her everything, and there was a lot. He left her a note, thanking her for being so kind to him."

He was touched, despite his distaste for Ida.

"Maybe she's not all bad."

"Nobody is all bad, Mr. McGuire," she replied. "Some people have worse lives than others, is all."

He shrugged. "Seems so."

She smiled gently. "You still missing Mina?"

He smiled back. "A little. But she and Cort and the baby are happy in Texas. I'm glad for them. I keep in touch with them through her dad, who's managing their family ranch outside town."

"You're a good loser."

"Not much choice about that," he replied. His pale silver eyes were sad. "You can't make people love you."

"Isn't it the truth?" she agreed.

HE WENT OUT to get into his car and spotted Ida standing by her Jaguar with her cell phone to her ear. The Jag had a flat tire.

"Yes," she said wearily. "Yes, I know, but it's going to

take two hours to get somebody out here, and I have to be at the doctor's by two!"

Jake paused beside the car.

She stared at him, surprised.

"I can run you to the doctor. Leave the key with Cindy Bates, inside, and tell whoever you're talking to where they'll be. Have him lock the car and give the key back to Cindy when he's done."

She was just standing there, surprised at how easily he organized things. A voice was coming over the smartphone.

"Oh, sorry," she said into the receiver. "Listen, I've had the offer of a ride. I'll leave the key inside the café with Cindy. She can give it to you and you can hand it back to her when you finish. That work? Great. Thanks so much. I'm really sorry… Of course. Thanks."

She hung up. She glanced at Jake warily. "You're sure it's not out of your way?"

He shook his head. "Give me the key."

She handed it to him. He gestured to a red Mercedes and used his own smart key to unlock it. "Go ahead and get in. I won't be a minute."

He didn't wait to see if she complied; he turned and strode back into the café. Ida stared after him with mingled discomfort and appreciation. He was very handsome. Tall, fit, muscular without it being overly obvious. He had beautiful manners and eyes that seemed to pierce all the way to the soul. If she'd been able to find a man attractive, he'd have been at the top of her list. As it was, that was impossible.

SHE WAS SITTING in the passenger seat with her seat belt fastened when he climbed in beside her.

"I've never driven a Mercedes. Are they nice?" she asked, to make conversation.

"They're immortal and almost never break down. Where are we going?" he added abruptly.

"Sorry. Aspen Street, just past the bakery."

He nodded, cranked the big car and pulled out of the parking lot.

She held her bulky purse in her lap and dug her nails into it. He couldn't know how difficult it was for her to sit with a man who was more or less a stranger. He disliked her and made no secret of it. Jerking out of his arms and running at that party they'd attended separately had just made things worse.

She stared out the window as he drove, not even trying to make conversation.

She directed him to the parking lot of a group of orthopedic surgeons. He didn't comment, but she was young, or seemed to be. He associated orthopedics with elderly people.

"Thanks for the ride," she said quietly.

"You'll need a ride home," he replied. "Give me your cell phone."

He spoke with such authority that she handed it over without thinking.

He took it and pulled up her contact list. It was blank. He looked at her with a faint scowl.

She swallowed, hard. "Why do you need my phone?"

He pulled up a screen and put his own contact information into it. He handed it back. "That's my cell phone number. Call me when you're through here and I'll drive you back to your car."

"I can get a cab…"

He just looked at her.

She bit her lower lip. "It will be an imposition."

She was fascinating him. The image of her he'd built up seemed nothing like the reality. She was uncomfortable with him, shy, withdrawn. He'd only seen her being vivacious, the life of the party. Was it a mask?

"I have to check in at my feed store and look over some accounts with the manager. It won't be an inconvenience."

"Well...okay, then. Thank you."

He shrugged. He turned off the engine, went around and opened the door for her. She actually flushed.

"Is that not allowed in our modern, too-liberal society? Opening doors for women?"

"I like nice manners, and I don't care if it's acceptable or not," she stammered.

He cocked his head and looked down at her with open curiosity.

"Thanks again. I'll be late," she added, glancing at the plain watch on her wrist. She turned and walked slowly toward the building.

It wasn't really blatant, but he could see that she limped a little when she walked. Odd. An old injury? he wondered. A fall or something? Not his business. But he was curious about her. Far more curious than he wanted to be.

IDA SAT IN the waiting room for her turn to see Dr. Menzer and tried to understand why Jake McGuire, who obviously disliked her, had been so kind to her. She didn't expect kindness from men. She pretended to be a wild woman, just to make men leave her alone. She exaggerated her reputation, let it be rumored that she had high standards for her bedroom and talked about fictional men she'd had affairs with to give the idea that she'd gossip about a man who didn't measure up to her expectations. As she'd expected, it kept her free of complications in her private life. Not many men had the ego to even approach her.

Cort Grier had, but she found an unexpected friend in the jaded cattle baron who'd had his own issues with women who wanted his wealth, not himself. They'd formed a friendship. She'd opened up to him as she hadn't been able to open up with any other man.

She was happy for him. He loved Mina and his son, and that was wonderful. But he'd been the only friend she had. When he married, she'd removed his contact information from her phone. She didn't want it to appear that she was after him even when he married. That left the screen completely blank. She had no contacts, because she only used the phone for emergencies and surfing the internet. Her attorneys had her home phone number, which had an answering machine. She had no idea how to set up voice mail on the cell phone, so it was better not to have people call the number. That was why her contact screen was blank, and Jake had noticed. She'd have bet that his own phone contact list was overflowing.

Well, she couldn't want a man that way, not anymore. And she had her own problems. Her ex-husband, Bailey Trent, was just recently out of prison and in hock to his gambling associates. How he'd gotten out was a mystery. She'd had him sent up for violent assault and battery. Shortly after his arrival, he'd lost his temper and killed another inmate, almost guaranteeing that he'd never get out. But he had gotten out.

He'd been calling her on her home phone, leaving threatening messages. She'd phoned her attorneys in Denver, but she wasn't even sure what they could do about him. He left no contact number. She didn't even know where he was. She tried a reverse lookup on her phone, but the number was blocked. What if he came after her again, the way he had the last time she'd refused to give him money, before he even went to prison?

Her hand went idly to her hip and she grimaced. She'd had a fractured pelvis and damage to her femur, injuries that had been catastrophic, to her mind. The orthopedic surgeon, a genius in his own right, had put her hip and femur back together like a jigsaw puzzle. Two surgeries, a partial hip replacement and a metal plate along her thigh with metal screws to hold it in place had alleviated most of her problem, but the pain continued and the visits to her orthopedic surgeon had increased in recent months. Oncoming cold weather usually brought its own set of complications. Secondary arthritis had set in to the damaged pelvis. She needed another prescription for the powerful anti-inflammatory medications she had to take, hence the visit.

She tried not to think about the injury her second husband had caused. He'd seemed like such a kind, sweet man. She hadn't realized that it was an act, all of it, to lure her in and get her to marry him so that he'd have access to her inherited fortune.

She shivered, remembering. It hadn't been a long fall, just over the side of a one-story parking garage. She'd landed on hard ground, not, thank God, on concrete. The pain had been something out of her experience. By the time the ambulance arrived, of course, Bailey was pretending hysterics and wailing that his poor wife had fallen despite his efforts to save her. It would have been her word against his, how it happened. Even in the hospital, he'd been the soul of remorse. No one realized that he'd caused the injuries, and she was too shocked and in so much pain that most of her hospital stay had been a blur. Rehab had kept her out of his hands for a while. But inevitably she had to go home. It was only a month later that he assaulted her in view of a witness, a severe beating that got him sent to prison.

She'd hoped he'd never get out. That was unrealistic. He could always talk people into things. He had a pipeline into drug trafficking and somehow he'd managed early release, probably by helping someone get access to controlled substances. The nightmare had begun all over again the day he was released from prison.

He was adamant about his confinement and her part in it. He was furious that she'd given up his name after the divorce and gone back to the surname of her first husband, Merridan. He was furious that he couldn't make her send him money for the pain and suffering she'd caused him. She owed him and he planned to collect. She had all that nice money and he was destitute. She could pay up or unpleasant things might happen, he suggested just before she hung up in his face and blocked his number. She remembered some of the unpleasant things that had already happened and she felt sick inside.

Cody Banks, the local sheriff, had been a sympathetic listener. He was one of the few people in Catelow who knew the woman behind the mask. He'd been kind to her. He promised that Bailey Trent wouldn't get near her. He encouraged her to take out a restraining order. She had, although the clerk had told her that they were very rarely worth the paper they were printed on. She phoned her attorneys in Denver and had them send an investigator out to keep an eye on Bailey. She could afford the expense, which might save her life. Bailey used drugs. He was dangerous even when he didn't.

She couldn't believe how naive she'd been about him. Coming from a marriage with a man who was a closet homosexual, she'd had no faith at all in her ability to attract a man. It wasn't until her husband took his own life and left her the note that she'd even known about his sexual orientation. She'd thought that she simply wasn't woman enough to appeal to him.

He'd been a kind, sweet man, always taking care of her, doing anything he could to make her life happy and easy. His loss was painful.

Then there was Bailey Trent. He was rugged, authoritative, a real he-man, at least to Ida's naive eyes. They'd dated and he'd been passionate with her, but he hadn't insisted on intimacy until they were married. That, too, she thought miserably, had been calculated. She'd been desperate to have him, in thrall to her senses for the first time in her life. He'd taken advantage of feelings she couldn't help to rush her to the altar.

And then had come her wedding night. Nothing in her young life had prepared her for the depravity some men reveled in. She had nightmares about what he'd done to her, that night and others, when she was too bruised and frightened to fight back anymore. That first week they'd been married was when he'd lost his temper and thrown her over the side of the parking garage. After her wedding night, it hadn't been much of a surprise, although the pain had been something far beyond what she'd already endured.

She'd tried to run away once, after she got out of the hospital. But he'd found her and convinced her protectors that she'd overreacted to what was basically just a sad accident. He loved her desperately. He couldn't live without her. He told everybody.

Ida knew better. He couldn't live without her money. But she was encouraged to forgive him and make her marriage work. Her sweet friends who'd taken her in had been happily married for twenty-five years. They had no idea what her life was like. And she was too ashamed to tell them.

"Mrs. Merridan?"

She lifted her head and came out of the reverie quickly. She smiled at the nurse as she got painstakingly to her feet and followed the younger woman back to the treatment room.

DR. MENZER EXAMINED her and grimaced.

"What did you do?" he asked.

She flushed. "It's autumn," she began.

"You can hire big strong hefty men to lift those heavy flowerpots from the patio into your sunroom," he said shortly and watched her flush. She did the same thing every year, just before frost warnings went out, getting her precious herbs and flowering plants inside. "You've no business trying to do it yourself."

She made a face. "I can't let my flowers die. And I love fresh herbs."

"Buy some at the store."

"It's not the same," she pointed out.

He drew in a breath. "Ida, there are things you just

can't do anymore. Heavy labor tops the list. You have to be sensible."

"Sensible." She sighed. "He's out of prison, you know," she added, her blue eyes poignant. "He wants money. He says if I don't give it to him, I can expect even worse than I had before he was convicted."

"Talk to Cody Banks."

"I have," she replied. "I took out a restraining order, as well. But if somebody wants to kill you, he can," she added.

"If he wants money, killing you isn't in his best interest, now, is it?" he returned.

"I guess not. I had a new will drawn up when he went to prison, guaranteeing that if I die, he inherits nothing." She drew in a long breath. "The nightmares came back, when he called me."

"You should be in the care of a psychologist."

She shrugged. "I tried. It didn't work." She looked over at him. "My first husband was gay, but he was a better, more loving husband to me than Bailey Trent could ever be."

He just smiled. "We all make mistakes."

"Yes, but most of us don't end up in intensive care when we make them," she replied with a faint smile.

"You survived, at least," he replied. "That's something."

"I guess."

"I'm going to have Melanie call in a prescription for stronger anti-inflammatories," he said, typing on his computer. "You'll take them for five days only, then ten days off. That way you'll be able to keep your liver and save your kidneys."

"Powerful stuff," she commented.

"Very. And don't take them and try to drive," he admonished.

"I won't. Thanks," she added. "For the meds. And for listening."

"Who else have you got?" he asked reasonably.

"Sad but true."

"You should come to supper one night," he told her as he got to his feet. "Sandy would love to make you that terrific meat loaf she does, along with some homemade bread."

"Your wife is a wonderful cook. And I appreciate the offer. But…"

He raised an eyebrow. "But?"

"Carl," she said, "anybody I associate with could be in the crosshairs when Bailey comes after me. I'm not putting you and Sandy there."

"Now, listen," he began.

"No," she interrupted. "But thank you. And tell Sandy one day I want her to try and teach me to do breads."

"I'll tell her," he replied. "Keep in touch with Cody," he added. "He'll watch out for you."

She nodded.

He hesitated. "For the record, Sandy and I are both sorry that we encouraged you to go back to Bailey. We didn't know about him then."

"You didn't," she agreed. "And I was too ashamed to tell you. That's all in the past. No worries."

"You take care of yourself."

She smiled. "I'll do my best."

"Some gentle exercise would help strengthen those muscles," he added.

"So you keep telling me. I bought a Tai Chi DVD," she added. "It's made for people with arthritis. So far, I've managed one whole form without falling over the coffee table."

He chuckled. "Keep it up."

She grinned. "I will."

SHE WENT TO the counter and got her next appointment set, then walked outside. She pulled out her phone and hesitated. She really shouldn't start anything with McGuire, she told herself. He didn't like her, even though he'd been kind today. And she hesitated to put him in the line of fire. She should just call a cab.

She pulled up the internet on her smartphone and started looking for the number of the only local cab company. Before she could copy the number, a red Mercedes pulled into the parking lot and stopped beside her.

CHAPTER TWO

IDA PAUSED WITH the phone in her hand and her mouth slightly open as she stared at the man sitting in the big car beside her.

He powered down the window. "Calling somebody?" he asked. "A cab, perhaps?"

She felt a shiver inside. How had he known?

"Get in."

She was too unsettled to argue. She climbed in beside him and fastened her seat belt. "How could you possibly know?" she asked.

He shrugged. "I get these wild notions sometimes. I don't know where they come from. Well, that's not quite true. An ancestor of mine ran afoul of the authorities in Salem, Massachusetts, in the sixteen hundreds."

She pursed her lips and whistled softly.

"So I come by it honestly. I knew my parents were going to die. I dreamed it."

"That must have been a hard gift to live with."

"It still is. Do you have a prescription to pick up?"

She nodded. "I'll check and see if it's ready. You're sure you don't mind?" she added worriedly.

Silver eyes met hers and slid away. "If I minded, I wouldn't be here."

"Okay, then. Thanks."

She phoned the pharmacy and spoke to Carol, a clerk she knew well. She asked about the prescription, smiled and thanked her.

She put the phone away. "She said they're already working on it. They have the drug in stock."

"What sort of drug?"

"Ibuprofen," she replied and told him the milligrams.

"Good God, you'll destroy your liver," he muttered.

"Five days on, ten off," she replied. "And you take it with meals three times a day." She drew in a long breath. "It isn't my first walk around the block with this drug, although it's been a couple of years since I've needed such a dose. We tried other meds, but they weren't working."

He scowled. He knew that such a massive dose would indicate an equally massive problem. "Broken bone?" he asked.

She nodded. There had been several fractures, but he didn't need to know that.

He glanced at her, curious. Away from people, she was a different woman. He was curious about the change in her.

"You don't talk much," he commented.

She was staring out the window. "I'm not used to people," she confessed. "I keep to myself."

"When you're not hosting orgies."

She tautened all over and couldn't force herself to look at him. It wasn't true, but she didn't know him and she didn't trust him. She turned her purse over in her lap and looked out the window.

He noticed her lack of response and put it down to acceptance. After all, she could hardly deny what she was. Everybody knew. He couldn't understand why he was ferrying her around in his car, looking after her. It wasn't like him to get mixed up with a promiscuous woman. God knew there had been enough of them when he was younger. But as he grew older, he grew more jaded, more disgusted. What sort of woman sold herself for trinkets?

He frowned as the thoughts ran through his mind. She was independently wealthy. Why would she even need to sell herself?

He glanced toward her set features with undue curiosity. There was one other possibility. Maybe she just liked men.

His broad shoulders shrugged. It was a modern world. If men could do it, so could women; he supposed that was what passed for equality. The days were long gone when a woman was sanctified for her impeccable reputation. But he wondered about the effect it had on children. His little mother had been sweet and kind and faithful to her husband. There had been no cheating. On her part, at least. He didn't like thinking about his father.

His mother had been vocal about modern women and their lack of morality. Her life had been free of scandal. Jake's had been, also.

He recalled the conversation he'd had with Cindy in the café. He'd been in high school when the community had turned against a woman whose little girl was in the fifth grade locally. Bess Grady's mother slept with every man she could get. Bess, a shy little thing, went to school with some of the children of men her mother had seduced. Jake's best friend had a brother in Bess's class. He said she'd been punished day after day by those other children. Jake wondered if the girl's parent even cared about making her part of the sordid mess she'd brought about.

When the scandal broke, because one of Bess's mother's lovers had been a well-known local politician and the affair cost him a state senate seat, the publicity had been terrible. Bess was shy and quiet and introverted. Being made a scapegoat for her mother had broken something inside her, done it very quickly.

A few days after the publicity became red-hot, Bess had taken several of her mother's sleeping pills, and when they started to take effect, she'd slashed the artery in her neck with a butcher knife. Her mother came home the next morning, very early, after a night out on the town in Denver with one of her rich Catelow lovers, to find her daughter on the bathroom floor in a pool of blood.

For once, the mother was the source not only of scandal, but also of hatred from the community. It came out in gossip that the poor little girl had been tormented by the children of her mother's lovers, for the breakup of their families. The funeral had been well attended, but not one local person except the minister would even speak to the mother. Her grief had been visible, along with her guilt, but small communities had their own manner of dealing with people who flaunted the rules and hurt the innocent.

One powerful family had gone after the scandal-ridden mother with everything they possessed. The errant mother, deserted by her local lovers in the face of so much bad publicity, had lost her home and her job, had been frozen out by people in every business she frequented. In the end, she'd given up and moved to Denver, apparently to live with one of her lovers.

Jake had heard that she died of an apparent drug overdose. He didn't mourn. His best friend's brother had a crush on Bess, who had suffered so much because of the hateful woman. It had been a hard blow for the boy.

He was also remembering Mina Michaels's mother. Mina had endured her promiscuous mother's lovers, some of whom had brutalized her. That had been years after Bess killed herself, however, and had no connection with Mina's family. What a life it must have been for Mina. Poor little thing. He still missed her. He was happy because she was happy, living with Cort Grier and their son, Jeremiah, in Texas. But her loss still wounded him. He'd had great hopes when he'd started dating her. Sadly, her heart had belonged to Cort almost from the day they met.

Cort had been going around with the merry divorcée sitting beside him, which spoke volumes about her. Cort Grier had been a notorious rounder before his marriage, and he'd spent plenty of time with Ida Merridan while he was in Catelow visiting his cousin.

Jake wondered why he was bothering with this woman in the first place when he didn't even like her. His pale silver eyes narrowed on the road ahead.

Ida, with no idea of what was going through her companion's mind, noted the dark scowl on his handsome face.

"Listen, I can come back later and go to the pharmacy..." she began uneasily.

He took a sharp breath and glanced at her. "I don't mind. Sorry. I was remembering the Grady girl."

She winced. "Oh, that poor little thing," she said quietly. "I remember her, too. She was in my grade at school, here in Catelow."

He glanced at her. "I thought you grew up in Denver," he prevaricated, because he didn't want to admit he'd been talking about her to Cindy at the café.

"I did, but we lived here until I was in fifth grade. Bess was one of my friends." She turned her eyes out the window. "We all hated her mother. Bess was shy and sweet and never hurt anybody. We did what we could to protect her, to shield her from the angry kids. But children can be so cruel. It was a shock, what she did. I mean, how many fifth graders do you know who commit suicide with pills and a knife?"

"There was an article in the local paper, a wire service article, that mentioned the death of a prominent man back East," he remarked. "It was very detailed about how he killed himself. My best friend's little brother was sweet on the Grady girl. He carried guilt for years because he told her about the story. He always figured she remembered it when she decided to end her life."

"He shouldn't have felt guilty," she replied softly. "We all have a certain time on earth, things we're supposed to do, purposes we fill. God decides when lives end and how. People may facilitate that, but in the end, we don't really choose how we die."

He was taken aback. He'd never pegged her as a religious person. "You don't strike me as a religious fanatic," he said abruptly.

She just smiled sadly. "My first husband was very religious," she said. "We went to church every Sunday, when we first married. He kept lists of members of the congregation who were poor, who had bills they couldn't pay. He made anonymous gifts to so many people who never knew who their benefactor was. He was the kindest man I've ever known."

"He was gay," he began.

"Yes," she replied. "That isn't a choice, you know,"

she said and glanced at him. "People don't wake up one morning and decide to be gay. It's something about the way their brains are wired. Cort Grier is married to Willow Shane, the author," she added, surprising him. She must have heard that he'd dated Willow, whose real name was Mina Michaels.

"I know her," he said.

"She told a mutual friend that writers don't think like normal people do. Their brains are connected differently. They see the world in ways that most people don't, and it affects the way they write. It got me to thinking," she continued. "Maybe our brains are constructed in such a way that it predisposes us to certain professions, certain personal ways of life." She laughed. "I used to think that everybody had thought patterns like mine. When I think, I picture things in vivid color. I see people and things in my mind. But I learned that not everybody does."

He glanced at her. He'd never considered that.

"Engineers think in terms of diagrams. Mathematicians think in terms of mathematical equations. Some people see abstract images. The point is," she said, "that when we think, it's an individual way of interpreting data." She smiled shyly. "It really fascinates me."

He cocked his head. "Did you go to college?"

She nodded.

"What was your major?"

She flushed and averted her eyes.

Now he was really curious. "What?" he persisted.

She swallowed. "Physics."

He almost ran the car off the road. "Excuse me?"

"I absolutely revered Albert Einstein," she said. "I loved math. I was very good at it. I wasn't sure what I wanted to study, but I wasn't really interested in the arts. I spoke to a faculty adviser, and he put me in a schedule that included higher math and chemistry and physics. I made straight As. My husband encouraged me," she added. "My first husband, that is. He was very educated. He inherited his wealth, but he graduated from Yale with an honors degree in business. He encouraged me to go to MIT. I came home for the summers and on holidays." She sighed. "Now that I look back, it was probably more to keep me from seeing too closely into his privacy than to educate me. But I felt obliged to make good grades, to justify the expense."

"And you're living in Catelow, Wyoming, instead of teaching at MIT."

She laughed softly. "Well, I can't really relate to most people. I had this incredible degree but I didn't really want to go into theoretical physics or quantum mechanics, so it's sort of occupying a drawer in my bedroom." She shrugged. "I love art and opera and I can write with either hand, so I guess I'm a conundrum."

What she was would fill a book. He was intrigued. "Art and opera," he mused.

"In between, I think about a unified field theorem," she murmured dryly.

He actually laughed.

"You have a degree in business, haven't you?" she asked.

He nodded. It was fairly well-known locally. "That, and I minored in finance. I wanted to know how to manage what I had. Too many businessmen go under because they trust the wrong people to manage their holdings."

"I have Edward Jones for my first husband's investments," she said. "And a team of super lawyers in Denver who keep up with the properties."

"How long were you married, the first time?"

"Five years," she said. She smiled. "They were good years. Charles Merridan was a kind, gentle man, and he loved to help other people. He taught me about art. And opera."

He pulled into the parking lot at the strip mall where Catelow's pharmacy was located. "What did your second husband teach you?" he asked idly.

"How to duck."

He parked the car and turned to her, scowling at the sudden paleness of her pretty face. His eyes narrowed. "Would he have anything to do with that broken bone you're taking high-powered meds for?" he asked abruptly.

She cleared her throat. "Proprietary information, Mr. McGuire," she said, but managed a smile. "I won't be long," she added as she unfastened her seat belt.

He was out of the car and around it before she retrieved her purse from the floorboard, holding the door open for her.

"Nice manners," she said absently.

"My mother was a stickler for them," he replied. "She was a sweet, unselfish little woman who always put her family first."

"So was mine," she replied quietly. "I miss my parents."

"I miss my mother."

She turned toward the pharmacy. "I'll be as quick as I can."

"No rush," he replied.

SHE DIDN'T HAVE to wait. The clerk had it ready when she got to the counter.

"Don't forget to put food in your stomach before you

take those," the pharmacist said as the clerk took her credit card and ran it.

"I won't. Five days on, ten days off," she repeated.

He gave her a thumbs-up and a smile, and went back to work.

"High-powered stuff," Carol remarked as she handed the prescription and the credit card back to Ida.

"I usually only need them in the winter," Ida replied. "I guess this isn't going to be my best year. It's just October."

Carol just smiled. Unlike most local people, she knew Ida very well. She knew that the divorcée's wild image was just a mask that she wore to protect herself. They had a mutual in-law who was kin to Ida's first husband.

"Thanks," Ida said.

"If you need me, you know my number," Carol said softly.

"I do. You know mine, also," came the smiling reply.

"We look out for each other."

"Harry looked out for me, when I really needed it," Ida said. "I do miss him so."

"Me, too," Carol replied. "He was so different from what people thought he was."

"Isn't that the truth?"

"You be careful driving."

"Oh, I'm not. Jake McGuire took me to the doctor and brought me by here." She flushed and looked around, to make sure nobody had overheard.

"We're almost empty today. Jake, hmm?" Carol teased.

"It's not like that. He doesn't like me at all." She sighed. "Which is just as well, with my history."

"We heard that your second husband got early release,"

Carol said, lowering her voice. "You keep your door locked and put Cody Banks on speed dial. Just in case."

"I thought they'd keep him forever," Ida said heavily. She shook her head. "He killed a man and hardly served any time for it. Now he gambles away everything he can steal. He's made threats…"

"I meant it, about putting our sheriff on speed dial. You live out in the sticks."

"I like my privacy."

"Maybe you should invest in some protection. A big mean dog?"

"My attorneys in Denver suggested a bodyguard."

"A constructive suggestion," came the quiet reply. "You should take it."

Ida nodded. "I guess so. I just don't like the idea of having somebody watching me all the time."

"If the bodyguard doesn't, your ex will be," Carol said. "You be careful."

"I'll be careful."

JAKE SAW HER coming and had the door open when she reached the car.

"Thanks," she said. "For everything."

"We all have these odd impulses from time to time," he replied.

She fastened her seat belt while he got under the wheel and cranked the car.

"Anyplace else you need to go while we're out?" he asked.

She shook her head. "I've inconvenienced you enough for one day."

"I didn't mind," he said and surprised himself by realizing it was the truth, not just a polite rejoinder.

"I can drive," she said, leaning her head back. "But it's my right hip that's most affected, and that's the one that gets used most, on the gas pedal and the brake. But these—" she indicated the medicine sack "—will get me back to normal."

"Do you take other pain medicine, as well?"

She laughed. "I'm allergic to most of it. I had a very mild prescription pain medicine that contained just a trace of codeine. I broke out in hives and almost ended up in the emergency room." The memory was painful. She glanced out the window. "My ex-husband thought it was hilarious. I had to drive myself to the allergist. He was watching a movie and couldn't be bothered…" She flushed scarlet. "Sorry."

"People have died from allergic reactions like that," he remarked, angered out of proportion by what her former husband had done.

She drew in a long breath. "He wouldn't have minded. All my money came from my first husband. My second didn't work. He said I had plenty of money for both of us. As long as I gave him what he wanted, things were just fine."

"And if he didn't get what he wanted?"

Her hand went absently to her hip. "It was a long time ago," she lied.

He reserved judgment. She had a scarlet reputation, but she was a beautiful woman. He wondered what sort of man would hurt her physically.

"How long have you been divorced?" he asked.

"Three years." She didn't add that he'd been in prison that long.

He glanced at her. Close-up, she was older than he'd first thought. "How old are you?" he asked abruptly.

She glanced down at her purse. "Twenty-six."

"Twenty-six." He was doing math in his head. "You married at eighteen?"

She sighed. "I'd just lost my mother. She went on one of those cruises in the Mediterranean and left me with friends—Dr. Menzer and his wife. He's my orthopedic surgeon. He and his wife moved here shortly before I came back here." She drew in a breath and looked out the window. "They said my mother fell overboard. She was out on the deck when it was storming and she was swept over the side." She looked down into her lap. It was a painful memory. "They never found her."

"That would be hard."

She nodded. "I grieved and grieved. I never even had a place to put flowers. So I went and bought one of those ornate urns that they put cremains in, and I put some of her favorite things in it and sealed it. It sits on my mantel." She smiled sadly. "So I put flowers next to it on holidays and her birthday. Next best thing to a grave."

"Not a bad solution."

"Not the best, either." Her eyes had a faraway look. "I kept thinking, maybe she washed ashore somewhere and lost her memory. Maybe she was still alive and didn't know who she was." She smiled. "There was this movie I always loved, about a female CIA agent who was shot and lost her memory. She ended up in a small town with a baby, and years later, her memory came back."

He chuckled. *"The Long Kiss Goodnight,"* he quoted.

She gasped. "Yes!"

He grinned. "I have it on Prime video," he mused. "Samuel L. Jackson's finest performance, until *Captain Marvel*," he amended. "He's one of my favorite actors."

"Mine, too," she said. "And I loved Geena Davis in the role of the schoolteacher mother who turned out to be an assassin."

He glanced at her. "You have an adventurous nature."

"I can't do adventurous things, so I'm an armchair pirate and superheroine and explorer and mercenary."

"Pirate?" he mused, and his pale silver eyes twinkled.

"I'd love to have a pirate ship and sail it on the local lake. It would have black sails and a skull-and-crossbones flag, and I'd hire men to sail it dressed up like Blackbeard."

"Why not do it?"

"Oh, I've given Catelow plenty of reasons to talk about me. No need to add even more," she added and regretted saying it when she saw the amusement leave his handsome face. It closed up. She grimaced. She had a knack for alienating people.

"Where are we going?" he asked.

"Oh! Sorry!" she blurted out and gave him directions.

HER HOUSE WAS OLD. It had been a bigger ranch in earlier days. It had belonged to a great-uncle who'd left it to her father. The family had lived there, barely scratching out a living, before her father had been offered employment in Denver at the same graphics firm whose owner Ida later married. It had been sold, but Ida's first husband bought it back and put in a ranch manager. Ida should keep the place for her heirs, he'd said gently, before she knew that there wouldn't be any with him. It had been a kind gesture, from a kind man.

Now it was a horse ranch. Ida kept a small herd of palominos and two part-time cowboys who did nothing but look after them.

"My dad worked as a typesetter for the local newspaper," she commented. "But we lived here. It was a hard life. We had a cow for milk and butter, and chickens for eggs."

"No beef?"

She shook her head. "It was hard enough providing for a milk cow and the chickens. We couldn't afford fencing for beef."

He frowned. He hadn't considered that her people had been poor. So had his. He was in his midthirties, over ten years her senior. It was probably why he didn't remember her from school.

"I grew up poor, too," he said quietly. "I mostly lived with my mother and her parents. We had a ranch only a little more prosperous than yours. Plenty to eat, but no luxuries. My grandfather drove a ten-year-old car with eighty thousand miles on it." He chuckled. "He used to say that any car that had less than eighty thousand miles would be as good as a new one to him."

"We had a twelve-year-old pickup truck with brakes that needed constant relining. My dad had a heavy foot."

"How old were you when he died?"

"Ten," she said softly. "He was the best dad in the world. I loved him so much. So did my mother. I almost lost her when he was gone so suddenly. She grieved until she died. She never even looked at another man."

"My mother was like that."

She glanced at him, curious. She wanted to know what sort of man his father was. But she was wary of asking. There was a look on his face that was puzzling.

He was aware of that curiosity. He didn't indulge it.

He pulled into the long driveway that led to the Victorian house in a grove of lodgepole pines, with the Tetons sharp and snowcapped in the distance. "Nice view," he commented.

"It is, isn't it? I sculpt, for a hobby. But I've always wished I could paint."

"I can see why." He frowned. "It's pretty remote."

"I like it that way," she said. She drew in a breath. "I don't…mix well."

"I have to," he said. "Business requires it."

"I suppose so. Watch for Butler," she said quickly as he pulled up close to the steps.

"Butler?"

In response, a huge yellow cat came trundling off the porch, rubbing up against the steps.

"He's not afraid of cars," she said. "I live in terror that somebody will run over him."

"Most cats are intelligent."

"I got the stupid one," she laughed. "He's old and arthritic, but he's so sweet."

He came around and opened her door. The cat curled around his slacks.

"Don't let him do that. He'll get hairs on you," she said quickly, trying to shoo Butler away.

"I have a German shepherd named Wolf," he replied. "I've got dog hairs everywhere, despite the best efforts of my housekeeper. You've got cat hairs. Hairs are hairs," he added with a faint smile.

"I guess so." She glanced up at him. It was a long way, and she was at least medium height. "I know you don't like me. Thanks for driving me around in spite of it."

He scowled. "How many surgeries have you had on that hip?" he asked abruptly.

"Two…" She blurted it out without thinking and then flushed, high on her cheekbones.

His pale silver eyes narrowed. "Two. It must have been one hell of a break."

She swallowed, hard, remembering. "It was. My hip was fractured and the femur was, too."

He wondered if she'd been in a car wreck. She didn't say any more about it and flushed, as if it embarrassed her to have said even that much.

"I got caught in the cross fire when I was fighting in Iraq, over ten years ago," he said quietly. "Three hits in the chest. One would have been fatal, but the medics were quick. I got sent home." He shrugged. "I would have gone back, but they discharged me. I guess three bullets qualifies you for retirement." There were other injuries, as well, but he wasn't sharing those.

She grimaced. "It must have been very painful."

"It was." He stuck his hands in his pockets. "The scars remind me, every time I look in a mirror." He laughed sarcastically. "I never take my clothes off in the light when I'm with women. I made that mistake just once."

She turned scarlet and averted her eyes.

He was stunned. She was embarrassed. It was so obvious that it was unmistakable. She was a rounder who slept with anything in pants, but it embarrassed her to hear a man talk about what he did with women.

"I have to go in and take these," she said, holding up

the bag of pills from the pharmacy. "Thanks again for the ride…"

"I gave Cindy my number," he interrupted. "When they finish with your Jag, I'll have one of my men come with me to bring it home."

"But you don't have to do that," she protested.

"I don't have to do anything," he said, "except pay taxes."

She got the point. "Well…thank you."

"You hate being obligated to other people," he guessed and saw her blue eyes flash. He nodded. "So do I. But it's not a bad thing to offer help when it's needed. You live alone."

"Yes." She drew in a breath. "I like…being by myself."

"Same." He studied her for another minute before he turned back to his car. "Watch your cat. I'll try not to run over him," he added.

"Come on, Butler," she called to the big yellow cat, who was trying to follow Jake to his car. "Butler!"

The cat looked torn, but he trotted back to Ida and followed her up onto the porch. She watched Jake drive away with mixed emotions. She couldn't think why he'd offered help, when it was so obvious that he didn't like her.

Jake didn't understand it, either. He went home, berating himself all the way for getting involved with the scarlet woman, even indifferently.

CHAPTER THREE

IDA HATED TAKING the huge ibuprofen caplets. They hurt her stomach, even when she took them with food, and she had to take an antacid just to tolerate them. But they did help with the inflammation and the pain.

Her car had required a part that had to be sent for, so it hadn't been returned the day Jake drove her home. It would be ready today, though. The mechanic, a former Jaguar mechanic at that, had told her on the phone. She didn't really mind. She couldn't take ibuprofen and drive anyway.

She scrambled some eggs and made a piece of toast to go with them. She didn't have much of an appetite. All she could think of was how dangerous Bailey was, and what he was capable of doing to her. The pain in her hip reminded her graphically what could happen when she refused him.

Over the few months of their brief marriage, he'd turned her from a happy, fun-loving woman into a frightened recluse who wanted nothing to do with men ever again. The trial had been quick, by judicial standards, and Bailey had sworn vengeance from the courtroom when he was convicted. Ida had been in the room, compelled to learn the outcome of the trial firsthand. She could never forget the look on her husband's face. Well, ex-husband.

She'd divorced him while he was in jail awaiting trial. Her attorneys had made him aware of what they could do if he refused to consent to it. So he'd consented, reluctantly. But he hadn't known that she was cutting him out of her will at the same time. She wondered if he knew even now.

She'd refused to go to his bond hearing when he was arrested, afraid of what he might do to her. The attorneys in Denver had concurred. One of them knew the assistant DA who tried the case. He'd made the man aware of just what had been done to Ida by the defendant, a drastically different story from the one the defendant had told. Bailey had no money of his own, no property for a cash bond, so he was forced to stay in jail until the trial. After the trial he went straight to prison. It was the first time in months that Ida had felt safe. She subsequently changed her surname back to that of Charles Merridan, her first husband. She didn't even want Bailey's name to be a daily reminder that she'd been stupid enough to marry him.

She'd told only a handful of people about the threats. Her attorneys had hired a temporary bodyguard for her. He was masquerading as a cowboy who helped with her small horse ranch. He lived in the old bunkhouse that she'd renovated as a guest cottage. Nobody thought anything about it, because of her reputation.

She grimaced. She hadn't told Jake. When he found out about the bodyguard, and he would, he'd assume that the bodyguard from Texas was just another lover, because he was young and good-looking. She was going to hate that. Jake was a good, kind man. She wished he thought better of her. But then, give a dog a bad name... And she'd given herself a very bad one, encouraging gossip that protected her from the attentions of local men.

She hated her own beauty that made her attractive to men. She downplayed it by not wearing makeup and going around in clothes that concealed her exquisite figure. But there was the occasional party and she dressed for those. They'd become an ordeal until Cort Grier had helped her out by pretending an interest in her.

At the party she'd been flirting with an older man deliberately, because she knew he was married and unlikely to want to start something with her. Sadly, her idea backfired. He became very aggressively interested, and his poor wife went to the restroom in tears. She backed off after that and ran into Cort Grier, who left with her when the party ended. She'd wanted so badly to apologize to the man's wife, but she hadn't known how to approach her. Very few people in Catelow knew the real woman behind the vivacious flirt with the sordid reputation. It wasn't the facts of any case; it was what people believed about it. Ida was a call girl who tried to steal other women's husbands. That was the latest gossip, after the notorious party.

Well, it was what she'd wanted, wasn't it, to be scandalous? She'd thought it was the best way to keep men at bay. It had worked, so far. She had no interest at all in another marriage or getting involved with a man. She was convinced that she didn't have the judgment God gave a billy goat, much less the ability to spot an abuser when she saw one.

She finished her meager breakfast and went into the living room, carrying a cup of latte from her European coffee machine along with her in a delicate blue-and-white bone china cup and saucer. She put it on the coffee table and just stared at it.

She drank too much coffee. It kept her awake at night.

That would have been a problem if she hadn't had the daily pain that ensured that she actively avoided sleep. She hated it when the lights went out, because that was when the bad dreams came. Horrible dreams, full of violence only half remembered when she awoke.

So she avoided sleep. She avoided men. She avoided almost all contact with other human beings. Her only companion was old Butler, curled up in his kitty bed, sound asleep.

There was a wide-screen television, the latest model, with every satellite channel known to man on it. But the centerpiece of the room was a grand piano. Ida's first husband had played beautifully. He had her taught.

She was a quick study, too. She'd always loved music. Piano came as naturally to her as breathing, to his utter delight. She memorized his favorite pieces and played them for him when they were at home together, which wasn't often.

Leaving the coffee on the table, she went to the piano, positioned the bench, sat down and put her right foot near the pedals on the floor.

Her very favorite song was an old one that her grandmother had loved. She'd had several recordings of it by different singers and groups, but it was the one by Steve Alaimo that was her favorite. Ida had grown up hearing it, loving it. Her hands went to the keys and she began to play, her eyes closed, the music filling up all the empty, frightened places inside her.

She was oblivious to everything around her when she played, even to the sound of the doorbell. It did finally get through to her. She stopped in the middle of a bar, jumped to her feet and moved as quickly as she could to the front door.

Jake McGuire was standing there, watching her curiously.

"Sorry, I didn't hear you drive up."

"One of my men drove my Mercedes over here. He's waiting for me." He studied her. "Your radio was pretty loud," he said. "No wonder you didn't hear the cars. My grandfather used to play that song. What's it called?"

"'Cast Your Fate to the Wind,'" she replied.

"Catchy tune."

"It is," she agreed, without telling him it was she, herself, playing it.

He handed her a smart key on a key ring with a silver leaper, the Jaguar symbol, attached. "It handles like a dream," he remarked. "I might even consider getting one of my own."

She smiled. "Thanks for all the trouble."

"It wasn't. Trouble, I mean," he replied.

She stared up at him with conflicted emotions, feeling things she didn't want to feel. He was only being kind. It was indifferent kindness. He didn't even like her, for God's sake!

He was having the same kind of issues. His perception of her had changed. She wasn't the wild woman he'd thought she was. He was curious about her. He didn't want to be.

Just as the tension reached flash point, there was a quick tap on the door and a tall man with dark hair and even darker eyes came into the house.

"Sorry to interrupt," he said curtly, "but we've got a problem with one of the horses."

"Which one?" she asked at once. "Not Silver?" she added worriedly.

"No, ma'am, not him. It's the palomino mare. The one that foaled last week."

She sighed. "Gold. She's had so many problems since we delivered that colt," she replied sadly. "What's wrong with her? Do you know?"

"She's got deep cuts on both her flanks," he said without inflection. "Bad ones." He had a closed expression as he spoke.

"But she's only been out in the pasture," Ida exclaimed. "And there's nothing that could have injured her there!"

"I know," Laredo replied quietly. "I checked." His dark eyes were saying things to her that she didn't want to share with Jake.

She just sighed. "Call the vet and see if he can come at once."

"I'll get right on it." He went out without another word.

Jake's eyebrow rose. "An employee?"

"One of my new cowboys," she replied, but she was lying and she didn't do it well.

He smiled. It wasn't a nice smile. "Have a nice day."

"Thanks for bringing my car to me," she said quietly.

He just shrugged and kept on walking.

And so much for wild dreams, she told herself as she went back inside and closed the door.

SHE WALKED OUT to the barn where the palomino was stabled. The mare, Gold, was standing, but long, bloody cuts were visible on her hindquarters. Even Ida could see the pain the animal was in. The new man, Laredo Hall, was kneeling beside the horse with one of the ranch's cowboys at his side. The mare shied away from him.

"Oh, Gold, my poor baby!" Ida said worriedly. She

went into the stall and drew her fingers down the mare's soft mane. "My poor girl!" She looked at the cuts. "This was no accident," she said icily.

"Looks like somebody did this on purpose," Laredo said. His eyes narrowed.

Her heart ran wild. Was Bailey here? Or had one of his shady friends come right onto her ranch and damaged her horse? It was the sort of low-down, sneaky, mean thing he would do, and she knew it. Laredo, judging by his demeanor, was thinking the same thing.

"Have you called the vet?" she asked.

He nodded. "He's on his way."

SHE WRAPPED HER arms around herself and winced at the horse's pain. Gold was still shying away from Laredo, and she was making nervous whinnies. Nearby, she heard the palomino's colt whimpering, as if he understood that his mother was ailing. Ida had become fond of the mare since she'd been living in Catelow. She rode her occasionally, as she rode Silver, another of her small herd of palominos with a beautiful white mane, and the colt's sire, but the cowboys mostly took care of the horses. She'd always loved to ride, but now she was afraid of large animals, afraid of any more injuries that would require surgery. It had been so painful…

The sound of a truck pulling up outside gathered everyone's attention. A young veterinarian came in the door, straight to the patient.

HE GREETED IDA, introduced himself as Dr. Mulholland and spent a few minutes examining the animal. He winced.

"Well, I don't find any more injuries, just these cuts. Who would have done this?" he added angrily, turning to Ida.

"At a guess, somebody sent by my ex-husband, who just got out of jail," she said tightly. "He's made threats."

The vet's eyes blazed. "He should be arrested and put back in jail."

"Chance would be a fine thing," she said sadly. "I can't prove he was responsible. Not yet, at least."

"If you can, I'll be happy to testify."

"Thank you," she said sincerely.

He applied locals and stitched the cuts, then gave the animal an antibiotic injection, just in case, to prevent infection.

The vet sighed as he put up his tools. "If you don't see any improvement, or if you see evidence of infection, call me, anytime. I'm always available. So is my wife, Ashley."

"Thanks a million," Ida said sincerely. "I love my horses."

He smiled. "We both love anything with fur. Or without it." He laughed. "I have one patient who's twenty feet long and weighs over a hundred pounds."

"Twenty feet long?" she exclaimed.

"He's an albino python. Lovely creature, with white and yellow scales and red eyes."

She shivered delicately. "I'm not a reptile person. I like warm-blooded things," she laughed.

"It takes all kinds," he said and smiled. "You call if you need us, okay?"

"That's a deal. And thanks for coming so promptly."

"SHE'LL BE ALL RIGHT, I think," Laredo told her later when they were alone, in his deep, calm voice. "I'll make spot checks out here at night. But our biggest problem is going to be who did it. You know who I suspect."

She sighed wearily. "Yes, I know. I have the same suspicion." She grimaced. "Why would anyone hurt a helpless animal?"

"Some men love it. They get a feeling of power. They get off on hurting things." He wasn't even looking at her. His hands were jammed in the pockets of his jeans and he was staring sightlessly across the pasture, reliving some trauma in his past, perhaps.

"What about Silver and the other horses?" she asked miserably.

"I've got a remote camera set up, and I sleep light. I'll be watching."

She nodded. "Do whatever you have to."

"That I will."

As she walked back to the house, she remembered what he'd said about men who hurt animals loving power and being aroused by it. Maybe something had happened to him, in his past, that had prompted his odd comment. But she didn't want to get personal, even with a bodyguard, so she put it out of her mind.

A WEEK LATER there was a dinner party that she was invited to. She hadn't really planned to go, but the hostess, Pam Simpson, was almost aggressive about it, pleading.

"You have to come. The numbers won't work, and nobody else is free," she lied. "Just for me, Ida. Please?"

Ida felt those words like bricks. Pam wasn't malicious, but it was obvious that she needed a female body in place, not a friend.

"That was tactless," Pam amended. "I could find somebody else, but I want you to come. Would you?"

"I'll be accused of trying to hook somebody's husband and there will be a firefight," Ida sighed.

"No. I promise, that won't happen. Please?"

"Oh, all right," Ida said heavily. "But I really can't stay long. I'm in a lot of pain. My orthopedic surgeon has me on powerful anti-inflammatories and I can't drive when I take them…"

"No problem at all! I'll send somebody to pick you up and take you home. How's that?"

Ida gave in. She laughed. "Pam, you're hopeless. But yes, I'll come."

"Thanks! You won't regret it. Honest." She hung up.

SO IDA DRESSED in a tasteful black cocktail dress, with cap sleeves, that fell to her ankles, with her beautiful back uncovered and a neckline that came above her collarbone. She looked elegant and beautiful, her pretty face accented by red lipstick and only a hint of powder. She put a black rhinestone clip in her short black hair and picked up her small evening bag.

She'd checked on her poor horse every day. Gold, as she was called, was doing well, but she was nervous, even when her colt was with her. The wounds were healing, but slowly. The mental ones, Ida considered, would be worse than the cuts. At least, Ida thought, Gold would live. That was enough. Now came the worry about whether or not Bailey had been responsible for her injuries. But Laredo had the house and yard wired like bombs, and he had outdoor cameras everywhere, along with sensors that would alert anyone listening about intruders. Bailey was going to have a hard time hurting any of her animals again, she thought angrily. But she wished he'd try, so she could have him arrested and sent back to prison.

SHE'D WONDERED WHO Pam would send for her. She was nervous of men. Pam knew that, but not why.

The doorbell rang. She slid into her long black leather coat with its epaulets and leather belt and opened the door.

She was at a loss for words. Pam had sent a rather disgruntled Jake McGuire to pick her up. He was glaring when she opened the door, but the horrified look on Ida's face, and the beauty of her face and her slender figure in that dress, left him momentarily speechless.

"I didn't ask Pam to send you," she stammered. "I don't even know who else she invited. She said she invited me just to make the numbers fit. I didn't want to come!"

Her embarrassment touched something deep inside him that had been frozen since Mina Michaels married Cort Grier. He reached out a big, lean hand and touched his fingers to her soft mouth to stop the words.

"It's all right," he said gently.

Tears, visible, stung her eyes and she averted them. "Thanks," she almost choked.

He was entranced. Her reputation would put any decent man off, but when he was alone with her, she was nothing like that reputation. She was a puzzle.

"We'd better go," he said gently. "Careful. There's snow on the ground."

"It's okay. I don't mind snow. Ice scares me."

"No ice. Yet."

She locked her doors and hesitated at the steps. She had on heels that were barely an inch high and stacked, the only sort she could bear with her old injury. The snow would come up over them.

Jake suddenly swung her up in his arms and started down the steps to his car, parked right in front of the house.

Ida was like a board in his arms, frightened and too shy to tell him why.

He turned his head and looked down at her when he reached the passenger side of the big Mercedes. He stared straight into her frightened blue eyes, his own silver ones narrow and assessing while the snow fell on his wide-brimmed hat and was funneled away from her face.

She just stared up at him, vulnerable, fragile, uncertain.

"You little fraud," he said in the softest tone she'd ever heard from him.

"Wh-what?"

He just chuckled. He put her down, opened the door and eased her inside. He didn't elaborate on what he'd said, but he was getting some interesting information about the wild divorcée without a word being spoken. She didn't act like any promiscuous woman he'd ever known, and there had been a few in his youth. She was far more like an actress playing a role in public to keep people from seeing the woman behind it. She was damaged somehow. He wondered who'd made her so afraid of men. Cindy had said something about Ida's second husband. Ida had intimated that the man had been responsible for her injuries. It angered him, remembering that.

He got in beside her, glancing sideways to make sure her seat belt was fastened before he put his on.

"Is there a big crowd there?" she asked, to make conversation.

"Five couples," he said. "We'll make six."

"Pam didn't say she'd invited you," she said after a minute.

His chiseled lips pursed. "Same here."

She drew in a long breath.

"She and Cindy, from the café, are friends," he mused as he pulled out onto the highway.

Which made things very clear. Cindy had told Pam about Jake taking Ida home and coming back to get her car. The two women sensed a romance and Pam was acting to help things along.

"Oh, dear," Ida said worriedly, and her long-fingered hands with their red fingernails crushed her small purse.

"Gossip only works if you let it," he said.

"So they say."

He glanced at her as they stopped at a traffic light. He could see the faint flush in her cheeks. It amused him, but he didn't let her see it.

"How's your mare?" he asked, unwillingly reminded of the handsome cowboy she'd hired.

"Gold? We had to get the vet. Somebody left deep lacerations all over her hindquarters, on both flanks," she said, her voice tinged with remembered outrage.

"How the hell did that happen? Did she take a fall?"

She bit her lower lip. "We're not sure what happened."

He gave her a long sideways look before he turned onto the road to Pam's house. "Not sure."

"I can't talk about it," she said. "I'm sorry."

His heart jumped. She was saying something without voicing it, and he knew it. Someone had hurt the horse. Who? Why? He was eaten up with questions and she sat there like the Sphinx, saying nothing, giving away nothing.

He pulled up in front of Pam's house. The driveway had been cleared of snow, so Ida walked in under her own power, with Jake just behind her after he parked the car in front of the house.

"Welcome!" Pam exclaimed, hugging Ida and Jake. "I'm so glad you could both come. We have a lovely dinner. Cook's been in the kitchen all day."

"I'm starved," Jake drawled. "Well, starved of home cooking, for sure. All I can make are scrambled eggs and toast."

"Don't you have a cook?" Pam exclaimed.

"I haven't been in town long enough to hire one, actually," he confessed. "I've been in Australia, helping Rogan assess the damage and deal with the fires. Rain would be damned welcome, I'll tell you that."

"We all heard about the fires," Pam said as she led the way to the elegant dining room. "Such a tragedy. So many animals lost."

"So many arsonists caught," Jake replied. "I hope they lock them up forever."

"So do I," Ida said quietly.

He glanced at her covertly, remembering her old cat and the damaged mare. She loved animals.

"Come on to the dining room. We're starting a little early, but I have a surprise for later," Pam said with a covert and amused glance that Ida didn't see.

"I love surprises," Jake teased.

Pam laughed softly. 'You'll really love this one. I promise."

Dinner was a delicately prepared chicken-and-shrimp carbonara with a crème brûlée for dessert.

"It was delicious," Ida told her hostess with a warm smile.

The other couples echoed the sentiment. Two husbands were openly staring at Ida while their wives, a little less attractive than Jake's dinner partner, glared.

Ida ground her teeth together. Pam noticed where she was looking and announced that they would all retire to the living room while the cook cleared away the dinner plates. She added that coffee would be forthcoming for any who wanted it.

JAKE WAS LESS than friendly as he stared at Ida covertly, noting the husbands who were almost falling over each other in an attempt to sit beside her.

He took Ida's arm and, to the husbands' irritation, moved her to a couple of upholstered chairs near the sofa, all the furniture facing an enormous, polished grand piano on a platform. The piano was obviously the centerpiece of the room. Everyone knew that Pam had been taking lessons.

Jake sat down beside her.

"Thanks," she said under her breath.

He glanced at her and scowled. Her hands in her lap were shaking. Her face was pale, her posture stiff and reserved. His mind went back to the orthopedic surgeon Ida was seeing, the massive amount of anti-inflammatories she was taking. Something had happened to her. Something traumatic.

Without voluntary effort, his big hand slid over one of hers, finding it cold. His hand closed around her fingers, shocking her into looking at him.

His pale silver eyes glittered as they registered her

delicate features, her soft mouth and exquisite complexion. "You're safe," he said quietly, without understanding why he said it.

She jerked a little, as if she hadn't expected the words. She averted her face, embarrassed.

Their hostess came into the room, followed by a server with a silver tray laden with coffeepot, china cups and condiments. "Coffee for anyone who likes," Pam announced with a smile as she directed the valet to a beautiful mahogany side table.

She turned. "I promised you a surprise. But it's going to come as a surprise to my guest." She glanced at Ida. "Would you?" she asked, indicating the grand piano.

"Oh, please, I'd really rather not…" Ida began.

Pam gently took the hand that had been under Jake's and tugged. "Come on, chicken."

Ida flushed. But Pam had been kind to her, after all.

The piano was beautiful, Ida noted as she sat down at the keys after positioning the bench where she wanted it.

"What will you play?" Pam asked, while Jake stared with barely concealed shock at his dinner companion.

Ida smiled. "This is one of my favorites."

And as her fingers touched the keys, the exquisite melody of Stephen Sondheim's "Send in the Clowns," from the 1973 musical *A Little Night Music*, filled the room.

Ida's eyes closed as she played from memory, her heart full, brimming over, as her thoughts drifted to the past, when her mother listened with a rapt face to this song, sung by Judy Collins. It had been her mother's favorite.

She played with all her skill, feeling the music in every cell of her body as it rose to a crescendo and, slowly, faded into a stunned silence.

Her eyes opened. She blinked. And suddenly there was furious applause, even from Jake.

"You play beautifully," Pam said. "You should do it more often."

Ida got up, a little self-conscious. She smiled. "Thanks."

"And now that I'm through putting you on the spot," Pam teased, "coffee?"

Ida laughed. "Please."

"IT WAS YOU PLAYING, when I brought your Jaguar home that day," Jake mused as they drove away from Pam's mansion.

"It was," she confessed. "The piano has gotten me through some very bad times."

"Where did you learn?"

"My husband, my first husband, had me professionally taught," she replied with a sad smile. "It was something we shared, a love of beautiful music. He played like an angel. I loved to sit and listen to him."

"Didn't you wonder, when you were first married?"

"You mean at the lack of physical contact?" She laughed. "I worried myself sick. I was certain that I smelled bad, or that I wasn't pretty enough, or that he just wasn't attracted to me at all. It was a relief, in some ways, to discover the truth."

"You didn't mind?" he persisted.

She studied the purse in her lap. "People are what they are," she said simply. "He was a good and kind man who never beat me or gambled away what we had or embarrassed me in public, the way many men do to their wives. He was fun to be with. He was very educated. We liked the same things, had similar tastes in music and politics and even religion." She sighed. "He was the best man I ever knew, regardless of how he felt about his place in life."

He smiled. "You're not what I expected."

She shrugged. "Who is, really?"

HE PULLED UP at her front door. "Your horse. How was the mare injured?"

She was taken aback by the question. She couldn't even think up a plausible lie.

"You think it was done deliberately," he persisted.

She hesitated, drew in a breath, then nodded.

"By whom?" he asked.

She looked at him with wide, pained eyes in the light from the map reader. She grimaced. "I...can't talk about it."

"Your second husband," he guessed. "Was his name Merridan?"

"Oh, no," she said quickly. "It was Trent. When I divorced Bailey, I reverted to my first married name, Merridan. Most of my stocks and bonds and my land holdings were still in that name anyway. I changed my will, too," she added darkly, not choosing her words, "so that when I die, all my holdings go to various charities. He won't get a penny."

"There's gossip that he was in prison."

Her pale face turned to his. "Was. Yes."

His face went bland. "So he's out now, is he?" Jake asked.

She bit her lower lip.

"Out for blood, too, unless I miss my guess."

"Blood. Money. It's all the same to him," Ida said.

"You think he hurt the horse?"

"I don't know. Laredo, he's the new man, he's set up cameras outside, just in case…"

"Is he really a cowboy?" Jake asked.

Her small breasts rose and fell with her inner torment. "My attorneys felt that I needed some protection, on the ranch," she blurted out.

He didn't say a word. But he was assembling puzzle pieces in his mind. It all became clear quite rapidly.

"Why was he in jail, Ida?" he asked quietly.

"Proprietary information," she replied, her voice barely audible. "Thanks for transporting me back and forth to Pam's."

"Thank you and good night?" he mused.

She sighed and forced a smile. "Something like that." She started to open the car door, but she was slow.

He beat her to it, opening it for her. She struggled to get out. Her back was painful, like her hip. She ground her teeth together at the pain.

"You okay?" he asked and sounded concerned.

"It's going to rain, or snow, or something," she predicted. "My bones hurt really bad when the weather changes."

"A complaint I hear from my cowboys," he replied. "They have all sorts of injuries. Working around livestock carries its own dangers."

She nodded. "My father was thrown from a horse when he was very young. He broke a rib, which punctured a lung. They barely got him to the hospital in time."

He walked her to her door. "Are you going to be all right?"

"A heating pad and one of those horse pills will ease the pain. Thanks for asking."

He tilted her face up to his with a big hand under her chin.

"You really are beautiful," he murmured as his head bent, his coffee-scented breath going right into her mouth seconds before his chiseled lips moved down and settled right on it.

CHAPTER FOUR

IDA'S ONLY RECENT memories of kisses came with terror and pain. She was wary of Jake this way, and it showed.

She felt as stiff as a board under the big, warm hands that settled on her shoulders as his hard lips brushed her soft ones.

He lifted his head and looked down into her eyes under the porch light. His own eyes were shuttered under the wide brim of his Stetson. "You're frightened," he said softly. "No need. I don't have to beat a woman to make me feel like a man." He said it with absolute disgust.

Her lips parted and the breath she'd been holding sighed out. "Sorry," she bit off. "I've…I've had some problems."

"With a brutal husband."

She hesitated. Then she nodded.

"So you wear a mask, to keep men at bay, so they won't know that you're afraid of them."

She shifted restlessly under his hands. "It usually works."

"You've damaged your reputation in the process. Doesn't that matter?"

"I was…rather desperate at the time, when I first came back here. Everywhere I went, men came on to me. Not in droves, but even one was frightening. I wanted to be left alone. I tried to tell them, but of course, nobody believed it. So I developed this personality…"

"The happy hooker," he mused and actually laughed softly.

"Something like that. You know, I'm so good in bed that I judge men, and almost all of them come up lacking, and then I gossip about them." Her blue eyes twinkled. "It really worked."

"Almost too well," he said under his breath. He cocked his head. "Are you afraid of me?"

"Not so much anymore."

His fingers smoothed over her cheek. She had exquisitely soft skin, and when she was vulnerable, like this, she made him ache.

"That's nice to hear."

As he spoke, his fingers were toying with her mouth, teasing the top lip away from the bottom, arousing her.

She barely recognized the feelings. She'd only really had them for Bailey before they were married. Then, so quickly after the ceremony, he'd brutalized her over and over during their brief marriage. She didn't trust desire. It had already betrayed her once.

She started to step back, but Jake went with her.

Her long-fingered hands pushed at his shirt with leashed fear.

"I won't hurt you. Not ever," he whispered, one big hand covering hers where they rested on the soft cotton of his shirt.

Under the shirt she could feel hard muscle and curious indentations. She recalled that he'd been shot and that he never took his shirt off with women. She blushed at the memory, which had embarrassed her with his telling of it. There was something soft over the muscle. Hair?

Unconsciously, her long nails were teasing his skin

as she stood there in the circle of his arms, nervous but trusting.

"I really like that," he said, his deep voice husky. "So it might be a good idea to stop."

"Stop?" She looked up with wide-eyed curiosity.

His hand pressed hers closer. "What you're doing with your nails."

She realized belatedly that she'd been exploring him. She gasped. "Oh, my gosh!"

He stilled her backward movement with a soft chuckle. "Don't panic," he said gently. "It wasn't really a complaint. I'm being protective. Of course, that's frowned upon in our enlightened modern society."

"I...don't mind it," she replied.

He cocked his head and smiled. "You don't?"

"I'm not really conventional. At least, I used to be that way. I was always happy, always laughing. I loved life..." Her face clouded.

He put his thumb over her lips. "Bad memories can be nudged aside by good ones," he pointed out.

"Good...ones?" she repeated. Her heart was racing madly. Her breath was coming in little gasps. Did he know?

He knew. He was experienced and she certainly wasn't. Not in this. One husband who didn't like women, a second who made her afraid of men. And this was the result, this quiet, inhibited woman who was frightened of physical contact with a man, any man. But she was reacting to him in a normal, healthy way, and he loved it.

His head bent again. "You know," he breathed against her parted lips, "the only certain thing in life is its uncertainty."

"It is?" She was staring at his chiseled mouth as it came closer, not really listening to what he said.

"You never know what to expect."

She nodded, but she was still staring at his mouth.

He smiled gently. "You haven't heard a word I've said."

"Haven't heard," she said, nodding.

"What the hell," he whispered, and his lips gently parted hers, hesitating when she stiffened, moving closer when she relaxed. Her fingers dug into his chest as he drew her closer, as his mouth grew slowly more invasive in the cold darkness, where he was the only warmth.

He felt her breath catch and knew it wasn't prompted by fear. But a good horseman didn't rush his fences, and a smart man didn't grow overly ardent with a damaged woman. He drew away from her, very slowly.

She was staring at him, her heart beating like a butterfly in her chest, her china-blue eyes vivid, wide, fascinated.

His fingers trailed down her cheek. "What you know about men, Ida," he said and watched her react as he spoke her name for the first time, "could be written on the head of a match."

She was still staring at him, transfixed.

He put her away gently. "I'll call you in a few days. We might go out to eat."

She flushed. "Really?"

He stared down at her and hated the men who'd made her feel inadequate, when she was a treasure waiting to be discovered. "Really."

She smiled. It was like the sun coming out. "I would... I would like that," she stammered.

He chuckled. "I know some great restaurants."

"I love good food."

"So do I. You've still got my number on your cell, right?" he asked suddenly.

"Yes."

"If you need help, use it," he said.

She drew in a breath. "I don't want to involve you in my trouble."

His heart jumped. It was a very protective attitude. He liked it. "If I minded, I'd never have offered," he explained.

"Okay, then. Thanks."

His eyes narrowed. "Or if you wake up screaming in the middle of the night, you can call me," he said abruptly. "I don't sleep much myself."

She turned red. "Cindy told you," she said self-consciously.

He nodded. "She worries about you."

Her eyes lowered.

"It must be one hell of a bad memory," he said after a minute. "We'll make some better ones. Supper. Next week. I'll text you."

She looked up at him with a feeling akin to rebirth. Her breath sighed out and she smiled. "Next week," she whispered.

He was tempted to pull her close and kiss the breath out of her, but she was going to need gentle handling. She was damaged. Odd, how much he wanted to protect her. It was a feeling he hadn't indulged since Mina had been part of his life.

He smiled, tipped his hat mischievously and walked back to his car. "Lock the doors," he called back.

She laughed. "You lock yours, too."

He threw up a hand.

She went inside and locked the door, leaning back against it with a long, sweet sigh of pure delight.

THE DELIGHT WAS gone in an instant when her cell phone rang and she answered it absently.

"New man in your life, huh?" came an insulting, angry voice over the line. "Well, you belong to me, and he's not getting you. Nobody's getting you."

"We're divorced," she said icily.

"A divorce you obtained through fraud, by blackmailing me," he shot back. "I can prove that, in court. You owe me!"

She hung up on him, shocked and terrified. The phone rang again, but she darted to a side table where she kept pens and paper. She wrote down the number and phoned her attorney, Paul Browning.

"Calm down, now. It's okay. Do you have Laredo's number?"

"Laredo."

"Your bodyguard," he prompted.

"Oh. Him." She drew in a breath. "Yes."

"Call him right now and tell him what happened," he replied. "I'll get the wheels turning here. If Bailey Trent wants trouble, he can have it. I'll talk to you tomorrow. Try not to worry. The laws are in place to protect you. There's a restraining order. If he steps over the line, he'll go back to jail. He knows that."

"It doesn't stop him from phoning me and terrifying me," she blurted out. "I should get a new number!"

"He'd just find it out. He has a friend who works as a

skip tracer for a detective agency," he added. "Changing the number will do no good."

"I feel so helpless," she blurted out.

"Take a pill and go to bed. Make sure your doors are locked and sleep with the cell phone. Wouldn't hurt to talk to the local sheriff, as well, and the parole officer on your husband's case. I'll do the latter. His parole officer is in Denver, where I am."

"Thanks, Paul," she said.

"We'll take care of you," he said warmly. "Try not to worry too much. It's just a tactic. He thinks he'll frighten you into paying him off."

She didn't tell him that it was working. But it was. "Okay," she said instead.

"I'll be in touch."

The line went dead. She looked around her with wide, frightened eyes. It was one thing to deny Bailey money, but she knew all too well what he was capable of. Would she never be free of him? She forgot to mention her injured mare to Paul. She'd have to call him in the morning and tell him.

Meanwhile, she phoned Laredo in the bunkhouse and told him what had happened.

"He can call you all he likes," Laredo drawled, "but if he sets foot on the place, I'll have him in jail so fast his head will spin. Don't you worry, Mrs. Merridan. I'm on the job."

"Okay. Thanks. Listen, do you think Bailey hurt my mare?"

There was a pause. "Well, anything's possible. But I can guarantee you he hasn't been on the ranch. I've got wildlife cameras placed in strategic locations and I monitor them. Uh, they went on your account at the local hardware store. Hope that's okay."

"I told you to get whatever you needed," she replied.

"Fine, then. I'll keep an eye out. Good night."

"Good night. Thank you," she added.

He hung up.

She put on her gown and climbed into bed, still worried and upset.

Her mind went back to the dinner and Jake McGuire and the gentle, soft way he'd kissed her at the end of the evening. She could feel the hunger in him, and she sensed that it wasn't the way he usually was with women. She didn't think he'd ever be brutal. But then, how did she know? Men were different behind closed doors. She'd learned that the hard way. It was a lesson she was never going to forget.

THE FOLLOWING WEEK Paul Browning had investigators looking into her allegations about the threats Bailey had made, and she was getting ready for a dinner date with Jake.

He'd phoned her Thursday night. "I know this sweet little fish place in Galveston," he began lazily. "It's only a couple of hours away by jet. How about it Friday night?"

She laughed, delighted. "Oh, I love seafood."

"So do I. I'll pick you up about five. That okay?"

"That's fine." She hesitated. "What should I wear?"

"Suit yourself, but I'm going in jeans and a warm jacket. I hate dressing up when I don't have to."

She smiled. "So do I. Jeans it is."

"I'll see you then."

She was trying to think up a sophisticated reply, but

he'd already ended the call. Just as well, she thought. She wasn't good at conversation anymore.

HE WAS WEARING jeans and a chambray shirt with a sheep-skin jacket and a Silverbelly Stetson. He looked comfort-able, but the jeans and boots were designer ones, and the sheepskin jacket probably cost more than the diamonds in Ida's dinner ring.

"Ready?" he asked with a gentle smile.

"Ready. I fed Butler and left him plenty of cat food. He's always starving."

He put her into the car. "How did you end up with a battered old cat?" he wondered.

"He was a rescue," she said. "I found him in the woods with a string tied tight around his neck, and welts all over him. I never knew exactly what had happened to him. He was afraid of me at first. But I coaxed him out of hiding and took him to the vet. When they had him back in good condition, I adopted him and took him home. He's been my family ever since."

"You like animals."

She nodded.

"How about cattle?" he mused.

She laughed. "Well, I haven't been around them very much. I love horses. I guess cattle are similar." She glanced at him. "But I do love a good steak," she added ruefully.

He chuckled. "I don't run beef cattle on the property here, but I know a few ranchers who do." His eyes met hers for a few seconds before they went back to the high-way. "I can cook a steak."

"So can I," she said.

"I might let you prove that one day down the road."

She hesitated. It was early days yet.

"No rush," he added, as if he understood.

She let out a breath. "Okay, then."

They drove in silence to the small airport at Catelow. It had a runway long enough to accommodate a small jet, but it was mostly for small aircraft. A lot of cattlemen used airplanes to help herd cattle. She wondered if Jake did.

He pulled up to a beautiful white aircraft with soft, elegant lines. "My goodness, it's beautiful," she said softly.

His eyebrows arched. "Didn't you fly around on private jets with your first husband?"

She laughed softly. "He was terrified of flying. He wouldn't even go on a conventional airplane if he could drive. I flew commercial, when I was in college."

"You aren't afraid of flying?" he asked.

She shook her head. "When I was younger, we had a friend who rebuilt aircraft for resale. I rode in a home-built one and was strapped in with a jet harness. It was one of the most exciting things I ever did. Well, except for the skydiving thing."

"Skydiving." He stared at her. "Skydiving?"

"Oh, it was a rush," she said, laughing, and her china-blue eyes sparkled with feeling. "I loved it!" The smile slowly faded. "Something I won't ever be able to do again, I'm afraid," she said, and the sadness was in her face as well as her eyes.

"I can't ride bucking horses," he said, after he'd introduced her to his pilot and they buckled themselves in for takeoff.

She looked at him curiously. "Did you use to do that?" she asked.

He nodded. "I won belts for it in my teens," he replied. "After Iraq, it became impossible."

"You have more than just bullet wounds," she guessed quietly.

He hesitated. Sighed. Then nodded. "I have a metal rod in one of my legs."

"Oh, my goodness," she said softly. "The pain must have been terrible."

He stared at her, surprised. He'd told a date about it, some years back, and she'd remarked that it must look absolutely horrible. Ida was more concerned with how much it had hurt him.

He studied her curiously. "How do you know that?"

She grimaced. "I have a metal rod and a plate and many screws holding it all in place."

"My God," he whispered.

She looked down at the purse in her lap. "It took two surgeries," she remarked, "because I had complications." She looked up. "How many did yours take?"

"Just one," he said. "But mine was prompted by shrapnel from an IED. How did you get that much damage to your body?"

She managed a smile.

"If you say *proprietary information* again, I won't feed you," he threatened, but with twinkling eyes.

She shrugged. "I had an accident."

"What sort of accident?"

She glanced out the window as the plane suddenly took off and shot up into the sky. "Your pilot is very good," she remarked.

"Yes, he is," he said. "I usually fly myself, but I'm having some issues with my joints," he added curtly. "And you're changing the subject."

Her china-blue eyes met his and she smiled. "Glad you noticed."

He chuckled, defeated. "Okay. I get the idea. What sort of seafood do you like best?"

"Fried oysters," she said at once.

He laughed. "I have to confess, that's mine, too."

"My dad used to cook them," she recalled fondly. "It was one of just a handful of things he could cook, but he was good at it. My mother taught us both how to cook." Her eyes were sad. "I still miss her."

"I miss my own mother. Nobody else is ever as proud of your accomplishments."

"Or loves you as much," she agreed. She sighed. "If she'd died in her bed, or in a wreck, maybe it would have been easier to handle. But falling overboard on a ship," she added sadly. "You never really know."

"I like what you did," he said. "Putting her favorite things in an urn and setting it on the mantel. It's a novel solution."

"I'd forgotten that I told you that."

He cocked his head. "What did she look like?"

"She was beautiful," she said, her eyes bright with memory. "She had pale blue eyes and jet-black hair, wavy and long, down to her waist in back. She was always laughing."

He frowned. "Then where do your china-blue eyes come from?"

"From my dad," she said, laughing. "He was blond, believe it or not."

"Genetics are fascinating."

"I know. I might have had blond children, if…well, if I'd married someone with a recessive gene for light eyes and hair…" Her voice trailed off.

"You wanted kids."

She nodded, her eyes on the clouds drifting by the window. "A forlorn hope. One man who didn't want children, and another who was one step short of homicide." She sighed. "I can sure pick 'em."

"Everybody makes mistakes," he remarked.

She glanced at him. "Even you?"

He averted his eyes. One big, beautiful hand smoothed over the fabric of his jeans, where he had one leg crossed over the other. "I was young and rich, and it never occurred to me that some women would do anything for money. I got mixed up with what I thought was a poor but honest girl who was being tormented by a boyfriend." He laughed shortly. "It turned out that the boyfriend was actually her husband and partner in crime. He took some incriminating photos and tried to blackmail me."

Her eyes widened. "What did you do?"

"I gave him the mailing address of one of the better tabloids."

"What?" she burst out and laughed.

He grinned. "He was shell-shocked. I also asked for copies that I could frame for my wall at home. He was very unsettled. So was she."

"You should have given their names to that show that does the segments about especially dumb criminals."

"They were both young and stupid," he said simply. "My mother's attorney was able to convince them that it would be safer to forget the whole thing and provide them with the negatives. Which they did."

She was listening, fascinated. "Did money change hands?"

He shook his head. "They were too relieved not to be going to prison to think about demanding money."

"Good grief," she exclaimed.

"I had my attorney recommend counseling, and I paid for it. The young man is now a rising attorney in a Houston law firm, and the young woman graduated with honors and is now teaching history at a high school in San Antonio."

She whistled.

"My mother always looked for the good in people, not the bad," he said. "The counseling was her idea. She kept in touch with both of them while they were going to the psychologist. I learned a lot from her about how to deal with people."

"How did she die?" she asked softly.

His eyes were wounded before he averted them. "She had a horse that she loved dearly. She was an expert rider. But it had been raining the day she went out on her favorite mount. The horse missed its footing on a hill and rolled on her." He winced. "She loved Clydesdales."

"One of the biggest breeds of horses," she realized.

"Yes. I wanted to have the horse put down. I was grieving, raging, drunk as a skunk. My foreman hid the horse until I calmed down enough to listen to reason. He was a lay minister in his spare time." He smiled. "He sat me down and explained life to me. Things happen for a reason. We all die. Nobody gets out alive. We have a purpose. When it's our time, it's our time. Things like that." He shrugged. "I finally listened. He was a good man."

"Is he still your foreman?"

He shook his head. "He was like me. Patriotic. We enlisted together. I came home. He didn't."

She winced. "I'm so sorry."

"So was I."

She frowned, watching him. "You enlisted after you lost your mother," she guessed.

He nodded.

"Didn't your father object?"

His face hardened. "I don't speak of my father. Not ever."

"Oh. Sorry."

He drew in a long breath. "It was all a long time ago. Except for the war wounds that ache when it rains, I'm pretty much over it."

She smiled sadly. "I wish I could say that." Her hand went involuntarily to her hip.

He saw that. "Painful?"

She nodded.

"Do you have something to take for it?"

"Ibuprofen," she replied. "But it makes me drowsy, and I'd prefer not to try to eat while I'm sleeping."

He chuckled. "Idiot. How can you enjoy food when you're in pain?"

"I don't have much appetite as a rule anyway."

"Do you have the ibuprofen in your purse?"

She made a face.

He reached into a compartment beside him and came out with a soft drink. "Take the pill."

She sighed. "I would, but I don't dare take it except with food."

"I forgot."

"I'll take the soft drink, though," she added with a smile. "I'm thirsty."

He chuckled. "Me, too." He handed her the can and got another out for himself.

"You don't drink beer?" she asked, noting that what he chose for himself wasn't alcoholic.

"I hate alcohol," he said, and his eyes reflected it.

She wondered at the violence in his tone as he said it and she wondered if he had an alcoholic parent in his background. It couldn't be his mother; he'd loved her dearly. It had to be the father that he wouldn't talk about.

Well, after all, she was reticent about her ex-husband and the way he'd treated her. It was too early in their relationship for buried secrets.

"I'm not fond of it myself," she said belatedly. "I don't like the taste and it's not a good idea to take it when I'm on powerful anti-inflammatories. Like drinking battery acid," she added with an amused smile.

He smiled back. "I get your point."

"Do you take anti-inflammatories?" she asked.

He nodded. "Very few, though. My injuries weren't in joints."

One side of her pretty mouth pulled down. "Mine were. My hip and my thigh. It messed up my knee, too, but not badly enough to need rebuilding."

He frowned. "It must have been one hell of an injury."

She thought back to the fall, to the agony she'd felt until she'd been found and transported to the hospital. Then the endless hours of tests and surgery and recovery, and then more surgery due to complications following the first surgery.

"It was," she said flatly.

His pale silver eyes narrowed on her face. She looked as if she'd visited hell and come away with memories that wouldn't die. He knew how that felt. But it disturbed him that someone had deliberately hurt her. He was fairly certain that it had been her second husband, who was now out of jail and after her.

"Did he hit you with something?" Jake asked her abruptly. "To cause those injuries," he added.

She met his eyes. "No."

"Then how…?"

She swallowed, hard. "He picked me up and threw me over the side in a parking garage, onto the ground below," she said finally.

CHAPTER FIVE

JAKE STARED AT her with absolute horror. "He what?" he burst out, enraged.

She shrugged. "He said I deserved it. We'd been to a party and the hostess's husband danced with me. He was twenty years my senior. Just a very nice man, nothing out of the way. Bailey was livid. We'd been married less than a week, at the time."

"Did you have him arrested?"

"Nobody saw it," she said simply. "He was at the hospital every minute, telling everyone how guilty he felt that I'd accidentally fallen and he couldn't get to me in time."

"What a piece of work," he muttered.

She sighed. "He was very good at lying. He could convince people that black was white. I had no comeback. I'd been so crazy about him that I could hardly believe he'd done it. But the feelings I had for him were already long gone, completely gone. He tortured me, in ways I don't even like remembering. Then after the fall, when I got out of rehab, I was trying to recuperate from the surgery, but that didn't save me. So I had to have another surgery, to repair the new damage." Her eyes closed. "I tried leaving once, but he brought me back and made violent threats about what he'd do if I tried it again. I was terrified of him.

I knew he meant it. I was so weak and in so much pain that I didn't have the strength to try again." She stared down at her hands. "A few months after we married, I smiled at a man in a restaurant who'd been kind enough to pick up the purse I'd accidentally dropped. When we got into the parking lot, Bailey drew back his fist and knocked me winding. But this time there were witnesses. They had to pull him off me," she added, shivering. "I thought he was going to kill me. The police came. He was arrested and taken to jail. I refused to bail him out. I called my first husband's attorneys and they handled the divorce." Her eyes closed. "I've been afraid of men ever since."

"No damned wonder." He was outraged. "What sort of weasel does that to a woman?" he asked angrily.

"A coward," she replied simply. "He was afraid of other men. He wouldn't say a word to someone who made him mad. He'd come home and take it out on me. At least there was finally proof of what he was doing to me. It was such a relief to be able to go to sleep and not worry if I'd live until morning."

"They should never have let him out of jail," he bit off.

"He served his time. They had to let him out." She looked back out the window. "At least I have people watching out for me on the ranch."

"Yes."

"I'm sorry," she said, noting his hard face and glittering eyes. "I've ruined our dinner before we even got to it."

His eyes caught hers. "I'm sorry for what he did to you," he said quietly. "I'm glad you told me the truth."

She smiled sadly. "I don't lie well. I was raised to believe that lies are evil."

He chuckled. "I was raised that way, too, but there

are times when lying is an absolute virtue. I mean, if a woman asks you if a dress makes her look fat, and it really does…"

She burst out laughing. "I guess that would be one of those times when lying is the right choice."

"Absolutely." His eyes twinkled. "I like hearing you laugh."

She flushed. "I don't do it much anymore."

"You will when you taste this seafood. We're coming into the airport at Galveston right now, in fact," he said, indicating the view in the window as the pilot turned toward the landing strip.

"Fried oysters," she said, almost dreamily.

"Not to mention the best hush puppies in three states."

"I can't wait!"

He chuckled. "Me, too."

THE RESTAURANT WAS a tiny little place in a strip mall. A stretch limo had been waiting for them at the landing strip. The driver let them out at the front door and went off to park so he could settle in with a good book until he was paged.

"I love this," Ida remarked, her eyes on the fishnets and small anchors and other nautical stuff that adorned the walls.

"So do I. It's one of my favorite restaurants. Not a lot of people know about it, either, so it's not overcrowded."

"I like that best of all," she remarked as the waitress came to lead them to a table in a corner.

She took their order for drinks, which was coffee, and provided menus while she went to get the coffee.

"Decisions, decisions," she said, shaking her head as she read down the menu.

"Oysters," he reminded her with a chuckle.

She sighed. "Yes. Oysters. But there's so much more!"

He watched her enthusing over the menu with pleasure. It was such a simple thing to bring that smile to her lovely face. He liked the woman he was getting to know. He hoped that he wasn't being taken in by her charm. It was hard for him to trust people. She really knew very little about his own background, although there were still a few people in Catelow who had known his father. His face hardened just at the memory. He'd never forgiven his father for what had happened. He was certain that he never would.

Ida wouldn't understand how he felt. Her parents had been, apparently, very much in love with each other and happy together. His earliest memories were of violent arguments that became physical. Eventually they became tragically physical. He knew more about domestic abuse than she realized. But he didn't trust her enough to tell her. Not yet. He kept secrets.

She peered over the menu and saw the anger and hurt in his expression before he could wipe them away.

"Have I said something wrong?" she asked at once, assuming that if he was troubled, she'd caused it.

What a hell of a life she'd had, he thought. "It's nothing to do with you," he said gently. "Bad memories."

"Oh." She smiled faintly. "I have those, too."

"Where is he now? Your ex-husband."

Her face clouded. "He's in Denver. My attorneys are having him watched. Just in case."

"You mean, just in case he comes after you," he guessed.

She sighed. "Something like that."

"Has he spoken to you?"

"If you can call threats speaking," she conceded. "He thinks that because I have so much money, he's entitled to a share of it."

"After what he did to you?" he asked, startled.

"Oh, in his mind, it was all my fault," she replied. "I caused him to lose his temper by flirting with other men." She looked at him evenly. "I never did it deliberately in those days. I was too afraid of Bailey. I only do it now to keep men from coming too close. It usually works."

"Usually." He smiled.

"There's always the rare exception, like that man at the party Pam Simpson had for Mina Michaels, before she married Cort Grier," she added. She grimaced. "I thought it was safe to flirt with him, because he was married. His poor wife! She was in tears and I felt so miserable about it. I didn't know what to say to her, how to explain what I'd done. I truly could have kicked her husband," she added coldly.

"You created a reputation for yourself," he reminded her. "It's hard for people not to take you at face value."

"I was afraid," she said heavily. "So afraid that if I'd find someone else, that I'd be tempted again. There was a journalist, after I divorced Bailey," she recalled, not noticing the suddenly stiff posture of the man across from her. "He was kind and sweet, but he liked danger. He was drawn to combat zones, and he said he could never settle to a nine-to-five job." She lowered her eyes. "I ran. I was very attracted to him, but I'd lost the ability to judge character and I couldn't trust my own feelings." She looked up. "He was killed in one of the incursions overseas, following a story for his magazine. So maybe it was just as well, the way things worked out."

He fingered his hot coffee cup without looking at her. He'd felt a skirl of jealousy. He wasn't happy about it.

"You went around with Cort Grier before he got involved with Mina."

She laughed. "Yes. He wasn't what I expected at all. He was nice. He didn't even make a pass at me. We just sat and talked about life and played chess occasionally."

Both eyebrows arched.

She saw that. "Yes, I know, I fall into bed with every man who asks, and Cort was a known playboy..."

"I didn't mean to be insulting," he said. "Mina's still a sore spot with me." He grimaced and sipped coffee. "I kept hoping she wasn't serious about him. She liked me, but not in the way I wanted her to. She was the most unique woman I'd ever known."

"She really is unique," she said, fighting down waves of jealousy. He hadn't gotten over Mina at all, and she'd better remember it. "I read about some of her exploits. I hope Cort's going to be able to keep her close to home."

He chuckled. "The baby's doing that," he said. "She really doesn't want to go crawling through jungles with a child to raise. So her commandos go out on missions and come back and tell her all about them." He shook his head. "I met them at the christening. They're a great bunch. Most have families of their own."

"Funny, you don't think about commandos having families. I mean, it's a high-risk profession, right?"

"Very high risk." His eyes took on a faraway look,

full of remembered horror. "We found one of them at an outpost we were occupying. The insurgents had…" He stopped abruptly before he told her what had been done to the man. It wasn't fit conversation for anyone who hadn't been in combat.

"It was something very awful, I gather?" she asked.

"Very awful," he conceded.

She smiled. "Thanks for not sharing it. I don't have a strong stomach."

"You must, to be able to understand quantum mechanics," he teased.

She laughed. "It's mostly mathematics," she pointed out. "I had a good brain for that."

"So did I, years ago. Now my head is filled with weight-gain ratios and marketing strategies."

"It's still math," she reminded him.

"So it is." He studied her quietly. "You could still teach."

"What, quantum mechanics?" she teased.

"No. High school math. Or science. Or both."

She made a face. "It would require more education, and I don't want to bury myself in academia. I like having free time. Maybe it's frivolous, but I've spent a lot of years in what felt like confinement."

"Do you like to travel?"

"Oh, yes," she said at once. "When I was married to Charles, I climbed up to Machu Picchu in Peru, I walked all over Chichen Itza in Mexico, I followed in the steps of Zane Grey in Arizona, I stood at the ruins of Great Zimbabwe in Africa, and traced Rommel's advance in Algeria…"

"Whoa," he said at once. "Rommel?"

"World War II, North Africa campaign, 1942," she said.

"Well, damn!"

He was cursing, but he was smiling. "Is it an interest of yours?" she asked.

"My grandfather was with Patton's division in Africa. Rommel had already gone back to Germany, sick, but his strategies were still being followed. My grandfather came back full of stories about Rommel that he had from other soldiers and from German captives. It fascinated me as a boy."

She laughed. "My dad was a history buff. One of his relatives, not sure which one, fought in North Africa, as well." She smiled. "Small world."

"Isn't it?" he chuckled.

They finished supper. Then Jake had the driver take them out to a long stretch of deserted beach. They got out, while the driver settled in with his book.

Ida took off her shoes and walked barefoot in the sand, her eyes on the glistening waves, the half-moon bright in the distance.

"Pirates must have sailed here in the distant past," she mused as they walked along.

"No doubt. These days it's good for deep-sea fishing."

"I've never been. I can't imagine trying to pull in something that weighs fifty or sixty pounds."

He glanced at her. She had a small frame, although she was medium height, and her injuries would never allow her to do such a strenuous thing as deep-sea fishing. "It would be difficult for you. Those fish fight back, and it takes a lot of strength to land one."

She turned to him. "You've done it," she guessed.

He chuckled. "I have. I pulled in a marlin that weighed a lot more than sixty pounds. By the time I got him aboard,

I was sweating and shivering with strained muscles and all out of my best cusswords."

"Did you have him mounted?" she asked.

"I tossed him back in."

"You did?"

He laughed at her expression. "I don't take trophies."

She smiled. "I knew you were a nice man."

"Nice." He rolled his eyes and started walking again.

"It's not a bad word," she pointed out. "Would you rather be thought of as a scoundrel?"

"In my experience, scoundrels have a lot more fun than nice men."

"I don't know," she sighed. "I've pretty much had my fill of scoundrels." She moved forward, a little gingerly, but the ibuprofen was doing its job. So she danced in and out of the foaming surf, laughing, her face almost radiant in the moonlight, her pretty figure outlined without the coat she'd left in the car, which she hadn't really needed here. But the water was still cold, because it was October.

"You're going to catch cold," he told her. "It's too cool for wading."

"Spoilsport," she teased. "I'm having fun. Don't spoil it."

"When you're sneezing your head off and coughing…"

"I know, don't blame you. Don't worry. I won't." She laughed. "Life is short," she said, dancing back into the water. "I'm going to live it to the very fullest. Nobody is guaranteed tomorrow, you know."

He felt an odd sense of kinship with her. He'd lost his mother, whom he'd loved dearly. She'd lost her own parents. They were both orphans. Adult orphans without anyone to share their triumphs and tragedies.

She glanced at him, curious. "What's wrong?"

"I was just thinking that we're both orphans."

She stopped playing in the surf and came back to stand just in front of him, holding her shoes in one hand. "We are, aren't we?"

He bent, framing her pretty, flushed face in his lean, beautiful hands. "All alone in the dark…"

His mouth brushed over hers with a tenderness that brought stinging tears to her eyes. She stood very still, so that he wouldn't stop.

But he felt the tears in his mouth and lifted his head, shocked.

"Why?" he asked, worrying that he was going too fast.

"I'm not used to it."

"Used to what, Ida?"

She swallowed. "Tenderness."

He smiled. "You might not believe it, but neither am I."

"I'll bet you leave trails of brokenhearted women behind."

"I used to. Not anymore." He sighed. "I'm tired of buying the facsimile of affection with expensive gifts."

Her small hand went up to his cheek and drew it down. In the moonlight, she could see the anguish on his hard face. She was certain that he disguised it in humor with most people. But with her, he could let his guard down. It made her proud.

"We've both lived through tragedies," she said.

He caught her hand and pressed it to his mouth. He scowled. "How do you know that I have?"

"You have an expressive face, when you're not pretending," she said simply and gave him a sad smile. "I guess people who've known tragedy can see it in other people."

"Not many have ever seen mine," he said curtly. Not even Mina had noticed, and she was sensitive.

"Or mine," she agreed. "Most people have enough trauma in their own lives, without adding my bad memories to them."

He smiled faintly, fascinated by her. "That's the way I feel."

Her fingers traced his chiseled mouth. He dazzled her. "I don't think I've felt safe with a man since my first husband died," she said in a soft, husky tone.

He glared at her. No man wanted a woman to feel just safe. He wanted her to feel passionate, hungry, all those things.

She laughed softly. "Bad choice of words," she said, when she saw the irritation he wasn't bothering to hide. "Let me rephrase it. You're the first man I'm not afraid of."

"Oh."

It was only the one word, but his face relaxed and lost its brief anger.

"I know that you won't hurt me," she added. She smiled. "It may not seem like much to you, but it's a world of difference to me."

He cocked his head. "You don't flirt with me," he pointed out.

"You'd see right through it if I did," she replied. "You're a no-nonsense man most of the time. Hard, when you have to be, but compassionate and kind."

There was a faint ruddy flush on his high cheekbones.

"Now I've put my foot in my mouth again," she sighed, grimacing.

"You see too deep," he said simply.

"I get it," she replied. She smiled up at him. "No peeking under that mask you wear, right?"

"Right," he returned. She made him uncomfortable with her surprising insight. He didn't want people close. Not emotionally close. His only lapse had been Mina, whom he'd loved.

She studied his drifting expressions with fascination. "You don't want anybody close emotionally, do you?" she asked slowly. "I mean, I know you cared deeply for Mina. But you had to fight your instincts even with her. Somebody hurt you deeply, scarred you."

He withdrew his hand. He was glaring at her now.

She moved away discreetly and turned back toward the ocean. The moon made a trail of sparkling light in its wake. The waves ran into the shore noisily with whitecaps grasping the white sand only for an instant before the ocean dragged them back out to sea.

"It's so beautiful," she said, her back to him. "My first husband was fond of beaches, and he had houses in Jamaica and the Bahamas, where I could stay when I liked. I spent a lot of time wading in the surf, just like here." She ran back to the surf and danced in and out of the foaming whitecaps until her hip started to protest.

She made a face and turned, walking slowly back to Jake, who had both hands in his pockets. He was still scowling, but now his attention was on Ida, not the past.

"You're limping," he noted.

She made a face. "I know better than to go dancing

with waves," she said and laughed softly. "My hip won't permit much of that. Everything aches when I overdo."

He moved closer. "Hurting?" he asked softly.

She nodded. She bent to put her shoes down and bit back a groan.

"Here. Lean on me."

She did, while she got her feet back into her shoes. "Stupid, running through the waves like that," she confessed.

"Which I mentioned," he pointed out.

She drew in a breath. "So you did."

"Was it just your hip and thigh?" he asked quietly.

She sighed. "Mostly."

He was reading between the lines. A fall like hers must have produced a lot of injuries. More than she'd admitted to. "And they let your damned husband out of jail," he growled.

"Ex-husband," she reminded him. "Very ex."

"So he is."

She started to walk toward the car, very slowly and with obvious pain.

"Come here," he said gently. He bent and lifted her, holding her close while he walked.

She looked up at his square chin, nicely shaven, and the scent of expensive cologne wafted down into her nostrils. He was warm and very strong. She'd never felt so safe in her whole life. She curled into him, her arms around his neck, and laid her cheek on his broad chest.

That soft submission made his heart race, hardened his body. He was being drawn into a raging passion that he didn't want to feel. He still adored Mina. There was no room in his life for another woman.

But this one was soft, and cuddly, and damaged, and she appealed to him in ways he didn't quite understand. He was wary of her. She had a scarlet reputation and he didn't trust her. Was she pretending? But why would she need to? She had money of her own. She was rich. She wouldn't be chasing him for anything he had.

He was very quiet. She could feel his heart going at her ear, feel the wild beat of it. He was attracted to her. It made her feel like a girl again, all tingly and fascinated. But she was uncertain. Her second husband had been like this, tender and protective and kind. And once they were married, behind closed doors he became a monster.

Her arms loosened their grip and she stiffened, just a little. She couldn't afford to give in to desire. It was treacherous, even with a man who seemed safe.

Jake noted the stiffening. Apparently, she was as uncertain as he was. Just as well. He wasn't going in head-first again, not with a woman who drew gossip like this one did.

He put her down gently at the back door, which the driver was holding open for them. He helped her in and slid in beside her, nodding to the driver.

As THEY DROVE back toward the airport, he noticed the pain on her face.

"Do you have anything left to take for it with you?" he asked.

She turned her head, surprised.

"Any of the ibuprofen," he clarified.

She grimaced. "I only had one tablet with me. I left the rest at home. I didn't think I'd need it. I'm all right," she added quickly. "It's just a little twinge, nothing major." But she was lying through her teeth. She should never have run through the surf, no matter how tempting it was.

"It won't take us long to get home," he said. She worried him. He didn't like that. Most women left him cold. He'd been a rounder in his younger days, interested in women only for their bodies and not much more. Most of the females in his set were sophisticated and out for an evening of indifferent pleasure, much as he'd been.

But these days he was thinking about a family, a place to belong, a woman to belong to. He'd never wanted children until he'd gone around with Mina. He could picture her as a mother, holding a baby and loving it. Loving him. But that hadn't happened. He'd adored Mina. She'd liked him, but only as a friend.

It had made him bitter and sad when he lost her to the Texas cattle baron. All his wealth and power had meant nothing at all to her. Mina wasn't mercenary, as most of his casual affairs had been.

The woman beside him in the back of the limousine was much the same, he realized with some surprise. She had money of her own, but she didn't sport expensive clothes or expensive gems. She wore a gold ring with a small emerald on her right hand and a midrange watch on her left wrist. There was also a Celtic cross on a gold chain. Puzzling, for a scarlet woman to wear such a thing. But he was becoming convinced that whatever Ida was, it wasn't a scarlet woman.

"You don't wear your wealth," he said abruptly.

She laughed, surprised. "No. I'm not like the Navajo, who really do wear their wealth," she said quietly.

"They do. I served with a man who had a fortune in turquoise and silver on his person, antique jewelry." His face hardened. "He died beside me, in Iraq."

Her breath caught. "He was your friend."

He nodded. "It was a blow. There were plenty of others…" He stopped and glanced at her. "I don't like to talk about it."

She smiled. "I won't ask," she assured him. "I have my own bad memories. I don't speak of them, either."

He didn't know what to say. So he said nothing.

IT WASN'T A long flight. At least, it didn't seem long. Ida and Jake spent the time discussing the upcoming local political race. Both were surprised to note that they felt the same way about the issues. They moved on to national government, and still they were in agreement.

He laughed. "I never pictured you as a conservative," he said.

She grinned. "I don't act like one, do I? Appearances can be deceiving."

"Tell me about it." He studied her quietly at her front door, his head tilted to one side, his eyes hidden under the wide brim of his hat. "This was fun."

"It really was," she agreed. She was hurting rather badly, but she didn't show it. She didn't want pity from this man. "Thanks."

He shrugged. "We might do it again one day."

That was disappointing, because he sounded as if he

was putting her off. She just smiled. She had cold feet, too. "That would be nice."

"Well," he said, not moving closer. "Good night. I'll let you get back to your pain medication. I expect you're hurting."

She swallowed. "Quite a lot, I'm afraid. It was worth the pain. I loved dancing in the surf," she added softly.

"I enjoyed it all."

She smiled up at him. "Then good night."

She hesitated for just a second, but he didn't come a step closer. She unlocked her door and went inside.

He stood on her porch, his emotions in turmoil, his mind whirling. He'd wanted to kiss her good-night. So why hadn't he?

Because he didn't trust her. She could be the reticent woman he'd squired around tonight, or she could be putting on an act. Had her husband really been brutal to her, or was she not telling the truth about him? Suppose she'd fallen accidentally, as her ex-husband had claimed, and she'd had him sent to jail out of spite, or distaste, or for some other reason?

He didn't know her. She seemed to be a lot of things that appealed to him, but he was wary of traps. He'd had his adventures with women who seemed like one thing and were actually something much worse.

He turned and went back to the waiting limousine. Maybe he'd take her out again one day. Or maybe he wouldn't. Just as he got into the car, he noticed her new foreman loping up onto the front porch and knocking on the door.

He saw Ida smile at the man as she opened it and let him in. It closed behind them.

Jake told the driver to go on. He felt angry. She was having a visitor at this hour, behind closed doors. The man, her so-called bodyguard, was handsome and well built. She'd welcomed him, although supposedly in great pain with her hip.

He laughed coldly to himself. He was certain that he never wanted to see Ida again.

CHAPTER SIX

"WHAT'S GOING ON?" Ida asked Laredo as she closed the front door behind him.

"We've had a break-in," he told her quietly. "Somebody got past the security cameras and beat one of the horses. He's got deep cuts on his flanks, just like Gold."

"Again?" she exclaimed. "Which horse?" she added in horror.

"The one you call Rory," he replied. "The saddle horse."

She was sorry about Rory, but she was fondest of Gold and Silver, and she felt guilty at being relieved that it wasn't Silver.

"What have you done about it?" she asked.

"Had the vet come out," he said. "I figured that's what you'd want me to do."

"Of course," she said. She bit her lower lip. "Did you call Sheriff Banks?" she added.

He looked faintly irritated. "No."

"Well, do it," she said angrily. "Bailey isn't getting away with this! If there's evidence that points to him, the sheriff is the obvious one to look for it. He has an investigator. Ask him to bring the man with him."

"I'll do that," he said.

"Two horses with injuries within a month," she said, her eyes blazing with anger. "I want security cameras everywhere. I don't care what it costs! Get some of those trail cameras that hunters use. They're Wi-Fi capable and they record everything. Make sure they have Wi-Fi and color and night vision."

"Okay," he said.

"Damn," she bit off. "Any man who'd hurt a helpless animal should be put on the rack!"

"Wrong century," he pointed out.

She glared at him. "Jail, then, and for years."

He shrugged. "Some men don't like animals."

"Yes, but on this ranch, nobody is going to injure one. Get busy."

"Yes, ma'am," he said in his lazy drawl. "I'll get right on it."

He went out the door and Ida cursed until she ran out of bad words. It wasn't until she'd gone to bed that she realized Jake had still been sitting in the yard in his limousine when she let Laredo into the house.

She groaned inwardly. That was going to look bad. The bodyguard was well built and handsome, and Jake already didn't quite trust her. What had he thought? If he thought Ida had something going with Laredo, he might not come back.

That thought haunted her. She'd already become fascinated with Jake, who seemed to be everything a true man should be. But he didn't trust her, and that was part of any relationship; there had to be trust. She wondered how in the world she could win his.

THE PAIN HAD been bad. She'd gone out to see Rory, her saddle horse, and winced at the deep cuts on his flanks. She stood beside the vet while he used a local and stitched them, muttering about the inhumanity of some people. She agreed with him, angry herself that it could have happened twice. She mentioned that to the vet, who said that he'd be happy to testify if she could find the scoundrel who was responsible. She said she'd talk to the sheriff the very next day and follow up on Laredo's call to him.

Later, when she was certain that Rory would heal, and when she'd checked worriedly on Gold, recovering in a nearby stall from similar injuries, she'd taken the ibuprofen with a few crackers and cheese, and an antacid. It was helping. It didn't stop the pain entirely, but it was effective. At least it would deal with the inflammation.

There were narcotics that would have done a better job for pain, but Ida wouldn't ask for them. She had no wish to become addicted to something that probably wouldn't work for very long anyway. Anti-inflammatories were quite effective, and the pain was something she'd learned to live with.

She closed her eyes and finally fell asleep.

The next morning she was awakened by a knock at the door. When she opened it, in her long, concealing thick robe, she found Sheriff Banks on the porch.

He tipped his hat. There was a quiet, friendly smile on his face. The sheriff was ultraconservative and he'd known Ida only by reputation when she'd first moved back to Catelow. He'd talked to Cindy, who filled him in about her reclusive neighbor. And the night Cody had talked with her, when her screams had led Cindy to call the sheriff, a lot of his misgivings about the divorcée had been laid to rest.

Sheriff Cody Banks was tall, dark-eyed, dark-haired, a handsome man with a rodeo rider's physique. Authority sat on him like a mantle. He was afraid of nothing on earth, and he'd been sheriff of Carne County for over nine years, reelected every time he ran with a unanimous vote. He was incorruptible, which kept him in office.

Ida invited him inside.

"Your cowboy said you had a suspicious injury to a horse," he said without preamble.

"Yes," she replied, all business. She folded her arms over her breasts. It was still uncomfortable being alone with a strange man. She trusted no one these days. "First it was one of my palominos. Now it's my older saddle horse. Both have deep cuts on their flanks, but there's no way they could have been injured accidentally."

He pushed his hat back over his thick dark hair. "You think it was done intentionally?"

"Yes." She shifted uncomfortably. "I'm sorry. I have to sit down," she said after a minute. "I have metal screws in my hip and metal screws holding a metal rod into the bone in my thigh. This cold weather makes for a lot of pain." She sat down, grimacing as the simple act sent a bolt of pain right through her body.

Cody scowled. "You never told me what sort of injury would cause that much reconstructive surgery," he said flatly.

She sighed. "Being thrown over the side of a parking garage. It works quite well."

He looked shocked. "That's what your ex-husband did to you?" he added, outrage showing on his hard face.

"My ex-husband," she agreed simply. "All the wealth is mine. He felt he was entitled to half of it. I divorced him while he was in jail awaiting trial for assault. There were no witnesses the first time, when he threw me over the wall, but he made the mistake of slugging me in front of a witness a few weeks after I got out of the hospital." Her face was drawn with pain and bad memories. "He was supposed to serve five years for it, out of a longer sentence, but they let him out in three for good behavior." She laughed without humor. "He phoned me the day he got out, demanding money again." She looked up. The sheriff seemed unsettled. "He said some gangsters are after him for a gambling debt, and I owe him because he went to jail on my testimony." She gave him a sardonic smile. "The photos and X-rays of my injuries were fairly convincing to the jury that convicted him."

"Good Lord," he said heavily. He hadn't known all this about her. The bare facts he'd been told by her the night she was screaming from a nightmare were nebulous at best, not explicit. Despite all that, he was still just a little wary of her because of her reputation.

"I see," she mused, studying him. "You're still buying into my masquerade. It probably was a stupid idea, but at least it keeps most men at bay." She wrapped her arms around herself again. "I never want to end up in a relationship like that again, and I seem to have no judgment about men at all. So it's easier to keep them at a distance."

He cocked his head. "I don't quite get it."

She gave him a worldly look. "I'm just dynamite for all men, and I judge their performances and gossip about them. I'm very vocal about my so-called ex-lovers. Most men won't risk the damage to their reputations, so they find excuses not to pursue me. It's a double-edged sword, but it does actually work quite well as a deterrent." She put a hand to her back and grimaced. "Probably won't be necessary for a lot longer. I expect the pain or the anti-inflammatories will kill me one day anyway."

He was getting a very different picture of Ida than the one he'd carried. He did remember the screams when her neighbor called him and said Ida must be in danger. She'd met him at the door, very quiet and pale, and said that it was just a nightmare. He hadn't questioned it or said anything much to her. She'd told him about her ex-husband, but not a great deal. Now he began to understand the nightmares.

"So that was why," he murmured out loud.

"Excuse me?"

"The nightmares."

SHE RECALLED THE night he'd come to check on her. She grimaced and nodded. "Life with Bailey Trent was quite memorable," she replied quietly. "Beatings were only the tip of the iceberg." She looked up at him with cold eyes. "Men can be animals. Worse than animals."

"They can," he had to admit. "I've seen my share of wife beaters. I've locked up quite a few and sent several to prison. I hate a man who takes out his anger on a woman or a child."

She'd heard that he was notorious for his pursuit of such offenders. It made her feel safer. "Bailey has made threats," she said. "My attorneys in Denver have an operative who's keeping track of him, since he lives in the city. But they felt I was in more danger here, so they insisted that I have a bodyguard. The man who spoke to you about the horse, Laredo, is the man they hired on my behalf."

"A bodyguard." His dark eyes narrowed and he nodded. "Not a bad idea. You're pretty isolated here, and in bad weather, it might take us a while to get to you, even though we have chains and plenty of experience driving in snow. It's just that accidents multiply. Some people come here from warmer climates. They don't adjust quickly to bad road conditions."

"I know what you mean," she replied. "My first husband and I spent a week in the Appalachian Mountains, in north Georgia. It snowed just a couple of inches, and the local police were overwhelmed with collisions." She shook her head. "I wonder how in the world they'd fare out here, where snow is measured in feet."

"Badly, I expect," he said, and he smiled for the first time. "Your bodyguard, the law firm checked him out, of course?"

"I'm sure they did," she replied. "They've looked after me very well all these years. They manage my estate."

"They're civil attorneys, not criminal, right?"

"Right. Estate planners, things like that."

He didn't say anything, but he had a strange expression on his face.

"They have a firm of detectives that they employ," she said quickly, anticipating his next remark. "It's a very good one. They check out new employees for the firm, as well." She smiled.

He laughed. "You read my mind."

"Not so much." She cocked her head. "I wouldn't mind playing poker with you, Sheriff," she added.

He made a face. "I'd lose my shirt. I don't have a poker face, although I've tried to manage one." His dark eyes narrowed. "If you don't mind a personal question, how did your first husband die?"

"Suicide," she said simply.

"It must have been a shock," he said.

"He was a lovely man," she recalled with a tender smile. "He was educated, talented, loved the arts. He taught me so much. I'd have done anything for him." She drew in an angry breath. "When he died, his lover tried to sue the estate for pain and suffering. I turned my husband's attorneys loose on him. He ended up paying court costs. He lost his shirt. He ended badly, in another relationship. I must tell you, I never shed a tear. My poor husband. He never deserved to be treated so badly, when he was such a kind and generous man."

Cody was still assimilating all the information. It shocked him. Most women would have been furious when they found out about a husband who cheated on them. This one was outraged that her husband had been badly treated by his lover.

"As you might imagine," she mused, "I came away from my marriage untouched. And then I met Bailey." Her face hardened. "I was grieving for my late husband and Bailey was masculine and exciting and full of mischief. I thought he was the perfect man. I married him the second week we dated. And I learned the true meaning of physical abuse in ways I wish I could erase from my mind." She stared at her hands in her lap. "I never dreamed a man would treat me like that."

He was reading between the lines. He'd been in law enforcement for a long time. "After the fall from the parking lot, did you have him arrested?"

"He was at the hospital every day, bringing flowers, telling everyone how guilty he felt because he couldn't get to me in time to save me. He was very convincing. By the time I was through the surgery and out from under the anesthesia, he'd convinced everyone on staff, including my surgeon, that he was the perfect husband. Who would believe that he picked me up and threw me over the wall?" She sighed. "I was lucky, at that, that it was only one story up and not more, and that I landed in grass and not on concrete."

Cody cursed under his breath.

"So he made the mistake of attacking me again, in public. But this time there was a witness. He was arrested and prosecuted and sentenced. I divorced him while he was in prison, with a little help from my attorneys. And I also cut him out of my will. He may not be aware of that just yet. The injuries to my horses may be a veiled threat that I could meet with an accident that might be fatal. I wouldn't put it past him. Hence the bodyguard."

"I see your point. Your cowboys will know about the horses' injuries?"

"They will. Laredo especially. He's worked on ranches. He's good with livestock, although I don't think he's really crazy about horses like I am," she added. "He doesn't seem to get attached to them, and he does the job, but he's not, well, affectionate toward them."

He chuckled. "A lot of men have trouble expressing affection."

"My first husband didn't," she said softly. "He was always hugging me, bringing me things, spoiling me. I couldn't figure out why he never kissed me or wanted to be a true husband to me. I was very naive and very sheltered. I thought I must smell bad or look repulsive to him or something," she recalled with a sad smile. "I didn't know the truth until he died. He left me the sweetest note." She stopped, choking up. It took her a minute to recover, during which she averted wet eyes and a grieving expression. "He left everything to me, and there was a lot. Stocks, bonds, property, the business." She sighed. "I'd rather have had him."

He had a new image of her. She was charming him, without even trying. "How do you manage the business?"

"I don't. My degree is in physics, not business, so I hired a manager for the business and my attorneys handle everything to do with the property and stocks and CDs."

"Physics?" he burst out.

She flushed. "Well, yes."

"Where did you study physics?"

The flush deepened. "MIT."

"And you're living on a little ranch in Wyoming?" he asked, aghast.

"I don't like cities," she said, "and I'm no teacher. I loved math. I was good at trig and calculus, and I absolutely adored Stephen Hawking and Michio Kaku."

"Theoretical physics," he mused.

She nodded. "Albert Einstein was my idol when I was in college. Amazing, what he was able to conceive in his head."

"An extraordinary man," he agreed. He shook his head. "You're not what you seem."

She laughed. "Who is?"

He got up. "Well, I'll go talk to your cowboys. My investigator quit and went back East, and I've just hired a new one, but he's not due here until tomorrow. Meanwhile, I'm doing my own investigating and leaving minor duties to my undersheriff and my five deputies. It's hectic."

"Sheriff Banks," she said, worried that she'd told him so much about herself. "What I told you…"

"Is privileged information," he said, and with a smile. "I don't gossip."

"Thanks," she said. She drew in a breath. "I haven't spoken of it in years. Only a few people know. But I never went into detail." She looked up at him. "I know that people in law enforcement see terrible things. This isn't something I'd feel comfortable talking about, to most people." She smiled shyly. "Thanks for listening."

"It wasn't a problem," he replied.

She started to get up, obviously in pain.

"Stay there," he said gently. "You don't need to come with me. I'll stop by after I've spoken to the men, and I'll let myself in, if that's all right with you."

She swallowed, hard. He was a kind man. "Thank you."

"No problem." He tipped his hat again and went out the door. Incredible woman, he was thinking, and if her ex-husband set foot in Carne County, Cody was going to arrange to have him followed if he had to hire a man out of his own pocket. Nobody was hurting that woman again, not on his watch.

IDA WAS STILL sitting where he'd left her when he came back in after a perfunctory knock.

"Your men corroborated what you told me. Your bodyguard agrees that the injuries aren't consistent with accidental injury. I'm going to speak to your vet, as well, if you don't mind."

"I don't," she replied. "I worry about my breeding pair, Silver and Gold. Gold was the first to be injured, and she's still recuperating. Silver is her mate. They're special. I'm fond of all my horses, but those two..." She ground her teeth together. "I'm worried sick about Silver..."

"Let me take them both over to Ren Colter's ranch for you. He has state-of-the-art protection for his horses and he hates the thought of anybody who'd injure a helpless animal. He has J.C. Calhoun working for him. Calhoun, like a number of Ren's employees, is an ex-mercenary. They protected Ren's wife from a contract killer some years ago."

"It would be an imposition…"

He chuckled. "I took the liberty of calling Ren, out on the porch before I came in. He said he'd send his men over with two horse trailers for your palominos. He has a place for both of them in his stables. They're incredible. I've never seen such facilities in my life. I wouldn't mind living in them myself. And he has a twenty-four-hour guard on his horses. He runs a few breeding stallions and mares, worth a fortune."

"What kind of horses does he have?"

"The usual saddle horses, but he's become fond of Friesians, and he breeds them."

"They're beautiful," she exclaimed. "There's a breeder on YouTube who does videos about hers. I'm addicted to it."

"They're beautiful," he agreed. "You don't mind, that I asked him to send over the trailer?"

"Not at all. Thank you so much. And thank him very much, as well. I don't know him. It's a great kindness that he's doing, for a stranger."

"I'll tell him. I haven't mentioned this to your cowboys," he said abruptly. "And I don't intend to."

Her blood chilled. Her hands gripped the arms of the chair in which she was sitting. "You don't think…?"

"I don't trust anybody," he said flatly.

She drew in a breath. "I used to. Not anymore. I won't tell them, either."

He nodded. "I've got a couple of calls to make, but I'll come back over when Ren calls me with a time frame." He smiled. "Never hurts to have a badge around when you're doing covert things," he chuckled.

She smiled back, not a flirtatious smile, but a genuine one. "Thank you."

He tipped his hat and went out, closing the door behind him.

LAREDO KNOCKED AND walked in a few minutes later. "Sheriff had us all against the wall," he said with a short laugh. "He thinks we're all fugitives from justice, I believe."

She laughed, too. "He's just being cautious. And keep in mind that he doesn't really know any of you. It makes a difference. I vouched for you."

He lifted an eyebrow. "Thanks."

"So how are the other horses?"

"Doing fine. I can put somebody in the stable at night, if you think it's necessary. Just in case somebody comes in with ill intent. I know how fond you are of Silver, especially after Gold and Rory were injured. I'd hate for anything to happen to Silver."

There had been an odd note in his deep voice when he said that, but she put it down to strain over the sheriff's interrogation. "I think that's a good idea," she said, not mentioning the upcoming departure of her two favorite horses.

"Okay, then. I'll find a victim and tell him he's sleeping with the horses," he said and grinned.

"Good job."

JAKE MCGUIRE HAD been livid when he saw the new so-
called bodyguard going into Ida's house after he'd dropped
her off the night they returned from Galveston. He didn't
trust her, and he was suspicious about the handsome cowboy.

But a couple of weeks of silent deliberation brought a
thought to the forefront. If Ida was in so much pain that
she had to take heavy doses of anti-inflammatories, if she
was even unable to wear high heels due to her injuries,
how was she managing a covert sex life? He knew from
his own injuries how difficult it would be, although it was
information he hadn't shared with anyone. Not even with
Rogan Michaels, his best friend.

He finally decided that she was probably speaking to
the bodyguard about her horses. Maybe there had been
another incident. His heart caught. She was out there all
alone. Was one bodyguard going to be enough, if her ex-
husband sent more than one or two thugs out to injure
another of her horses?

He worried about it. He'd been out of town on business
twice, but he'd had time to check on Ida. He just hadn't
done it out of suspicion that she was playing around with
her handsome bodyguard. He phoned the sheriff, Cody
Banks, because he was concerned.

"No, it's just the one bodyguard," Cody replied, a little
surprised that he was getting a call from McGuire, who'd
been openly disdainful of the beautiful divorcée.

"She's alone out there, and she takes heavy doses of
ibuprofen for her injuries," he added.

Cody was surprised that the man knew that about her.

"Heavy doses like that put most people to sleep," Jake

continued doggedly. "And even bodyguards have to sleep. She's had one horse injured. What if it happens again?"

"It already has."

"What? When?"

Cody told him when. Jake realized with a start that it was the night they'd returned from Galveston. No wonder her bodyguard had been at the front door as soon as she arrived. It angered him that he'd rushed to judgment and ignored her for two weeks, when she had such trouble. He'd failed her. It really disturbed him, knowing that. He felt guilty.

"Somebody injured another of her palominos?" Jake persisted.

"No. Her saddle horse. Deep cuts on his flanks, just like the other one, and another visit from the vet to stitch him up and give him antibiotics."

"Damn. She must be worrying about the other one of those two palominos that she breeds, Silver. She loves him," Jake said heavily. "Gold is still recuperating. And her stable isn't all that secure."

"That isn't a problem anymore. Ren Colter sent over a man with two horse trailers to get Gold and Silver the day after the saddle horse was injured, and he had them both brought straight to his ranch. You know what sort of men he has, and how much security he deploys on his ranch. Also," he added with a chuckle, "he still has J.C. Calhoun working for him."

"I get it." Jake relaxed a little. "Do you think it's one of her cowboys doing it?"

"If I did, I couldn't tell you, Mr. McGuire," Cody said. "I can't discuss an ongoing investigation."

"Couldn't you pretend I'm one of your deputies and tell me anyway?"

Cody chuckled. "Afraid not."

"Then you don't mind if I ask Ida?" he returned.

Cody smiled to himself. "I have no control over Mrs. Merridan," he said.

"She's not what she seems," Jake said quietly.

"I noticed."

Jake didn't like that note in the sheriff's voice. Ida was very attractive... "Well, thanks for telling me what you could."

"No problem."

Jake hung up and went out to his limousine, phoning his driver on the way. Fred came running out of the house behind him, shrugging into a jacket and fastening his shirt. He was new to the job. Doing okay so far, though, Jake thought.

He opened the door for Jake, panting from the supreme effort to wake up and dress in a flash.

"You'll get used to it," Jake told him with a sardonic grin. "I'm impetuous."

"Yes, sir."

"Take a minute to finish getting dressed," Jake said before he closed the door. "I've got a few texts to send before we go."

The driver chuckled. "Yes, sir. Thank you."

Jake sat in the back seat, idly pulling up screens and sending text messages to two managers about problems at the companies he headed. By the time he finished, his driver was inside, cranking the car. Fred was still adjusting to his impetuous boss. His former driver had quit rather suddenly, citing a sick relative back home in

Montana. This one had come through an agency, but he seemed trustworthy, and he was an excellent driver.

"Where are we going, Mr. McGuire?" he asked.

"Ida Merridan's place," he said.

"Yes, sir."

BELATEDLY, JAKE TEXTED Ida and asked if it was all right for him to come over. He had something to discuss with her.

She didn't answer. He stared at the screen, wondering if she was avoiding him because he'd ignored her for so long, or if she was in trouble, or if she'd gone riding. He knew she took her saddle horse out when she wasn't hurting too much. She could be out on her property. That worried him. Her ex-husband had made threats. He should have been looking out for her. More and more, he felt responsible for her. She was more vulnerable than any woman he'd ever known. He didn't like it, but he couldn't help caring. He didn't trust women. Not even Ida. Especially Ida.

HER JAGUAR WAS sitting in the driveway. Nobody seemed to be around. The driver opened the door for him, and Jake went up on the porch and knocked.

Nothing stirred inside. He paused, not certain what he was going to do next, when a shadow moved inside.

There was the sound of a cane, and he saw Ida coming slowly down the hall to the front door. She opened it.

"You look like hell," he said abruptly.

"Thanks," she bit off. "You look charming yourself."

He turned to the driver. "Go read something. I'll page you when I'm ready to go."

The driver laughed. "Yes, sir."

Jake entered and closed the door behind him. He

propped Ida's cane by the door, picked her up and started for the living room.

"I didn't…" she began indignantly.

He bent and kissed her eyes shut. "Hush," he said softly.

She was startled by the tenderness, something she'd never really had from any man except this one, and tears stung her china-blue eyes, overflowing.

He sat down in a big, cushy armchair with Ida in his arms and proceeded to kiss all the tears away. Which only made them fall faster.

"Now, now," he said gently. "What's been going on over here?" he added, pretending innocence.

"Somebody came over here and took something like a quirt to my best saddle horse, Rory," she choked. "His poor flanks had deep cuts. I called the sheriff. He's investigating. But I know it's Bailey. He called me last night, again, and said I could pay him off or there might be more little accidents!"

"Damned idiot," he muttered.

"I told the sheriff. He's going to get a warrant for Bailey's phone records." She looked up at Jake with wet eyes. "I was so worried about Silver and Gold, even though Gold seems to be healing well…"

"We can take them to my place," he said and waited for her to tell him what he already knew.

"That's so kind of you," she choked. "But Ren Colter had them taken to his ranch. He has state-of-the-art security. Bailey would be crazy to go over there and make trouble."

"He would," Jake agreed. "Ren has J.C. Calhoun on the payroll." He shook his head. "Not a man you'd want to meet in a dark alley if you had bad intentions. He's calmed down a bit since he married, but he's still a force to reckon with when he's on the job."

"So I've heard." She let her cheek lower to Jake's chest and she forced her painful body to relax. She closed her eyes with a sigh. She always felt so safe with him.

"Did your ex-husband admit that he'd hurt the horses?" he asked at her ear, his chin on the top of her head.

"He didn't come right out and say anything," she said wearily. "But he did mention that he had mob ties and that he wasn't afraid to use them, despite my bodyguard and the hick sheriff. Those were his exact words." She looked up at him. "Mr. Banks is no hick sheriff. He's a good man. I don't think he believed me at first, but he listens. I think I convinced him."

"You did," he said sourly.

Her eyebrows arched. "How did you know that?" she asked suspiciously. "How in the world did you know?"

Jake's face drew up as he searched for an answer that wouldn't get him thrown out of the house.

CHAPTER SEVEN

"YOU CALLED SHERIFF BANKS," she accused.

He made a face. "Well, I was concerned," he said curtly. "It finally dawned on me that your bodyguard wouldn't have been practically waiting on the doorstep when we got home, without a good reason."

That went right by her, that insinuation of jealousy. "Yes. My best saddle horse had been injured, with deep cuts on his flanks, just like Gold. He came to tell me about it."

"Your ex-husband needs a few more years in stir, just to give him the idea that he hasn't the right to maul helpless animals," he said.

"He doesn't care. Not about animals or people. I don't think he's capable of it. I spoke to a friend from college who's a forensic psychologist. She says there are people who have no sense of compassion, who don't feel sympathy. They're self-centered. The only feelings they're concerned with are their own." She shook her head. "It's a hard concept to wrap your head around."

"Yes," he agreed. His lean hand smoothed up and down her bare arm unconsciously. "When I was overseas, we had a guy in our unit who worked as a sniper. He laughed when he killed an insurgent. Laughed." He sighed, his face hard with anger. "I killed men. I had to, to save my own men. But I never laughed. It's hard to live with, taking a life. Any life."

"We're raised to believe that killing is a sin," she said. "Then they put people in uniforms, send them overseas, give them a gun and tell them to kill people. It's a painful contradiction. Some people just snap."

"They really do," he said. He leaned back in the chair, shifting Ida into a more comfortable position against him. "We had an officer who watched two of his men get torn up by gunfire in a night attack. He ran into the gunfire, screaming, before any of us could stop him. He was killed instantly."

Her small hand smoothed over the soft fabric of his shirt. Her eyes, wide-open, looked across his broad chest to the window. "Everybody has a breaking point," she said. "Poor man. Did he have family?"

"A wife and a new baby, a son. He was so excited when the baby was born. He stopped total strangers to show them the digital images of the little boy." He drew in a short breath. "What a hell of a way to die."

"Yes."

His big hand smoothed over hers, where it lay on his chest. "Did you want children?"

"Oh, very much," she said quietly. "With my first husband. He wasn't particularly handsome, you see, but he had wonderful qualities. A child with such a parent would have been blessed. But that was never meant to be. With Bailey, I used birth control from the beginning. He said that he didn't want children. When we were first married, I was tempted to forgo the pills. Thank God I didn't!"

He could feel the torment in her. She was so different from the person he thought he knew months ago.

"Do you want children?" she asked absently.

His heart jumped. He'd wanted them with Mina, wanted them almost desperately. He drew in a breath. "I did," he said finally.

She smiled sadly. "With Mina," she guessed.

There was a cold hesitation. "Yes."

"I'm sorry. I shouldn't have asked…"

"It's all right," he said, surprised at her empathy.

"I'm a private person, too, as a rule, Jake," she said, using his name for the first time.

He was surprised at the hunger it kindled in him. Surprised and shocked.

There was a long silence. His big hand smoothed gently over her short hair while they just sat quietly together.

Jake had been something of a playboy in his younger days. He still liked taking beautiful women around with him. This woman in his lap was beautiful, but she was also fragile and gentle and kind. He'd taken her at face value, as so many other people in the community had. He felt the long-fingered hand flat on his broad, muscular chest with disturbing sensitivity. He felt her sigh. He didn't need to look at her face to know that she trusted him. It must be very hard, he decided, for a woman with her past to even let a man hold her. It touched him, in unexpected ways.

"Have you had lunch?" he asked abruptly.

"No," she said. "I was going to make a sandwich…"

He lifted his head and tilted her chin up. "Still up for some fried oysters?"

"Oh, yes," she said, her blue eyes wide and curious as they looked into his silver ones.

He pursed his sensual lips. "I know a great little place in St. Augustine."

Both her eyebrows arched. "Florida? St. Augustine, Florida?"

He shrugged. "The jet makes good time. It's comfortable. There's even a bed, if you need to lie down."

Her lips parted on a soft breath. "It would be a lot of trouble."

He smiled.

She smiled back, enchanted.

He got up and gently set her back on her feet. "Then grab your purse and a sweater and we'll go."

She hesitated. She was wearing jeans and clogs and a blue-and-white buttoned blouse. "I should change..."

He chuckled. "It's just lunch. You might notice that I'm not wearing a suit."

He wasn't. He had on jeans and boots and a nice chambray shirt that had been soft under her fingers.

She grinned. "Okay."

HE WAITED WHILE she told Laredo she was going to be gone for the afternoon. He wished her a pleasant day, nodded at Jake and went back to work.

Jake put her beside him in the back of the limo and instructed his driver to take them to the airport. He punched numbers into his cell phone and called his pilot, having him meet them at the airport.

Ida was in awe of him. Even her first husband, who owned a business, hadn't been so efficient at getting things done so simply. She mentioned it.

"I grew up being regimented. My father was career military," he said a little stiffly. "He retired as a captain in the army and came back here to manage the ranch when his father died. It wasn't much of a ranch, deeply in debt, and my father only had his military pension to keep the wolf from the door. He didn't like working cattle. Got his hands dirty, you see." He smiled sardonically. "My mother's father had the money. She became an oil heiress when he died. I inherited from her."

She was fascinated. "Was she kind?"

He nodded. "Kind and gentle, the sort of woman who kissed bruises and baked cookies." His face hardened. "My father resented her family's wealth."

She could feel the pain that she saw in his tanned face. "And made her pay for it," she said without thinking.

He stared at her blankly for a minute. "Physics, huh? Are you sure you didn't study fortune-telling?" he probed, but he was smiling.

She laughed softly. "Sorry."

"Yes, he made her pay for it, over and over, until I was old enough and mean enough to make him stop." His face hardened. "There's nothing in the world I hate more than a woman beater."

"You and the sheriff, from what I hear," she said.

"His mother was the victim of an alcoholic father," he replied. "Cody had an older brother who was sensitive and kind. He loved his mother, but he was afraid of his father, who hit him, as well. He tried to interfere with his father just once, when he was hitting his mother, and he was beaten bloody for it. Two days afterward Cody's brother took his own life. Cody said his father didn't even go to the funeral."

"Oh, the poor man!" she exclaimed, and her sympathy was obvious and not pretended. "And he's so kind!"

"Yes, he is," Jake replied. He was trying to cope with a bad memory of his own, of a brother he'd had and lost to tragedy. He understood how Cody had felt.

"What happened to his father?"

"Died of a heart attack when Cody graduated from high school and joined the army."

"Just as well. His mother?"

"She was always frail. One winter she caught pneumonia, viral pneumonia. She was alone in the house because Cody was overseas, and by a quirk of fate, the distant cousin by marriage who was supposed to be staying with her didn't show up. His mother died."

Ida just shook her head.

"As you might imagine, he and the cousin never speak. I understand that she tried to explain, but he wouldn't listen. She was only sixteen at the time. I always felt that Cody rushed to judgment. People usually have reasons for what they do, and the girl wasn't flighty or mean-spirited."

"He blamed himself, but it was easier to blame the cousin," she murmured.

His intake of breath was audible. "Do you always do that?" he asked.

She looked at him with both eyebrows raised. "Do what?" she asked, all at sea.

"See things that most of us miss."

She averted her eyes from his piercing silver ones. "I suppose I've become introspective from spending so much time alone."

"No boyfriends, in other words."

She shook her head. "Never again," she said, the words rough and angry.

He frowned. "Ida, there are kind men in the world."

"Maybe they look that way," she said. "Even act that way. Then they get you behind a closed door…" She stopped abruptly and drew in a breath. "Where are we going exactly?" she asked with a social smile.

She was far more damaged than he'd realized. He wondered just what else her ex-husband had done to her and was surprised that he cared.

"This little fish place I know," he replied after a minute. "Best fried oysters on both coasts."

"And you'd know this, how?" she asked with a little smile.

He grinned. "Because I've eaten at most of them. I can pick a restaurant."

"Can you, now?" she chuckled.

"Wait and see," was all he said.

THE RESTAURANT WAS a tiny little hole-in-the-wall in a strip mall, right on the ocean. There was a back patio where people could sit at a small table and eat while they watched the waves come in, foaming on the white sand.

"This is absolutely charming," Ida exclaimed when they sat, waiting for their order. "They could make money just renting the tables!"

He laughed softly. "I agree. It's a beautiful place."

"I lived in Massachusetts while I was going through college," she recalled. "I loved the ocean. My husband actually bought a hotel on the ocean near Boston so that I'd have a nice place to go on weekends and holidays."

He felt a pang of something he couldn't quite identify. "Kind of him."

She smiled. "He was like that. He sent me to Paris on our first wedding anniversary and had a personal tour guide take me everywhere I wanted to go. It was the grandest trip! I'd never even been out of the country. I saw Versailles and the Eiffel Tower and the Louvre…"

"He didn't go with you?"

"No." She sighed. "I never knew why until he died."

He was thinking of Paris, how exciting it could be. He'd been in love once, with a model who'd worked there. He'd followed her to Paris, and they'd had an exciting few months while the affair lasted. Sadly, she was just getting over a failed affair, and just when Jake was ready to give her a ring, her old boyfriend came back and she was gone, just like that. It had left him with a bad taste in his mouth and an undeserved prejudice against the City of Light.

"You're brooding," she said.

He snapped out of it. "Sorry. Bad memories."

She cocked her head, pondering that.

His dark eyebrows drew together. "No mind reading."

She held up both hands. "I know nothing."

"I'll bet," he murmured under his breath, because she was the most perceptive female he'd ever known.

"No, really, I know nothing." Her blue eyes twinkled. "You might decide to take me home before the oysters get here, if I open my mouth."

That provoked him out of his brief bad mood and he chuckled. "Point taken."

"THESE ARE…UNBELIEVABLY DELICIOUS," she moaned as she dipped a second delicately fried oyster in red sauce and popped it into her mouth. "Even better than the ones in Galveston, and those were out of this world!"

He grinned. "I told you so." He was eating his own with as much gusto as she was. "The owner could open a franchise if he wanted to. The spices are a very old family recipe, and he has a deft hand with breading, which he does himself. But he's very content to carry on here."

"A happy man," she replied. "And very lucky."

He drew in a breath and sipped cappuccino. "Happiness is a rare thing."

She nodded. "Exactly."

He studied her while she ate, his eyes going from the deep circles under her blue eyes to her long-fingered hands.

"Is my hair on crooked?" she asked after a minute, both eyebrows arched.

He laughed out loud. "No. I was just noticing the dark circles under your eyes," he said honestly. "You don't sleep much, do you?"

She grimaced. "It's a little unnerving," she said finally. "Bailey made some pretty bad threats." She looked up. "He doesn't really threaten. He does what he says he will." She shivered a little, remembering some of them.

Jake winced, but he didn't let her see. "You've been through a lot."

"Oh, yes, but everybody has problems," she replied and smiled. "Mine are no worse than someone else's. You just put one foot in front of the other and keep going."

"Sound advice."

They finished the oysters and had a second cup of coffee with a delicate little torte that was one of the specialties of the house.

"What is this?" she exclaimed when she'd taken a bite of it. "My goodness, it's awesome!"

"Almond torte," he chuckled. "It's good, isn't it? Mack makes these himself, too. He has a cook, but the man spends a lot of time twiddling his thumbs. Mack loves his kitchen."

"You know him," she guessed.

He nodded. His face hardened. "He was overseas with me, when we went into Iraq the second time."

She grimaced, because that hard face was briefly vulnerable. "I'm so sorry."

His eyes lifted to hers and he scowled. "About what?"

"Bad memories," she said quietly. "They show." Before he could pull up an angry retort, she added, "I have them, too."

Which curtailed the hot words on the tip of his tongue. He drew in a breath and laughed. "You have a knack for disarming me."

"I've been through the wars, too, even though I've never been in combat. It...hardens you," she said after a minute.

He could have retorted that it had only made her more vulnerable. She saw deep inside him. He wasn't sure he liked it. Most of his dates, with the exception of Mina, had been shallow women, with eyes for diamonds and high living. None of them had Ida's ability to feel the emotions of people around her. It was a true gift. He wondered if she even realized it.

AFTER LUNCH IDA expected him to head for the airport. Instead, he caught her hand in his and walked her out to the beach behind the strip mall.

The feel of his big hand holding hers made her feel awkward just at first, but it was warm and strong, and after a minute, she relaxed.

He felt that, smiling inwardly.

"I love the ocean," she said softly. "I collect beaches." She laughed. "My favorite was in Morocco. I spent a couple of weeks in Tangier. There were camels dancing in and out of the surf," she recalled with soft eyes.

"I've been to Tangier," he replied. "Fascinating city. Did you see the church that the Berbers gave to the Christians?"

She laughed. "Yes. It was a surprise." She sighed. "But what I loved most about the city, even more than the bazaar and the wonderful food, was the call to prayer broadcast over the loudspeakers. I don't know why, exactly. It was beautiful."

The hand holding hers was suddenly stiff. She recalled that he'd fought overseas, probably fought some of the people who would have loved those calls to prayer. She stopped suddenly and looked up at him. "I'm sorry."

His eyes were like steel plates, but he wasn't looking at her. His eyes were on the ocean, and he didn't speak.

She never touched men voluntarily. Not since Bailey. But she moved, hesitantly, closer to Jake and slid her arms around him, laying her cheek against the soft chambray of his shirt. She held him, just held him. After a minute she felt something like a shudder go through his powerful body, and his arms closed around her a little roughly.

She didn't mind. He was familiar to her, in a way that she didn't understand. She closed her eyes and drew in a long breath.

He stood holding her, letting her hold him, while the anguish of memory slowly faded. His hand smoothed up and down her spine.

"You can't live in the past," she said after a minute.

"No matter how painful it is, you have to keep moving forward."

"You stole that line from *Meet the Robertsons*," he chided at her temple, because she only came up to his chin.

She laughed unexpectedly. "Don't tell me you watch cartoon movies!"

He smiled. "One of my vice presidents had a little boy, about seven at the time. It was his favorite movie. I'd go to his home for supper occasionally, and the whole family gathered around to watch the movie with him." His hand stilled. "He was the sweetest kid." He broke off.

She drew back and looked up at him. "What happened?"

"His father was late getting to work. He jumped into the car and didn't realize that the little boy was standing behind it."

"Dear God," she whispered reverently.

"He lost his mind," he said. "Quit his job, left his wife, ended up on the streets and died of a respiratory infection one winter as an indigent. I tried to find him after he left my mining company, but he didn't want to be found. He went back East to New York City and just lost himself in the crowds. He was identified through his fingerprints— I'd made all my employees submit theirs, so they were kept on file. It was a wrench. I had him brought back to Billings, where he was buried."

"What happened to his wife?" she asked.

"She went to live with a sister in Phoenix," he said. "She came to the funeral." His face hardened. "I don't think she ever remarried. She loved him, right up until the end. She forgave him. But he couldn't forgive himself."

She didn't say a word. She put her cheek back on his shirt and just stood there, with the breeze whipping around them and the sound of the surf curling on the beach and the infrequent cry of a seagull.

"You're restful," he commented after a minute.

She smiled. "That's a new adjective."

He chuckled. "You have a knack for calming me down. I lean toward extremes of emotion."

"I used to be like that."

"What happened?"

"Ibuprofen," she murmured dryly.

He didn't laugh, as she meant him to. He drew back. "Is your hip hurting?"

She grimaced. "Just a little. No, I don't want to go yet, please?" she asked. "I love beaches, too." Her blue eyes pleaded.

"Okay. Just for a few minutes."

She grinned.

THEY WALKED ALONG the beach, hand in hand. It was invigorating, the sound of the ocean, the whip of the wind, the foaming churn of the surf dancing in and out of the beach.

"Oh, look, a shell!" she exclaimed and pulled away from him long enough to pick it up.

"It's just a seashell, not a treasure," he teased.

She turned it over. It was a simple shell, but perfect, with the softest pink inside and gray perfection outside. "I'll keep it as a souvenir," she said.

"I can get you something from one of the shops…" he began.

She looked up, surprised. "No," she said. "That's not… well, it's not really a souvenir, is it? I mean, things in shops come from everywhere." She turned the shell over in her hands. "This came from here, from this beach." She made a face and lifted soft blue eyes to his. "I'm not putting it well."

"Yes, you are," he replied. He looked at her hands. They were bare. No diamonds, no jewelry of any sort. She was worth millions, from what he'd heard, but she didn't wear her wealth. Not even a small part of it. "Don't you like jewelry?" he asked abruptly.

Her thin eyebrows arched. "Excuse me?"

"You aren't wearing rings or bracelets."

She studied his face quietly. "I don't like rings and bracelets," she said. "They get in my way when I'm working clay."

His own eyebrows arched. "Clay?"

"I like to sculpt. It's a hobby I started when I was in high school, before my mother died. She used to throw pots, but I like making busts." She laughed. "It's great exercise for my hands."

He shook his head. He'd never met such a complex person. "Physics and sculpting." His silver eyes twinkled. "Starships and canoes," he murmured absently.

"Freeman Dyson," she retorted immediately.

He burst out laughing. "Yes. Dyson. It was a great book. He was quite famous for his theory."

"The Dyson Spheres," she agreed. "I wonder if our civilization will ever advance to the point that we might actually employ them?"

"Between the two of us, I seriously doubt it. There have been some massive, civilization-ending events in the past. They weren't even discovered until late in the last century. When they noticed a layer of iridium that went all the way around the planet, and deduced that it was from a collision between the earth and—"

"An asteroid," she finished for him.

He grinned. "Exactly. Luis Alvarez proposed the theory in the early 1980s, noting that a layer of iridium marked the Cretaceous-Tertiary or K-T boundary. Since iridium is a very rare element on this planet, but fairly common in asteroids, Alvarez proposed the asteroid theory." He stared at her with admiration. "You're constantly surprising me."

"I have geek issues," she returned with a little laugh.

"Geek issues." He sighed. He caught her hand back in his and they walked some more. "Do you know what true geekdom is?" he asked lightly.

"No. Do tell."

"It's when you look at your weather apps to see if it's raining, instead of opening the curtains and looking out the window."

She burst out laughing. So did he.

"Do you do that?" she asked.

He shrugged. "Once in a while."

"Me, too."

"I live on apps that cover weather, space, volcanoes, earthquakes, that sort of geeky stuff, when I'm not up to my neck in business matters."

"I have five earthquake apps, two volcano ones and about six weather apps," she confessed.

He beamed. "Well!"

"I guess it comes from spending so much time alone."

"How about social media?" he asked.

"Twitter."

He named a few others.

She shook her head. "I don't mix well," she replied. "And I wouldn't air my dirty linen online, no matter how popular it is."

"I feel the same way."

They walked some more. She still had her pretty seashell in one hand. She turned it over in her fingers and looked at it. She knew that she'd keep it forever. And every time she looked at it, she'd remember walking on the beach in St. Augustine with Jake.

THEY WERE ALMOST back at the restaurant when he spotted something in the surf. He let go of her hand to retrieve it.

His was a tiny spiral seashell, but it also had the delicate pink coloring inside. He gave it to her.

"It's pretty," she said.

He took it back, to her surprise. "Souvenir," he said absently and stuck it in his shirt pocket without further comment.

She felt odd. Happy. Safe. But her emotions were in turmoil. She wasn't sure what was happening to her. She wasn't sure she liked it, either.

They went back home with a strange silence between them. It was pleasant, but disturbing. The ease of speaking to one another seemed to have been replaced with an odd restlessness. Ida didn't understand why. But she smiled and made small talk just to relieve the tension.

JAKE'S CHAUFFEUR WAS waiting for them at the Catelow airport. He drove them back to Ida's small ranch.

They sat apart in the back seat.

"Thank you so much for lunch," Ida said as the ranch

house came into view. "It was kind of you to ask me along. I've never tasted food that was so good."

"Same here." He was being pleasant, but there was something different under the surface, like currents under a calm sea.

The limo pulled up in front of her door. The lights were all off. The house looked lonely and cold and somehow foreboding.

Jake came around to help her out of the car and walked her up onto the porch.

She hesitated. She didn't know why. She felt something, like a shiver going down her spine.

Jake looked down at her with eyes she couldn't see. His face was in shadow, but she felt anger in him.

"Thanks again," she began.

He stuck his hands in his pockets. It kept him from doing what he wanted to do. "No problem."

"Good night," she said.

He just nodded.

She turned and started to unlock the door. She hesitated. "I know I locked it..."

He moved her back and pushed open the door, searching for the light switch at the same time.

What met his eyes made him furious.

CHAPTER EIGHT

JAKE WAS SO silent that Ida moved up behind him and looked past him at her living room.

"Oh, my God!" She moved forward, but he caught her. "Butler! No," she sobbed. "No!"

Jake went around her, following the thin blood trail to her big yellow cat. Butler was lying on a throw rug, not moving.

"I wish I knew a hit man!" she sobbed. "I'd send him after Bailey Trent this very minute! He killed my cat! He killed my baby!"

Jake had a hand on the cat. He caught his breath. "He's still alive. Can you go and have Fred open the back door of the limo? I'll carry him. We'll get him to the vet right now!"

"Still…alive?" she choked, tears rolling down her cheeks.

"Yes!"

THEY GOT HIM in the back seat. Ida didn't bother to lock the door. Whoever had injured her cat hadn't been stopped by a lock, after all.

Fred, Jake's driver, was a wild man when he was given the green light to break speed limits. They pulled up in front of the vet's office in scant minutes, where they were

met by the vet himself, who'd come from home after
Jake's phone call from the limo.

"Bring him right in," the vet said quickly.

Jake took the cat, wrapped up in the throw rug on Ida's
lap, and carried him inside. He put Butler on the exami-
nation table and then slid an arm around Ida, who was
in anguish.

"He's all I have," she sobbed. "Please, Doctor, can you
save him? I don't care what it costs!"

The vet, Donald Mulholland, was still examining the
cat. "There are some deep lacerations, not fatal, but con-
cerning, and what feels like a broken rib. Probably a broken tail, as well, here at the tip." He turned to her and
smiled gently. "Not fatal injuries. I'll need an X-ray…
There's Ashley," he added with a smile at the young
woman coming in the door. "My wife," he said, introduc-
ing them, "and my partner in the practice. She's smarter
than I am," he added in a loud whisper.

Ashley chuckled. "Liar. What have we got?" she asked,
moving to stand beside her husband, while he updated her.

"We'll get him right back to X-ray. Are you going to
stay…?"

"Oh, of course," Ida said at once, biting back another
bout of tears.

The doctor picked up Butler and, followed by his wife,
went back to the X-ray room.

"You don't have to stay," Ida began, looking up at Jake.

He bent and kissed her eyes shut. "Hush," he whispered. Which did nothing to stem the tears but induced
more of them. Tenderness was still new to Ida.

He held her gently while she wept, and then mopped
up her face with a spotless white handkerchief.

"I didn't think men carried handkerchiefs anymore," she said, her voice hoarse from crying.

"My mother thought that any decent man should have an ample supply," he teased.

She smiled. "Thanks. For everything."

"Someone got into your house, and it didn't look like a forced entry," he said quietly.

She drew in a long breath. "Yes, I noticed that." She looked up at him. "Laredo has a key," she said hesitantly.

Jake pulled out his cell phone and called Cody Banks.

"But I'm not sure…" she began.

"You can't afford to hesitate," he interrupted curtly. "A man who'd do that to a cat would do it to a human. Or a horse," he added angrily. He recalled that her horses had similar injuries to the cat, which might indicate that one perpetrator was responsible for damage to all three of her animals.

She sighed. She nodded.

"Banks," came a curt voice from the other end of the line.

"Jake McGuire. Someone got into Ida Merridan's house and almost killed her cat. The door wasn't forced. Her so-called bodyguard has a key."

There was a very bad word from the sheriff. "Where are you, at the house?"

"At the vet, with the cat," Jake replied.

"Call me when you take her home. I can be there in less than five minutes."

"I'll do that. Thanks."

He hung up the phone.

She breathed a sigh of relief. "I should have known," she groaned. "I should have suspected that anything I

cared about would be in the line of fire. Anything or anyone…" She broke off with a look of horror as she stared
up at Jake.

He gave her a sardonic look. "I lived through a tour of
duty in one of the worst hellholes in existence, and you
think a man who's cowardly enough to torture animals
is a threat to me?"

"Anybody can get caught off guard," she began.

His eyes were as tender as his smile. "You worry about
me, do you?" he asked.

She flushed scarlet.

The vet came out just in time to spare her more embarrassment.

"Two broken ribs," he said, "and some nasty cuts. His
tail has a break just at the tip." He shook his head. "Anybody who'd hurt a cat like this…!" he said, angry.

"I think he also hurt two horses," Ida replied. "They
have deep cuts on their flanks…"

"My God, I'd forgotten that!" the vet exclaimed. "I remember now. I treated your horses." The vet shook his
head. "You make very bad enemies, Mrs. Merridan."

"Her ex-husband," Jake volunteered curtly. "Fresh out
of prison for assault on her." It was a summary, but it
caused a visible reaction in the vet, who was cognizant
of Ida's bad reputation.

"A threat?" the vet wondered.

"I'm afraid so," Ida said, sighing. "I wish it had been
me, instead of my poor horses and Butler." She bit her
lower lip. "I rescued Butler when he was very young…
He'll be all right, you think?" she added, her china-blue
eyes wide with emotion.

"I can assure you that he will be." He studied her. "We

have burglar alarms here, because we keep pet medications on hand. If anyone tries to break in, the sheriff can be here in less than five minutes," he added deliberately.

She let out a breath. "What will you do?"

"Keep him for a few days, just to monitor him and make sure he's on the mend. Antibiotics, rest, careful diet, loving care," his wife said, joining them. She smiled. "You can call any time you like to check on him."

"Thanks," Ida said huskily.

"We love animals, too," the vet said gently.

Ida just smiled. She was worn out from worry and fear.

BUT AS THE chauffeur drove them back to Ida's home, she had another fear, and that was what Bailey might do next. The horses and the cat had underlined the threat.

"Maybe if I just paid him off…" she began worriedly.

"And reward him for almost killing Butler?" Jake asked tersely. "Over my dead body!"

She looked at him with wide eyes.

"I want a word with your bodyguard. I think the sheriff may want more than I do." He pulled out his cell phone and called Cody Banks.

The sheriff was waiting for them at Ida's front porch.

"We need to talk to the bodyguard," Jake said as he helped Ida up the steps.

"And chance would be a fine thing," Cody returned. "I just talked with one of your part-timers. Ironically, Laredo had a death in the family and had to rush back to Texas just before you got home."

"How convenient," Jake said icily.

"Isn't it?" Cody replied. "My new investigator started

today. He's doing a background check on Laredo with the agency that provided him."

"At this hour?" Ida asked.

"Oh, he doesn't mind getting people out of bed to answer questions," Cody said with an amused grin.

"It might be a legitimate thing," Ida began.

The sheriff's phone rang with a dull beep. He answered it. His eyebrows arched under his Stetson. "You don't say? Thanks, Dirk. Sure. Great work." He hung up and turned to Ida and Jake. "The agency your attorneys contacted had a bodyguard en route. Someone called, giving your name, and told them not to send him." He paused. "Apparently, your bodyguard was substituted."

Ida's lips fell open. "If I'd just checked…!" she said in anguish.

"If your attorneys had just checked," Jake broke in, angry.

"He won't quit, you know," Ida said sadly. "He'll just get somebody else."

"In which case, we'll both do a background check," Jake replied.

"It's all my fault," Ida said. "My poor horses. My poor cat!"

"We'll keep an eye out," Cody promised. He smiled at her. "I've got a deputy recovering from a gunshot wound. I can send him over to stay with you…?"

She shivered. "Thank you. No."

Cody and Jake exchanged a quiet glance.

"Pack a bag," Jake said. "You're coming home with me."

"I will not!"

He noted her scarlet blush and chuckled. "I have an elderly couple living with me. He wrangles horses, and she cooks. I also have a housekeeper who comes daily. I can have one of them live in the house, while you're in residence," he added meaningfully.

"Go with him," Cody said at once. "You're not safe here. Not until we do some investigating. I need the name of your attorney and his phone number. We'll arrange something between us."

"You're so kind," she began.

"Crimes have been committed," Cody replied. "And I'll tell you again that any man who mistreats animals won't hesitate to target a woman."

She looked torn.

"We can explore some more restaurants," Jake coaxed.

She hesitated.

"Restaurants?" Cody asked.

He nodded, grinning. "We've been to Galveston and St. Augustine, but I know lots more all over the country."

Cody laughed. "Sounds like fun. I like food, too." He moved toward the steps. "I'll say good-night. If you hear anything from your ex-husband, I'd like to know," he told Ida.

She nodded. "I'll call you if I do. And thanks very much, Sheriff Banks."

"Just Cody," he said, and with a warm smile that made the hairs on Jake's head stand up a little.

"Cody, then," she agreed, smiling back.

THEY WATCHED THE sheriff drive away. Jake went inside with Ida and paced while she got a bag packed. The blood trail was still on the floor. He frowned, bending down to look. There were two trails, one smaller than the other and thicker. It was, he decided, a smear, as if whoever injured the cat might have gotten clawed in the process and left the smear when dropping the cat.

He pulled out his phone and called Cody again, informing him about the blood.

"I'm turning around right now," Cody said. "I'll bring my investigator with me. If you're right, we can pull DNA from the blood smear."

"It might supply some interesting information about the bearer," Jake noted.

"Yes, it might."

CODY DROVE UP just as Ida was coming out of her bedroom. "I'm packing, but I needed to know how much to bring."

"Enough for a few days. Sit down," he told her gently, because she was limping again. There was a loud knock at the front door. "I'll get it," Jake told her.

She tensed. "What if it's one of Bailey's thugs?" she worried.

"It's the sheriff. I just phoned him."

"Why?"

"Wait and see." He opened the door.

Cody Banks came in with a tall, broad-shouldered man with silver-blond hair and cold gray eyes.

"This is Dirk Coleman." He introduced the other man. "I stole him from the Bexar County Sheriff's Office down in San Antonio, Texas. Jake McGuire and Ida Merridan."

Dirk nodded. His eyes went to the blood trail. He moved forward and went on one knee, intent on the evidence. He pulled out a blood collection kit.

While the investigator went about his task, Cody asked more questions, some he hadn't thought to ask before. One was about the other cowboys who worked for her.

"Just two part-timers," she said. "I only have a handful of horses, and they take good care of Silver and Gold and Rory and the other four. They're almost like family. They've been here since my first husband bought the family ranch back and renovated it. He thought I'd like to spend some of my holidays here, and I did."

"The palominos have been here for a while?" Cody asked.

She nodded. "About two years." She grimaced. "Gold's much better." Her eyes sought Cody's. "You don't think Bailey might send somebody over to Mr. Colter's to hurt her and Silver…?"

"If they did, and they ran into J.C. Calhoun, they'd be running for the border in no time," Cody said flatly.

"I know J.C.," Jake said. "We were in separate units in Iraq. He was a hell of a soldier."

"Not a bad merc, either," Dirk Coleman said without looking up.

"You know him?" Cody asked.

He nodded.

"And you'd know this, how?" Cody asked with faint suspicion.

"Oh, gossip."

Cody didn't add anything to that. His new investigator was very closemouthed. A good detective, but with a mysterious background. He never spoke of it, and his records only went back a good seven years. Before that it was difficult to find even a trace of him. It had puzzled Cody, but he was so desperate for help that he hadn't paid much attention to the omission. After all, if the sheriff in Bexar County had recommended the man, and he was working for them, they'd have done an exhaustive background check on him.

"Did you talk to Ida's lawyer?" Jake asked Cody.

"Yes." He sighed. "Ida, he's a really nice guy, and he has your best interests at heart, but he's a civil attorney. He's not really up on mob contacts and what they can mean in a situation like this."

"Damned straight," Dirk muttered as he finished collecting trace evidence. He bagged it and put his cell phone away—he'd been using it to collect visual evidence of the blood smear and the blood trail. He stood up. "I'd like to come back in the morning and talk to your part-timers," he said. "Just to cover all the bases," he added when she looked worried.

"You won't, well, make them feel as if they're under suspicion or anything?" she asked. "They're such good men."

Dirk cocked his head and looked down at her. Even with red eyes, she was beautiful. "I won't make waves. But we need to know if there's any connection. One of them might have a relative or a friend who'd do something for your ex-husband."

"Oh, I see," she returned, nodding.

He smiled. His gray eyes sparkled. He was very good-looking. "If your ex-husband was behind this, we'll find out. And he'll be very sorry that we did."

She relaxed and smiled back. "Okay. Thanks."

Jake moved closer and took her hand gently in his. "Yes. Thanks very much," he added pleasantly, but his pale gray eyes, just a shade lighter than the investigator's, were throwing off sparks.

Dirk laughed inwardly, wished them both a good night and went back out to the car with the evidence.

"He'll get the blood to the state crime lab office," Cody told them. "I'm almost certain there's enough to get DNA from. I'll let you both know when we get the results."

"Thanks so much," Ida said.

Cody smiled. "No problem. Good night."

JAKE GLARED AFTER THEM. He turned back to Ida and the frown was quickly erased. "Finish packing and we'll be off," he said softly.

"Okay." She smiled. "Thanks, Jake. I'm not comfortable staying here by myself, but I'd never have asked you…"

"I know that," he interrupted.

"But what about the rest of my horses?" she worried. "The part-timers go home at night."

"I'll take care of that. You just pack, okay?" he asked gently.

She smiled. "Okay."

He took out his cell phone and called his foreman, who said he'd have a man out at Ida's place within the hour, armed and ready.

IDA WENT SLOWLY back into the bedroom, puzzled by Jake's odd behavior when she was talking to the investigator. He couldn't possibly be jealous of him, of course. She felt a wave of pleasure wash over her as she processed the unlikely thought. No, she told herself firmly, he was only being kind. Of course.

She got together enough clothes for a few days and packed them in a suitcase. It was heavy.

She went out into the hall, grimacing as she walked. "Jake, can you get the bag for me?"

"Sure thing." He glanced around the bedroom as he picked up the piece of luggage. No frills, nothing fancy at all. The room was spartan. There was a bed and a chest of drawers, a bedside table with a lamp, several throw rugs, and a vanity with a mirror and a little chair. Nothing else. Not even a picture on the wall.

"You live simply," he remarked.

She shrugged. "I have paintings that I'd like to put up, but they need to be matted and framed first, and it's a long way to Casper."

His eyebrows arched.

"I can't really drive that far," she confessed. "And there's no frame shop in Catelow."

"I get it." He led the way into the living room, noting that she'd retrieved her cane and was using it. Most likely bad weather was on the way. People with joint injuries had a lot of pain just before a low-pressure system moved in.

"Can you make it all right?" he asked, concerned.

"I'm doing fine," she lied. The ibuprofen was wearing off. She stopped. "Jake, my ibuprofen is in the cabinet in my bathroom…"

He put down the suitcase and went to get it. The medicine cabinet had Band-Aids, antibiotic cream and ibuprofen. He palmed the bottle. "No toothbrush?" he asked when he rejoined her.

She laughed. "Packed," she said, indicating the luggage.

On his way back he noticed a box, open, with leads in it. "What the hell is this?" he asked.

"It's my TENS unit," she said.

"Come again?"

"It has electrodes. You put them where the pain is and turn on the power. It pulses electric shocks into the muscle to help relax it. Works pretty good, but it's uncomfortable to wear."

He smiled. "You learn something new every day," he chuckled.

"So you do." She smiled back.

"Okay. If that's the lot, let's go."

He led her out the door and she locked up.

The driver, Fred, was standing at the back seat of the limousine with the door open, smiling at them. "Everything okay?" he asked. "I hope they get the person who hurt your cat, miss," he added. "I have cats of my own."

She smiled. "Thanks."

Jake put her inside and climbed in behind her.

HIS RANCH WAS BIG. The limo drove down a paved driveway with white fences on either side of it. Even at night, it was impressive. The house sat far back off the highway in a grove of aspens and cottonwood trees. It was yellow brick with graceful arches and a lot of black wrought iron trim. There were two balconies. On either side of the house were what looked like flower gardens.

"It must be gorgeous here in the spring," she said as he helped her out of the car. "My goodness, it looks like it should be in Texas or Arizona..."

He chuckled. "It's called Spanish House locally," he told her, watching his driver get her bag out of the boot. "My grandfather was married to a Spanish lady. She was related to most of the royal houses of Europe, although her family shunned her when she came to the wilds of Wyoming to live on a poor cattle ranch. She was my mother's mother. My grandfather remodeled the house for her after some stocks he'd invested in made a huge profit. It was the only time he had money, but he never regretted spending it. He loved my grandmother to the end of his days. So did I," he added curtly, pushing back emotion. "When she died, my mother inherited a great deal of money and property. My father was dead by then."

"It's lovely," Ida said. "Are there flowers in the spring?"

"Oceans of them," he replied. "My mother loved them." He made a face. "My father mowed down every one of them, every single spring. I replaced them when he was finally gone, and it was just my mother and me. I've kept them just the way she left them."

"What a terrible man," she said.

"You don't know the half of it," he returned.

The driver opened the door, and Jake led her gently down the cobblestone path that led to the front door.

She was unwieldly on the uneven surface, depending on the cane to get her safely through what felt like a maze as she avoided the more prominent stones.

Jake looked back and realized belatedly how difficult it was for her.

"Here," he said, taking her cane and tossing it to the limo driver, who caught it neatly in the air.

Jake swung Ida up in his arms and carried her to the door, which was opened by his little housekeeper, Maude Barton.

She smiled at Jake and nodded curtly at Ida.

"I've brought Mrs. Merridan home with me for a few days, Mrs. Barton," he said. "Is the bed in the guest bedroom made up?"

"Yes, sir," was the guarded reply.

Ida sighed. Apparently, her reputation had preceded her.

She just smiled sadly at the older woman as Jake turned and carried her back down the hallway to an open door.

Beyond it was the sort of luxury she'd become accustomed to over the years. The guest room was done in soft pastels, peach and beige, with powder-blue walls and a matching carpet. The bed, king-size, was covered with a patterned blue-and-beige duvet.

"It's beautiful," she said quietly as Jake put her back on her feet.

"I'm glad you like it. Why don't you lie down for a bit, while I go over some paperwork and talk to my stock manager?"

She forced a smile, because she was hurting. "That would be nice, if you don't mind. And could you get out my ibuprofen and ask your housekeeper for something to take it with?"

"Sure thing."

He fished out the prescription meds and went to the kitchen to see Mrs. Barton.

"Can you make coffee and take a cup to Ida?" he asked.

Maude glared at him. "Why can't she come in here and get it?" she asked waspishly.

His pale eyes took on a steely shine. "If you don't like working here, Maude, you know where the door is."

She caught her breath. It was a very high-paying job. She'd never manage another like it. She gritted her teeth. "I'll take it right in, Mr. McGuire."

"I thought you probably would," he shot back. "And if you aren't polite when you deliver it, I'll know."

It was a veiled threat. She swallowed. Hard. "Of course, Mr. McGuire."

He nodded, a curt jerk of his head, and walked out the front door to have a word with his limo driver before he got to work.

MRS. BARTON CARRIED a tray into the bedroom where Ida was lying on the cover, propped on some pillows, her lovely face taut and pale with pain.

She grimaced at the sight of the tray. "Oh, please, Mrs....Barton, wasn't it? I didn't need that. Just some water, to take my medicine with."

Maude cocked her head. "Medicine?" she asked curiously.

Ida nodded. She sat up on the edge of the bed, swung her legs out, painfully, and opened the medicine bottle. It jumped out of her hand, scattering pills all over the spotless duvet. "Oh, damn!" she ground out, fighting tears. "First my horses, then my cat, now this...!"

Maude put the tray on the vanity and retrieved the medicine bottle, glancing at it with raised eyebrows as she put the pills back in it. "How many of these do you take?" she asked, in a much less hostile tone than Ida had expected.

Ida sighed. "Three a day."

"It's 800 milligram tablets," she noted.

"Yes. It takes a lot when the weather changes. I have a partial hip replacement and a metal rod with screws in my right leg, holding a broken femur bone in place. The whole works throbs when we have pressure systems moving in."

Maude handed the pill bottle to Ida, who shook out one pill and waited while Maude put the tray on the bed beside her.

"Do you take cream and sugar?" she asked politely.

"No. I drink it black. Thank you," Ida added when she

picked it up with an unsteady hand and took the ibuprofen with two sips of blazing-hot coffee.

"My cousin takes those for a bad back," Maude told her. "He says he can only take them for five days, then he has to wait for ten to take them again. He's also supposed to take them with food."

Ida sighed. "I don't feel like food. Somebody almost killed my cat. He's at the vet's…"

"Good Lord! Who would hurt a cat?" Maude exclaimed.

"The same sort of man who laughs when he tosses you over the side of a parking garage," Ida said with a sad smile. "At least I landed on the grass verge below or I'd probably be dead."

Maude scowled, wincing inwardly at the pain the injury must have caused the younger woman. "Well, you have to eat something or you'll do damage to your stomach," she muttered. "I'll scramble some eggs."

"Please don't go to any extra trouble…"

"It's no trouble," the older woman said curtly. "None at all." She put the little coffeepot and the napkin on the side table. "I'll take these back to the kitchen," she added, indicating the condiments on the tray.

"Thanks very much, Mrs. Barton," Ida replied.

"It's no bother." Maude didn't smile as she went out. But Ida didn't expect her to. The bad reputation she'd worked so hard to build was having sad consequences. It protected her from men but made her an instant enemy of most women she met.

Well, that couldn't be helped. She finished her coffee and put the cup down gingerly, lying back on the pillows with her eyes closed.

Only a few minutes passed before Mrs. Barton was back with a plate of scrambled eggs and two slices of bacon.

"You eat that," she said in a motherly tone. "It will keep those nasty pills from dissolving your innards."

Ida laughed in spite of herself. "Yes, I expect so. Thanks very much. I'm sorry to put you to the trouble…"

"No worries," Maude replied, and she even managed a brief smile. "You just sit that on the side table when you're through." She paused. "Why would someone attack your cat?" she wondered again.

"My ex-husband was sent to prison for abusing me," she said simply. "He's out and I have a lot of money and he has gambling debts. He says I owe him for what happened to him. He's already hurt two of my horses. I guess poor Butler was the weakest link in the chain. Poor old cat," she added heavily. "He had a string around his neck that had almost choked him when I found him out in the woods. He had welts all over him, as if somebody had hit him with a belt. I got the string off and took him home with me. It took almost two weeks for him to come out of hiding when I walked into a room. The vet said he looked as if he'd been tortured by someone. That's what I thought, too. He lived through that, and now this. Two broken ribs, a broken tail, welts all over him…" She stopped, swallowing hard. "There was a blood trail halfway across the living room when I got home. If Mr. Colter didn't have my poor horses, I expect they'd be victims all over again. They both had deep cuts on their hindquarters. My ex-husband said it was only a taste of what I could expect if I didn't put up some cash."

Maude whistled softly. "And I thought I had a hard life," she murmured. "He should be locked back up."

"If the sheriff can find anything to connect him to my babies' injuries, he will be," Ida returned, blue eyes flashing fire.

"You might be next," Maude said and grimaced.

"Yes." She looked at the other woman worriedly. "I'm putting you and Jake in danger just by being here!"

"No, you're not," came the firm reply. "Mr. McGuire has two cowboys who used to be mercenaries. He coaxed them away from Ren Colter. Nothing, and I mean nothing, gets past them. You're safe here."

Ida bit her lower lip. "Safe." She laughed hollowly. "I haven't been safe since the day I met Bailey Trent."

"Well, you are now. You eat those nice eggs before they get cold. And if you need more coffee, you just call me, okay?"

"Okay." She picked up her fork with a long sigh. "Thank you for the food. And the kind words. And for listening."

Maude flushed. "It was… You're very welcome." She smiled jerkily and went back to the kitchen.

Ida finished the eggs and bacon, put the plate up, sipped half a cup of coffee and lay back on the pillows. Minutes later she was sound asleep.

CHAPTER NINE

MAUDE MET JAKE at the door when he came back inside.

"I'm very sorry that I rushed to judgment about Mrs. Merridan," she said stiffly. "I didn't know her true circumstances."

"Gossip is a dangerous thing," Jake replied. "She has some serious issues."

"She told me." She grimaced. "What sort of monster was she married to?"

"One of the worst kind," he replied. "I think he'll put her in harm's way next. Her animals were a warning."

"Her poor cat," she replied. "She said she found him in the woods with a string tied tight around his neck and welts all over him. She took him to a vet and adopted him. She was very upset that he'd gone through something similar again." She lifted her eyes to his. "She's not what I thought."

"She's not what I thought, either, Mrs. Barton," he replied quietly. "She's like a chameleon. She pretends to be something she's not so that men won't hit on her. She's afraid of them."

"Poor child," she sighed. "What a life she's had."

He nodded. "She could have gone on in college and taught physics. Pity she didn't."

"Physics?" Maude exclaimed.

He chuckled. "She graduated from MIT."

"Well, you never know about people, do you? I fed her some scrambled eggs and bacon. Not a good idea to take medicine that powerful on an empty stomach. My cousin is on the same sort of dose."

"Someday, I hope, they'll come up with a treatment that works better and isn't as dangerous," he returned.

"And then they'll take ten years to approve it for general use," Maude muttered. "I'll just go clean up the kitchen. What would you like for supper, Mr. McGuire?"

"Just soup and salad. I expect that's all Ida will want, too. She's upset about her cat."

"I know how she feels. I have four cats at home. One got run over by a car and barely escaped with his life. They had to take off one of his legs, but he still runs pretty good," she added with a smile.

He nodded. "Lucky cat."

"That's his name, all right. I'll have supper on the table about six."

"Six is fine. How's Ida?"

"Fast asleep." She shook her head. "She's got such huge dark circles under her eyes. I don't think she sleeps well at all."

"She has nightmares," he returned.

"And that doesn't surprise me at all."

"If the vet's office calls here, if they can't reach me on my cell phone, take a message, okay?"

"I'll be glad to. And, sir," she added, a little shame-faced, "I'm sorry about the way I was when Mrs. Merridan came in here. She's not the woman I expected. Not at all."

He smiled. "She's not the woman anybody expects."

HE WENT IN to look at Ida. She was curled up on her side in the huge bed, her eyes closed, long black eyelashes lying on her cheeks. She looked beautiful like that. He had to force himself to leave the room.

When he recalled not only the sheriff's, but also the investigator's interest in her, he felt himself bristling. He had competition. He wasn't sure how he was going to handle it, which surprised him, because he'd been certain that Ida wasn't getting next to him. Apparently, he'd made a miscalculation. It gave him something to think about while he worked in the office.

IDA WOKE UP just in time for supper. Maude brought her a tray with soup and salad and homemade dressing, with a cream puff for dessert.

"I could have come to the table, Mrs. Barton," she protested. "This makes so much more work for you!"

Maude just smiled. "It's no work at all. I love to cook. And it isn't as if you're on the tenth floor of some apartment building, you know. You're just right down the hall."

Ida laughed softly. "So I am. But thank you."

"Very welcome. I hope you enjoy it."

She went back into the kitchen and dished up Jake's supper. He was sitting at the table reading a market bulletin and glaring down at it.

"Now, now, Mr. McGuire, reading all that political stuff is just going to mess up your mind and ruin your appetite."

He laughed hollowly. "True enough," he conceded. He folded the paper and moved it to one side.

"It's a good night for soup," she pointed out. "Viciously cold and they're calling for a foot of snow tonight."

"I know. I've been making phone calls to get things organized here. You'd better get on home while the road's still passable. We'll put the dishes in the sink when we're through with supper."

"Mrs. Danbury hasn't shown up yet, and her husband phoned and said one of the children was sick and she might not make it over here tonight," she remarked worriedly. "Are you sure you don't want me to stay?"

He just laughed. 'With Ida in her present condition, I don't think we'll present much of a scandal."

She grinned. "I should think not. I'll pass that along, by the way. Mrs. Merridan's had her share of problems. I'll see if I can help solve at least one of them."

"Thanks."

"I like her. She's nice."

"Yes," he sighed. "She is."

AFTER MAUDE LEFT, Jake retired to his study to look over the newest computer records on his purebred herd. His mind wasn't really on it, however. It was on his houseguest. He didn't trust her, not just yet, but was drawn to her in ways he didn't want to be drawn. She was an unknown quantity. He was trying to get over Mina. This was a bad time to ricochet to another woman. Especially one who was as fragile as Ida seemed to be.

HE PHONED THE man he'd sent over to Ida's place to monitor her remaining horses.

"Hey, Bob," he said pleasantly. "How's it going?"

"Fine, boss," came the reply. "I rigged up some sensors in the stable and put surveillance cameras around the place, like you told me to. Sheriff's investigator came by a few minutes ago with the same question you just asked. I told him you'd taken Mrs. Merridan over to your place."

Jake muffled a satisfied laugh. "She's asleep. She loves that cat. Vet says it will be all right with time and care."

"Takes a mean person to hurt a cat that way. Or especially horses," he added angrily.

"Yes, it does. Which is why you're over there and she's over here. Still packing that shotgun?"

"Oh, yeah," Bob replied. "I've got birdshot for warnings and double-aught buckshot for serious intruders."

Jake chuckled. "Nasty stuff, birdshot."

"Try rock salt," Bob replied in a drawl. "I was cow-tipping at a neighbor's in my late teens and caught a load to my backside. Hurt almost as much as my dad's belt when he found out from the rancher what I'd been doing. And on top of that, Mom had to pick the salt out of my hide."

"Ah, childhood," Jake replied on a laugh. "Such sweet memories."

"Those weren't sweet, boss," came the amused reply.

"Never ceases to amaze me, people talking about how wonderful childhood was," Jake sighed. "Mine wasn't that great, either."

"Nobody's was," Bob returned. "I think it's all fantasy myself, something to make your own kids think they should behave better, so they can have a similar childhood."

"You lucky devil. You've got three."

"Lucy and I love every one of them, too," Bob said. "Why don't you get married and have some of your own? You're not getting any younger."

"I am so," Jake said with mock haughtiness. "I'm taking courses in how to live forever, but I won't share them if you harp on my age."

Bob chuckled.

"Keep your eyes open. If there's any trouble, call the sheriff first and then me, okay?"

"Will do."

HE PUT THE phone down. Did Ida's ex-husband know that his troublemaker had run for the hills? Was he discouraged by the advent of lawmen after the cat was hurt? Or was he just biding his time, waiting to add something more traumatic to the mix than hurting Ida's horses and her cat? It was worrying.

While he sat at his desk, thinking about it, he heard movement in the hall. He went out to see what it was.

Ida stopped in her tracks. "Did I disturb you? Sorry. I wanted to see if there was any coffee. Your housekeeper said she'd leave a pot heating in the kitchen. I must have dozed off."

"You needed the rest, I imagine," he said, smiling. "I'd like a cup myself. Come on."

He led the way into the kitchen, noting that she was walking a little better. She was wearing jeans with a long-sleeved blue sweater that almost matched the color of her eyes. Her feet were in slippers. "Pain easing up?" he asked.

She nodded. "It fluctuates," she said. "I have post-traumatic arthritis in my hip from the injuries. They did a partial hip replacement, and they had to wire my femur back in place and almost rebuild it. Hence the rod and pins." She sighed. "I'm lucky it wasn't worse."

"You said you had damaged vertebrae, as well," he recalled.

"Two, in my lower spine. They repaired those." She laughed softly. "Of course, I have issues in my back, too." She shook her head. "All my own fault, I guess. I should have known that Bailey was too good to be true. But I was so stupid about men."

"You didn't go out with anyone while you were in college?" he asked idly as he poured the warming coffee into two mugs.

"I was married," she said with a quizzical glance.

He turned, grimacing. "Sorry. Wasn't thinking."

She smiled. "It's okay. My reputation follows me around. It was really a stupid idea, but I was so desperate to keep men at bay when I came back here. I didn't go out with anybody except girlfriends when I was at MIT. They thought I was nuts." She drank coffee and sighed. "I guess I'm out of touch with the modern world. I was sheltered all my life, then I married a man who sheltered me just as much. Then there was Bailey." She made a face.

"We all make mistakes," he pointed out.

"Some of us make more than others," she returned. "I was afraid I'd meet somebody else and go nuts over him and end up like I'd already done, twice. I have no sense about men, apparently." She didn't add the journalist she'd avoided, because he'd attracted her, too, before he died overseas. He might have been a good choice, but she didn't trust her own judgment anymore.

"You have to take into account that you were naive," he said. "Being street-smart takes time and hard experiences."

She cocked her head and studied him with vivid dark blue eyes. "Are you street-smart?"

"About women? Yes." He sighed. "I got rich all too quickly. When my mother died," he said, "I was left with a fortune."

"It didn't go to your father...?" She stopped dead, grinding her teeth. "Sorry, I didn't mean to say that."

But he wasn't offended. He looked at his coffee cup. "He was in prison by then."

She hadn't moved. She just sat there, staring at him.

"He was like your ex-husband, only he didn't get out for good behavior. He took a shiv and tried to kill a fellow inmate. He died instead."

"I'm so sorry," she said gently.

He sipped coffee, burning his lip to stop the pain of memory. "We didn't mourn him. My mother had a little over two years of peace and serenity before she died, at least. Her father had died soon after she married my father. It wasn't until my father was arrested and convicted that her mother died, leaving her the only heir to the family fortune. So she became an heiress. Up until then, we were poor. Grandmother would have helped, but my father refused any offer of it. He hated my mother's wealth. The money was on her side of the family, not his, obviously. When she died, I inherited the works." He smiled sadly. "I'd rather have had her."

She drew in a long breath. "I loved my mother like that," she replied. "But my father was just as special to me." She smiled. "I loved him very much." She sipped coffee and stared at him. She wanted to ask why his father had gone to jail, but she didn't want to pry.

Nevertheless, he saw the question in her eyes. The pain he felt pulled his face taut, kindled anger in his eyes.

"My father was beating one of our horses with a hammer," he said through tight lips. "I had an older brother, Dan. I'd tried to stop my father and been knocked down for my pains. Dan was furious. He loved me, but he also loved the horse our father was trying to kill. Dan went after Dad and got hit in the head with the hammer. He died on the spot."

"Oh, Jake," she said, wincing. "I'm so sorry!"

"So we had two family traumas at once. I had to testify. Not that I minded," he added curtly. "It was an absolute pleasure when the prosecuting attorney brought out the many 911 calls my mother had made to the local police because of my father's brutality to both her and her sons. But I lost my brother. That was the purest hell I ever knew, until my mother died not quite three years later."

She didn't say anything. She just looked at him, with soft, sad eyes.

"You'd know how that feels," he added, forcing a smile. "You've lost both your parents, as well."

She nodded.

"So I got rich overnight and I was already traumatized from losing my mother, not to mention what had come before it. I went wild. I bought a small jet, purchased a couple of mining companies, invested in growth stocks with an eye to the long haul, not short-term profits, and I got even richer." He laughed. "Women, some women," he qualified, "go nuts over rich men. I guess I found my share of them. Beautiful, cultured, talented—brains the size of a pea," he added with a grin. "But you know what? After a while, they—"

"All look alike," she finished for him. "That's what

Cort said. He got tired of being wanted for what he had, not what he was."

"That's me, too," he confided. "I'm tired of being a wallet with legs. I'm thirty-seven," he added quietly. "I've got everything. Except somebody to come home to. I thought Mina might fill that spot in my life." He grimaced. "But the Texas cattle baron beat me out."

"She loves him," Ida said gently. "It's not like you lost a competition. She fell in love."

"Were you ever in love?"

"I thought I was," she said after a few seconds. "But what I felt for Charles was gratitude, and what I felt for Bailey, at first, was just physical and mental infatuation." She looked up at him. "I don't know what love is. And I don't want to know. Not ever again."

His face was quiet and sad. "Neither do I."

"Two lost souls, drowning our sorrow in coffee," she mused, and her blue eyes twinkled. "What a pair we make!"

He chuckled. "Both of us alone and rich as pirates and nobody to talk to at midnight when the walls start closing in."

She nodded sadly. "I know just how that feels. Walls. Nightmares." She closed her eyes. "I used to think it would get better, that I'd get over it." She sighed. "You never get over trauma like that."

His eyes had a faraway look. "That's how I felt, when I came home from the army. I thought, I'm a grown man, I'm tough, I'll cope." One side of his chiseled mouth turned down. "I haven't coped. I've just gotten older." He looked around him. "All this," he said, indicating the wealth of antiques around him, "hundreds of thousands of acres of land on two continents, purebred cattle, more money than I could spend in two lifetimes. And I'm all alone in the dark."

"So am I," she said, her face stark with pain and bad memories.

He cocked his head and stared at her. "I don't want to fall in love again. Neither do you. Both of us are rich and alone. But we get along pretty well."

"We do," she said, sipping more coffee.

He took a deep breath. He'd had an insane thought. He didn't even know where it came from, but it felt right. "How would you feel about getting married?" he asked abruptly.

She blinked. She stared at him. "You mean, marrying somebody one day…"

"I mean, marrying me."

At first she thought it was a bad joke, except he wasn't smiling, and his silver eyes were flashing with feeling of some sort, narrow and piercing on her face.

Her lips parted on a shaky breath. She just stared at him, and her face tautened as she recalled how she'd been drawn to Bailey and what had come after.

"A marriage of friends, Ida," he said quietly. "Just that. We can explore the world together, in between raising cattle and looking after horses. I've had more than enough of women who want me for my bank account. You've had more than enough of men, period."

"Yes, but you're a man," she pointed out.

"God, I hope so," he said, and then laughed.

She laughed, too, but her blue eyes were somber seconds later. "It's just that, well, the physical thing…"

"We can leave the physical thing out of it," he interrupted. "I haven't felt much interest in sex since I lost Mina, not that we were ever even close to being intimate. She didn't feel that way about me. What I'm proposing is a platonic sort of marriage. Later on, if we both agree, we might consider altering the terms of the agreement. But for the time being, you'll have a separate bedroom and I won't make any sort of demands on you."

"That would be fine for me," she confessed. "I'm afraid of men, that way. But you...?"

"I'm feeling my age," he said heavily.

"Thirty-seven isn't old, Jake," she said softly.

He smiled. "You're good for my ego." He sighed. "Some men get raunchy as they get older. It's not that way with me. I like good food and good company to share it with."

"Well, when you put it like that," she said. She studied his lean face. He was very handsome. There were so many advantages to what he was proposing, the most notable being that she wouldn't have to worry about being hunted by other men, ever again. Jake would protect her. And if he was willing to forgo adventures in the bedroom, then that was an added bonus. She was uncertain that she'd ever be able to get over what Bailey had done to her.

"You're thinking about it, aren't you?" he asked after a minute.

She nodded. "If you think you could live with me, like that," she said. "Separate bedrooms, I mean," she added and flushed, averting her eyes.

"I can," he replied and meant it.

She drew in a long breath. "I feel very safe with you," she said gently. "I know that's probably not what a man likes to hear..."

He smiled. "It makes me feel good inside, that you think of me that way."

"You're a kind, gentle man," she said unexpectedly. "I'd be honored to marry you."

Sudden heat ran through him like molten lava. He felt his heart go up like a rocket, felt the blood rushing through his veins like a flood. He couldn't explain it or understand it, but hearing her say the words made him feel invincible. Strong.

"I'd be honored to have you accept, Ida," he replied.

She flushed, too, and then she laughed softly. "I suppose it's not an everyday sort of marriage."

"Nobody's business but our own, either," he pointed out.

She nodded.

"So," he said on a sigh and smiled, "what sort of ring would you like?"

IT WAS TWO days before the snow stopped and the roads were clear. Jake took her by the vet's office to see Butler, who was improving nicely, and then on into Catelow to the jewelry store.

Old Brian Pirkle had owned Catelow Jewelry Company for fifty years, and he was still around, although his son, Bill, waited on Jake and Ida. Brian's eyebrows went up, as silvery as his hair, when they walked to the counter that displayed wedding sets.

"You're not getting married, Jake?" Brian exclaimed.

Jake chuckled. "I wasn't. But I am now." He looked down at Ida, who flushed prettily.

"Well, congratulations!"

"Thanks," they chorused.

"What sort of ring would you like?" Jake asked Ida.

She was hesitant. Charles had bought her a diamond. Bailey had let her buy herself an emerald set.

She looked up at Jake. "You should decide, too," she said. "I'd like them to match. You'll wear one, too?" she added hesitantly.

"Oh, yes," he said, when he hadn't planned any such thing. He got lost briefly in her wide blue eyes.

"Then what sort of stones do you like?" she persisted.

He smiled gently. "My grandmother loved rubies. I have hers in the safe-deposit box. Among them is a small, very simple yellow-gold ring with a faceted ruby in a Tiffany setting that her grandfather left her. Legend says that it belonged to a royal member of Isabella's Spanish court in the fifteenth century. If you'd like to wear it as an engagement ring, we can get a band here to match it. Pigeon's blood rubies," he added, which were the most expensive.

"We should have an eighteen-karat yellow-gold band with rubies in that back section, Bill," the old man told his son.

"Yes, sir, we do. Here it is." He pulled the ring out and laid it on a cloth on the counter. It was an ivy pattern dotted with inlaid, faceted pigeon's blood rubies, the sort of ring that would become an heirloom.

Ida caught her breath as she picked it up. "It's the most beautiful ring I've ever seen," she said in a hushed tone.

"Here. Let's see." Jake picked up the ring and her left hand. He slid it gently onto her third finger, where it fit as if it had been measured for her. He looked down into her soft blue eyes and felt another unexpected jolt like a burst of electricity.

"Do you want it?" he asked her.

"Oh, yes, please." She searched his eyes. "You have to have one, too."

"There's a matching men's band, a little less ornate," Bill told them and pulled out a wider gold band with inlaid rubies just in the center. It wasn't fancy, and it was definitely a man's ring. "We have a designer who works with us. He's in New York, but he sends us mailings of his latest work. I wasn't sure why I bought these," he added, chuckling. "Honestly, most people just want traditional wedding sets with diamonds."

"I like something a little out of the ordinary," Jake said, smiling.

"Me, too," Ida agreed. Her eyes were on the ring. "It's beautiful," she repeated.

"I'm glad you like it."

"You didn't try on the man's ring," Ida said.

He picked it up and handed it to her, and then extended his left hand. He smiled as she slid it over the knuckle. It was a perfect fit.

"That's one for the books," the elderly man chuckled.

"A good omen," Jake said softly, smiling at Ida as he pulled off his ring and took hers, handing both of them back to Bill, to be boxed up, before he pulled out his wallet.

"A good omen, indeed," Bill said, smiling.

They went back to the ranch and he led Ida into the living room, to the safe on the wall behind a portrait of the grandmother he'd told her about who was Spanish royalty.

"She was magnificent," Ida murmured, gazing at the gentle smile displayed by the proper Spanish lady in the portrait, silver hair piled on her head, dressed in black with a high black lace collar and decked out in rubies.

"She was," he replied. He opened the safe and pulled out an elegant jewelry box, wood with inlaid jade. "This was her jewelry box," he added as he placed it on the coffee table and sat down beside Ida. He opened the lid.

She caught her breath at what was inside. "These are beautiful," she said, touching the spiderweb necklace of rubies with a tender hand, the filigree earrings that matched it, the bracelet and, finally, the little ring.

"Here." He picked up the ring and let her look at it, pulling out the bridal set they'd chosen and opening that box for comparison.

The way they matched, the engagement and wedding band, was uncanny.

"We couldn't have done better if we'd taken the ring with us," he mused, smiling as he watched Ida enthuse over the ruby solitaire.

"I love things with a history," she said softly. "Things that have stories attached. A ring you buy new isn't the same." She looked up into narrow silver eyes and grimaced. "That came out wrong. What I mean is, it isn't the same until it has a history of its own, after belonging to someone." She held out her right hand, palm down, indicating a yellow-gold ring with a cat's-eye setting. "That belonged to my great-grandmother," she said. "It was the only expensive piece of jewelry she ever owned, and my great-grandfather sold a milk cow and calf to buy it for her."

He smiled, understanding. "You appreciate such things a lot more if you know how it feels not to have anything."

"Exactly," she agreed. She turned the little ring over

and over in her hands. "I love this," she said. "I'll take wonderful care of it."

"I know you will," he said.

She handed it to him. "Will you...?" She held out her left hand.

He pursed his lips. "Even if it's to be a marriage of friends, shouldn't we do the thing right?" he asked.

While she was wondering what he meant, he went down on one knee in front of her, and he wasn't smiling.

"Ida Merridan, will you do me the honor of becoming my wife?" he asked in a soft, deep, tender tone.

Tears stung her eyes. "Oh, yes," she replied, and her voice wobbled.

He took her hand in both of his and slid the ring into place. It was an exact fit. He lifted it to his mouth and brushed it gently with his lips.

She looked down on his dark hair and knew quite suddenly that she loved him. It was a very bad thing to happen when they'd just promised to have a platonic marriage...

CHAPTER TEN

JAKE CHUCKLED AS he got to his feet, before Ida could embarrass herself by saying something sentimental.

"We'll put an announcement in the papers," he said as he dropped back down beside her. "Do you want a church wedding?" he asked.

She hesitated. She'd been married twice and she had an ex-husband still living. She bit her lower lip and looked hunted.

He scowled. "What is it?"

She looked at him uneasily. "Do you know a minister who'll agree to marry a divorced woman with my reputation?" She fought tears. "I've made so many stupid mistakes in my life. That thing about being a wild woman with men was the worst, the absolute worst!"

He caught her hand and held it in his. "Listen to me," he said gently. "Nobody's perfect. Well, except me," he drawled, and his silver eyes sparkled.

"And not a bit conceited," she agreed, rising to the bait.

He chuckled. "I know an unorthodox minister who'll marry us," he said. "His church isn't exactly conventional, but it's a church." He cocked his head. "Do you want to wear white satin?" he teased.

"I was married in a suit the first time and a purple silk dress the second time." She sighed. "I'm too old to wear white satin." She met his eyes. "How about a nice white wool suit with a big fancy hat with a veil?" she asked, and she smiled.

"I'm intrigued. And it sounds very nice."

"Can you fly me to Manhattan before we marry? I'd like to shop for it up there at one of the couture houses," she added.

"I have an account…"

She held up a hand. "Thank you, but I could endow a small country with what I've got in the bank. I'll pay for my own wedding gown." Her blue eyes twinkled. "You can provide the flowers, and I'll expect bushels of them, I'm warning you. I love flowers."

He chuckled. "Okay. We can tell everybody that you're marrying me for my money."

"We can tell everybody that you're marrying me for mine," she countered.

They both laughed. It was a wonderful start. They got along together, they enjoyed each other's company.

Ida was already crazy about him and worried about how she'd hide it, but she'd worry about that later. Right now her only ambition in life was to marry Jake McGuire and do everything in her power to make him happy.

There was only one real worry. "What if Bailey finds out?" she asked. "He might try to do something…"

"Let me worry about your skanky ex-husband," he said firmly.

Her eyes widened with laughter. "Skanky?"

"I heard that word on a talk show and appropriated it," he informed her. "I plan to use it liberally for the rest of my life, despite the fear of copyright infringement."

She laughed. "Jake, you're so much fun to be with," she said.

He smiled. "I like hearing you laugh," he said. "I'm amazed that you still can, with all you've gone through."

"Takes fewer muscles to smile than to frown," she pointed out.

"Yes, it does. Do you want a formal wedding, with a best man and a maid of honor?"

She grimaced. "Could we get married with just us and a couple of witnesses?" she asked. "I don't really have any friends, except the Menzers and Cindy, and Cindy can't afford the sort of dress she'd need as a bridesmaid. I'd buy her one, but she'd never let me. She's too proud. I'd have loved having her as my matron of honor."

Her thoughtfulness surprised and touched him. He wouldn't have even considered that a friend might not have enough money to buy a fancy piece of clothing to wear to a wedding.

"Just us sounds nice," he said. "I'd like that, too."

She nodded, her eyes full of dreams that she was careful to hide from him. "Just us." She hesitated. "Jake, do you like cats?"

"Of course I like cats! What did you think, that we'd leave Butler at your house? Which reminds me, I have to pick up Wolf from the vet. He's had a minor intestinal problem, so they kept him while he was being treated."

"I remember. We saw him at the vet's when we visited Butler. He's a beautiful dog." She sighed. "I hope he likes cats, and not as an entrée."

"We had a cat here, until just recently, when one of Maude's grandkids begged to replace his cat, which had just died. Wolf slept with it, in my bedroom," he added with a chuckle. "He moped around for a week after the cat left. He'll love Butler."

She relaxed. "That's great." It was a relief.

"No more worrying," he said. "You'll get wrinkles."

She laughed. "I'm bound to get more of those as we go along. I'm not keen on face-lifts."

"Neither am I," he replied with a smile. "We earn our years." He studied her jet-black hair. There were a couple of barely noticeable gray hairs. "And don't even think about coloring your hair. I think silver is very pretty."

She smiled. "You'll look very elegant with silver hair," she said softly.

He laughed. "Not for a few years yet, though. Okay. What about a small reception? A caterer?"

She just stared at him, poleaxed. She hadn't considered those things.

He drew in a breath. "Luckily for you, I'm a great organizer. I'll get right on it."

"Should we get engraved invitations or just email people?"

He pursed his lips and smiled. "How about engraved ones? I have a friend who runs a print shop. He owes me a favor. I'll phone him. I need your full name and your parents' names."

Her face tautened.

He moved closer, touching her cheek with a tender hand. "Ida, I'll have both my parents' names in the wedding announcement. You have to have yours, as well. Even though we're both orphans."

She relaxed a little. "It still hurts," she confessed. "Especially Mama, because of the way she died."

"I miss my mother, too. I'd like to think they'll be

floating around somewhere, watching," he added with a tender smile.

She smiled back. "That's a nice way to look at it."

He removed his fingers. Touching her was disconcerting. It was a bad time to remember how her mouth felt under his. He hadn't kissed her often, but the memory was unusually vivid.

"Your first marriage was from necessity. The second was a dead loss. So wear white, would you?"

"People would be outraged..." she began worriedly.

"The people who matter won't," he returned firmly. "You're wearing it for me. Not for the masses. All right?"

She felt lighter all of a sudden, as if several problems had just been neatly solved. "Well, if you're sure?" she said.

"I'm sure." And he smiled.

SHE WORRIED ABOUT MINA. It had been obvious that Jake wasn't quite over his feelings for her, and that he was still wounded from her rejection. You couldn't make people love you, that was true. But it was equally hard to get over unrequited love. It had surprised her a little that Jake hadn't been in love before. He'd confessed to a couple of infatuations with women who were totally out of his life experience, but they'd only been infatuations, soon forgotten. Mina had broken his heart.

It wasn't as if she was jealous, Ida assured herself. Then just as quickly, she admitted that she was, but only in the silence of her mind. She had no right to be jealous, was the thing. She and Jake were getting married because they had a lot in common and they were both alone. Looking back at her easy acceptance, she wondered if she was doing the right thing. She was only a bandage over a festering wound. He might never get over Mina. Worse, he might fall in love again, with a woman who loved him back, and there would be Ida, right in the way. It would be a gamble, and she was a woman who rarely took chances. Well, except for that time with the slot machines where she'd lost a rather small amount of money. It had taught her that gambling could be a slippery slope.

Jake had gone off to see to the arrangements, and Ida sat in the living room with the workbasket she'd brought from home. She loved to knit. It kept her hands and her mind busy. She was doing a yellow blanket with the smallest gauge of soft yarn, made especially for babies. She made these to give away. She didn't have friends anymore, but she knew people locally who were expecting. Yellow was a safe color, when someone didn't know the sex of their unborn child. And she loved yellow anyway.

Her hands were busy with the wooden needles when Maude stuck her head around the door. "Do you want lunch, Mrs. Merridan?" she asked. "I've got homemade soup and crackling bread."

"Crackling bread?" Ida exclaimed.

The housekeeper's face flushed as if she was worried about making a bad choice of foods to cook.

"I love crackling bread!" Ida exclaimed quickly and was glad to see Maude's face relax. "My father used to make it for us," she added softly. "It was one of the few things he could cook, but he made it wonderfully well!"

Maude smiled. "Then come on to the kitchen and have some. Unless you'd rather eat in the dining room?" she asked.

"Oh, no," Ida said at once. "The dining room is a bit

too formal for me. I always eat in the kitchen at home. We used to when my parents were alive," she added with faint sadness as they went into the kitchen.

Ida put the food on the table. "What would you like to drink?" she asked.

"Oh, I'll get the coffee. Go ahead and sit," Maude said.

Ida was hungry and hadn't realized it. She tasted the soup and the corn bread. "These are delicious! Even my dad couldn't have made the crackling bread any better."

Maude put a mug of black coffee in front of her along with cream and sugar in silver containers. "I'm glad you like it." She paused. "How long ago did you lose your parents, if you don't mind me asking?"

"I don't mind," Ida said. "Please, sit down. I know you've been on your feet all morning. Wouldn't you like a cup of coffee, too?"

Maude smiled. "Yes, I would."

She got herself a cup and sat down.

"My father died of a heart attack when he was still young," Ida said between bites of the delicious meal. "He was in the doctor's office at the time, and nothing they did could save him. My mother was devastated. Me, too. She stayed alive just for me, but she missed my father every day of her life. When I was eighteen, she went on a cruise. I was working at a business in Denver that my first husband owned." Her face tautened, just a little. "Somehow, Mama fell overboard. They never found her."

"That would be far worse than if they had," Maude said quietly. "It must have been hard on you."

"I was very sheltered," she replied. "I'd never even dated much. None of the men I knew ever thought about marriage and children. They just wanted to have a good time. I can't abide superficial people," she added quietly. She smiled wistfully. "My first husband was all sympathy and comfort. He married me. I thought it was odd that he didn't, well, want to sleep with me. He said that we would be soul mates, but not physically."

"Goodness," Maude exclaimed.

"I'd never indulged, you see, so I didn't really have those feverish urges people talk about." She sighed. "He was a good and kind man. He spoiled me, took care of me, pampered me. I adored him. We had five wonderful years together, just as friends. Then one day he left a note for me, went to the top floor of his building, onto the roof and jumped off." She swallowed, hard. It was a painful memory. "His lover, a younger man with an attitude problem, came to the funeral and pretended to grieve. I had him shown to the door. Then he sued for damages, saying my husband had mistreated him." Her dark blue eyes were spitting fire. "You know, corporate attorneys are very good at civil law. They pinned him to the wall and stuck him with court costs after he lost the lawsuit. He went on to a new lover, who, sadly, killed him a few months later." She looked at Maude. "I didn't grieve. Not at all. My poor husband!"

Maude was thunderstruck. She'd never known anyone who wouldn't have been raging about a man keeping that sort of secret from her. And here was Ida, with her scandalous reputation, furious because her husband had been hurt.

"You didn't suspect?" Maude asked gently.

Ida shook her head. She finished her meal and sat back to drink the strong coffee. "I heard other women talk about their husbands, of course, but I had no practical experience." Her eyes twinkled, just a little. "From some of the things I heard, maybe it wasn't so bad that my husband wasn't interested in me that way. Of course, then I was widowed, and I found Bailey Trent." She sipped coffee, her face showing the anguish of saying that name aloud.

"A bad husband?"

Ida's eyes, haunted, met the housekeeper's. "You never know what a man really is until you're behind a closed door with him." She swallowed, hard. "Bailey was a sadist, and I didn't know. He swept me off my feet. I'd had five years of no physical contact, and he kissed me coming and going. He was a little rough, but I put that down to his hunger for me. Was I wrong!" She shivered. "He was brutal. I was so afraid of him. He was insanely jealous. I smiled at another man and he turned around and threw me off the first level of a parking garage. If I hadn't landed in grass, I guess I'd be dead or brain-damaged. I hit in such a way that only my back and hip and upper thigh were impacted. It still took surgery and a long time in physical therapy to get me back on my feet." She laughed. "I limp when the weather gets stormy. They did a partial hip replacement, and I've got a metal rod and pins down my right leg where the femur was broken. At least it doesn't show. Not that I'm vain about it," she added. "I've had a bait of men. I never want anything physical, ever again."

"I can't blame you for feeling that way," Maude said. "But didn't you want children?"

"I would have loved having them with my first husband." She laughed. "He was overweight and balding and a little slow. I loved him with all my heart. His children would have been like him, gentle and sweet and kind…"

She fought tears and brought the coffee cup to her mouth. "I still miss him, after all this time."

"It just goes to show that looks don't matter much, if you love someone," Maude said gently. "The boss said your ex-husband abused your animals."

Ida drew in a breath. "Yes. I can't prove it, but I know he was responsible. He even made threats. My poor horses. Poor Butler…" She hesitated. "Mrs. Barton, Jake says you like cats?" she added.

"Well, yes. I have several at home," she said, puzzled by the question.

Ida grimaced. "Mr. McGuire wants us to get married…"

Maude actually smiled. "Hallelujah!" she said. "About time he stopped mooning around here miserable because Mina wouldn't marry him."

"It's not going to be that sort of marriage," Ida began. "We like each other, and we like the same things," she added. "He said we had enough in common that we could make a good marriage without the drama."

Maude chuckled. "The drama is what makes a marriage. My husband and I used to have little spats when we first got married. Oh, the making up! What fun!"

"I don't really think Jake is going to want that."

"Well, you never know, do you? Why do you want to know if I like cats?"

"Because if we live here, and I guess we will, Butler will come with me."

"He won't bother me," Maude assured her. "I've had cats all my life. Three of them pile into the bed with my husband and me at night. They've all got Maine coon in their ancestry, so they're huge. My male, Calipher, weighs almost twenty pounds, and he's just a baby!"

"Maine coon?" Ida asked, curious.

"It's an expensive breed of cat, if they're purebred. They were named for Captain Coon, who sailed to New England in the early eighteen hundreds. Apparently, there were Persian cats on board his ship who got loose and, legend says, bred with lynxes in the wild."

"What a fascinating story!"

"You might want to get one to keep your cat company," Maude suggested. "If you ever do, I know a good breeder who lives right here in town."

"Did you get yours from her?"

"Lord, no," Maude laughed. "They're horribly expensive. I got mine because one of Jessie's tomcats got loose and had a bit of fun with a neighbor's Persian female. Jessie sent me to the Persian cat lady."

"She sounds very nice."

"She is. Most of the people around Catelow are. You know that. You were born here, weren't you?"

"Oh, yes. I was away for a long time. But it was nice to come home. Or it would have been, except for Bailey trying to force me to pay off his gambling debts."

"You've had a hard time of it. But there are always rewards for living through hard times."

Ida beamed. "I've noticed that."

"You'll be happy with Mr. McGuire," Maude said. "He's easygoing and he never fusses. Well, he can raise the roof when he loses his temper, and his language gets a bit rough around the men if they do things he doesn't like. But he's mostly pleasant."

Ida, who'd never seen him in a temper, grew a little worried. Surely, he wouldn't be like Bailey, who was dangerous when he blew up!

She had to stop worrying, she told herself. It wouldn't change a thing. She could back out of the marriage, but she didn't really want to. She was drawn to Jake, loved being with him. She didn't have the strength to refuse. But she was wary of the future. If he'd never loved before Mina, then he might be a man who was only capable of loving once. The thought was so disheartening that she fought tears. She hid them in good humor and asked Maude about her cats. That was good for ten minutes.

JAKE CAME HOME SMILING. "All done," he told her as she sat knitting in a chair in the living room. His eyebrows arched. "I didn't know you could knit."

She smiled. "It gives me something to do with my hands," she said simply.

He sat down across from her, sailing his Stetson onto an end table with unnerving precision. "My mother used to make sweaters for my brother and me, when we were kids." His face hardened, remembering his brother and how he'd died.

"You shouldn't look back," Ida said softly. "I know how you must feel. I don't have any family left, either. But you have to go forward."

He made a face at her. "Optimist."

She laughed and bent her head back to her knitting.

"What are you making?"

"A baby blanket," she said, and then flushed and met his arched eyebrows, and blushed even more. "For a woman who works at my doctor's office, who's having a baby," she stammered.

Jake didn't say anything. He just stared at her.

She jerked her eyes back down to her knitting. She

was embarrassed, and she didn't understand why. She thought about their upcoming marriage, one of friends, with no physical contact. Was he reminding her of that, with his shocked expression? Did he think she was making a statement about her needs by knitting something for a baby, when they'd almost certainly agreed that they would never have one?

Her mind went flying to the image of a baby in a crib, one with jet-black hair and silver eyes, and she cleared her throat and put aside her knitting.

"Did you put the announcement in the paper?" she asked a little too quickly.

"Yes. I talked to the minister. And the florist," he added with a grin. "You'll need a weed eater to get through the massive pots of flowers in the church," he promised.

She laughed. "Okay. I won't mind."

"When do you want to fly up to Manhattan to get your wedding outfit?"

. She flushed. "Well, can we go tomorrow?"

"Sure."

"All right, then." She started making a mental list of things she'd need. In the middle of it, she remembered her cat. "I have to call the vet about Butler," she burst out.

"That's taken care of, too," he said gently and smiled at her. "We'll pick up Butler and Wolf this afternoon and bring them home so they can get acquainted."

"I asked Maude if she'd mind Butler being here and she said not at all, she's got some at home," she said.

He chuckled. "She spoils her cats. She'll spoil Butler, too."

"He'll need spoiling. Poor old cat," she said sadly. "He's never hurt anybody, but life has been hard to him."

"It will get better very soon. What about your place?
I know you don't want to sell it. You grew up there. Suppose we put in a ranch manager, somebody married, with
kids perhaps, and they can live in the house."

She smiled. "That sounds like a wonderful idea. It
would be nice if we could find some people who really
needed a job," she added thoughtfully.

"We can, and I have. I'll take you over and introduce
you to them tomorrow."

She relaxed. "Okay, then. If you like them, so will I."

His eyebrows arched. She only laughed.

THEY WERE A youngish couple, Tanner and Grace Lowell,
with three little kids, all under the age of ten.

"I just run all the time," Grace laughed, running down
her toddler whose diaper had come off. "We've had a hard
time making ends meet since Tanner got thrown at the
last rodeo." She grimaced at her husband's expression.
"Well, it's not like it's a secret that you got hurt, honey,"
she added softly.

He sighed. "No, I guess not."

"You'll be the foreman," Jake pointed out with twinkling silver eyes. "That means you sit and give orders."

"I won't always have a bum leg," Tanner promised. "I
go to physical therapy three times a week."

"It's wonderful, isn't it?" Ida asked gently. "I have a bad
hip. They did a partial replacement and there's a metal rod
and screws where my femur was broken, so I still have
trouble walking. But therapy is wonderful. I especially
loved the heat lamp," she added with a grin.

The Lowells, who'd heard bad things about Mrs. Merridan, were fascinated at this look at the real woman. Gossip, apparently, was way off the mark here, as usual.

"That heat lamp's not bad," Tanner agreed and smiled at his wife.

"You can start Friday, if you like," Jake told him. "House is rent free, utilities provided, and you get a salary. House comes with a kitchen garden that you can plant any way you like."

"There's a stable, too, for your horses," Ida added. "Mine will come to Jake's house with us when we're married." Her face tautened. "I've had two injured. They're staying with Ren Colter for the time being."

"Injured?" Tanner asked worriedly.

"My ex-husband wants money," Ida said quietly. "He has ways of trying to extract it from me that will get him arrested if we can prove it. And don't worry. I'll make sure he knows that I'm not living at the ranch anymore. Your animals and your family will be safe. It's only me that he's after."

The Lowells exchanged glances. They had a pretty good idea of how Ida's hip had been injured, but they didn't mention it.

"I'd love to start Friday," Tanner said, "if you'll bear with me while I get back on my feet."

Jake grinned. "No problem there. You'll want to take your furniture, so we'll need to move Ida's out."

"We can put most of it in storage, but I want my piano," she told Jake.

"You play?" Mrs. Lowell asked gently.

Ida smiled. "Oh, yes. My first husband had me taught. He played so beautifully. He was a kind man." She glanced at Jake shyly. "He plays, too."

His eyebrows arched. "And how do you know that?" he wanted to know.

"Maude."

He made a face.

"Why don't you have a piano?" she persisted.

"I did have one." His face closed up, but he didn't say another word, changing the subject to the issue of Tanner's duties.

LATER, WHEN THEY were alone, she started to ask him about the piano.

"I was taking lessons, when I was fifteen," he told her, his eyes glittery with memory. "My father said it was a sissy thing for a boy to do. I told him I was no sissy and that Mama said I could learn to play if I wanted to. So he went out to the barn, got his sledgehammer, came back inside and smashed the piano to bits. It had been my mother's grandmother's piano. She cried for days afterward, and I felt such guilt."

"It was your father's fault, not yours," she said gently. "And I know your mother never blamed you." She hesitated. "You don't mind if I bring my piano with me?"

He was withdrawn for a few seconds. Then his face cleared. "Certainly not. You play beautifully. I'll enjoy listening."

She smiled. "Okay. Thanks."

He sat down in the living room with her. "You do understand that I'm going to be on the road a lot?" he asked, because it needed to be made clear at the outset. "I do business all over the world, and I have holdings in Australia that I share with Rogan Michaels. I won't expect you to travel with me."

She would have volunteered to go, but something in his expression stopped the words in her mouth.

"I'll have things to keep me busy here," she replied and was rewarded by a quickly hidden relief in his hard features.

"Sculpting?" he asked after a minute and smiled.

She nodded. "Which reminds me, I have to have my clay and tools." She sighed. "I have twenty-five-pound bags of special clay." She put a hand on her hip. "And a ton of potted plants that have to come also, including a banana tree and a lemon tree and..."

"Well, well," he drawled and chuckled. He got up. "Come here. I want to show you something."

She followed him slowly down the long hall toward the back of the house. He opened the door, and there was a room, enclosed by glass, a huge room with lit trays that held scores of orchids of all different colors, along with dwarf fruit trees, flowering shrubs, hanging baskets of ferns and philodendrons, even a Norfolk Island pine and a huge bird-of-paradise plant.

"Oh, my goodness," she stammered, lost for words.

"I like plants," he said, hands in his pockets as he surveyed the enormous room.

She laughed. "So do I. Mine are mostly flowering plants, but I love orchids and bonsai trees..." She broke off as she spotted a table behind some ferns. Her breath caught. Pots and pots of bonsai trees of all sorts, from jade plants to cypress to miniature weeping willow trees.

"This must have taken you years!" she exclaimed.

"It did. Maude keeps it when I'm out of town. The orchids need a lot of care. They're misted every day and watered every other day. They don't like wet feet, so you have to be careful how much water you give them. And they need fertilizer periodically."

"I've always loved orchids. I've never been able to grow one, not even a phalaenopsis, and they're supposed to be foolproof."

"They need sun-spectrum light," he said easily. "Thus, the vertical trays with light fixtures."

She noted the chairs placed around the room. "This would be a lovely place to just come and sit and admire the plants."

"Which is what I do, when I'm restless or worried," he replied.

She turned and looked up at him. "You don't seem to ever get that way."

He sighed and smiled. "You don't know me," he replied. "Not yet."

She just nodded.

"But you will," he teased. "How about some more coffee? Then we'd better decide on how to store your furniture and see about getting your piano and your other possessions over here."

CHAPTER ELEVEN

IT WAS A rushed thing, getting all Ida's things together and moved, and bringing a happy Wolf and Butler home to roam the house, before the Lowells moved into her ranch house. But she and Jake between them managed to do it.

Her furniture had been placed in storage, all except the piano and her bed, which had a special mattress that helped her sleep. Jake had moved the bed and furniture in the biggest of the guest bedrooms into storage with Ida's things, to make room for her bed and its matching suite of furniture. She also had a huge alpaca rug that went beside her bed on the carpet.

Jake gave it a curious appraisal.

"It's a comfort thing," she murmured. "I like the way it feels under my bare feet when I get up in the morning."

"You're not allergic to fur?"

She shook her head and smiled. "My mother bought the rug at a mall when I was a little girl. It's sort of an heirloom. It reminds me of her."

He understood. "It's beautiful."

"I keep it clean," she said.

He looked around at the white French Provençal furniture that she'd had since her first marriage. The bed had a white plush duvet, and there was a canopy, white and ruffled, along with a skirt around the queen-size mattress. The curtains, Priscillas, matched the frilly bed-spread and canopy.

"Very feminine," he mused.

She laughed. "I suppose it is. We were so poor that I spent my young life coveting a set just like that. My girl-friend, whose parents were well-to-do, had a canopied bed and white furniture. I swore that one day, if I ever had enough money, I'd buy myself a set."

"It does suit you." He frowned slightly. "Do you have French ancestry?"

"I don't really know," she replied. "Mama said we had a relative who died in France two hundred years ago, but not who or how."

"You need to do one of those ancestry searches," he suggested.

She pursed her lips. "What a neat idea! There's some-thing to look forward to!"

He cocked his head. "What?"

"Well, it's something I learned just after I was injured," she replied. "The doctor said we all need goals, espe-cially when we're hurt and upset and afraid. We need little things to look forward to. A new piece of jewelry, a holiday, even just a special meal in a restaurant. He said that goals made the time go easier. And he was right. I've done that ever since. Little goals. Baby steps."

He smiled. "Not a bad idea." His pale eyes were thought-ful on her face. She was excited, and it brought an even greater beauty to her elven face. He felt a sudden wave of feeling for her and fought it. Theirs was going to be a marriage of friends. There would be no place in it for any-thing physical. It was a bad time to remember how sweet it had been to kiss her. He ached to repeat it but smothered the urge.

"I'd like you to come with me tomorrow to talk to the minister about details."

She turned and looked at him, lost in the past so that she hadn't quite heard him. "What?" she asked softly. "I'm so sorry. I was remembering when I was a child."

He moved a step closer and looked down at her. "You were poor," he recalled.

She nodded. "And now I could fund the treasury of a small country. So could you," she added.

He sighed. "Yes. Too much money, too much time, too many days and nights spent alone."

She flushed and averted her eyes.

He reached down and took her hand in his big one. He felt a jolt of delight. It was mirrored on her surprised face. "Listen," he said gently, "we're going to be married, but it's not going to be conventional." He hesitated, because she wasn't getting it. He let out a rough breath. "We won't share a bed, is what I'm trying to get across."

"Oh." She looked up at him with so many emotions clouding her mind that she could barely get a coherent thought. She flushed again. "It's going to be hard for you," she stammered.

"Why?"

"Well, you're…you're used to women, aren't you? I mean, intimately used to them."

His thumb rubbed against her wrist as he tightened his hand on hers. "I was," he confessed. "But since Mina, I haven't wanted that. I haven't wanted anything intimate, with anyone." He was surprised to recall how long he'd gone without a woman.

"If you find someone you can love, you'll tell me, yes?" she asked worriedly.

"Okay. And if you find someone…"

"Oh, no, it won't be me," she interrupted. "I've had my fill of men." She stopped dead and ground her teeth. "Not you," she added. "You're not like any man I've ever had in my life." She hesitated, flushed. "I mean…" she began.

He drew her to him very gently and put his arms around her, as a friend might do when offering comfort. "I know what you mean," he said at her temple. He liked the feel of her in his arms. She was soft and warm, and she smelled vaguely of flowers. He smiled. "We're going to get along fine," he said, his deep voice like velvet. "When you have problems with your hip, I'll take care of you."

She sighed, smiling against his warm chest. She could hear his deep, steady heartbeat under her ear. "And if you get sick, I'll take care of you," she replied.

His heart jumped. He'd never had a woman make that offer, not even Mina when he thought he had a chance with her. But then, Mina had wanted Cort, not him. He felt the rejection wound him, all over again. It was the first time in his life that a woman he wanted hadn't returned his interest.

She smoothed her hand over his breastbone. Under the warmth, she could feel thick, cushy hair. Under that was firm muscle. She knew that he worked on the ranch. That would account for the muscles she felt, because he wasn't the sort of man to sit at his desk and just enjoy his wealth. His hand stilled hers as it moved toward where his heart would be, but she was too content to think anything of it.

"Don't you want anybody at the wedding?" he asked suddenly.

She drew in a breath. They'd already discussed this, and she knew Cindy, her only real friend, couldn't afford a fancy dress and was too proud to take one from Ida. "I don't have family anymore," she replied. "I'd like Maude to come, though. And my two part-time cowboys. And Dr. Menzer and his wife."

"Okay. I'd like Rogan Michaels to come, and Cort and Mina, I suppose," he said, and Ida felt her whole body tauten. "But Rogan's still in Australia, dealing with the aftermath of the fires, so he couldn't come. And Cort and Mina took the baby to Jacobsville, Texas, to visit two of Cort's brothers." He didn't notice that she suddenly relaxed. "I don't have family, either." He looked down at her and grimaced. "I was going to fly you to Manhattan. Suppose we go to Los Angeles instead?" he asked abruptly. "I have to meet a businessman there about a potential investment."

"Los Angeles will be fine," she said, not minding at all. In fact, she'd dreaded the long flight to New York, even though Jake's baby jet was very comfortable.

"Anybody else you want to come?" he asked.

She looked up. "I thought about asking my attorneys, but it would be like tying the past to the present. There are too many connections with Bailey," she explained.

His fingers burrowed into her short black hair. It felt like silk against his skin. "You can tell them later that it was a rushed-up wedding."

She laughed. "They'll think I got pregnant and you had to marry me very quickly," she teased. "Catelow is so small that it still has people with those attitudes about the thing."

His heart had jumped wildly when she said that, because he immediately thought of how she might look, carrying his child under her heart. "I haven't thought about children since…" He broke off, because he knew she'd sense what he meant. He'd wanted a child with Mina, who didn't want him.

"Sorry," she said, having felt him stiffen. "I shouldn't have said that."

His hand tightened in her hair. "Why not?"

"If I offend you, you'll let me go," she said simply, and with an honesty that surprised him. "I haven't been hugged very often. Not since my first husband," she added.

That dragged a soft laugh from the man holding her. His arms slid all the way around her and held her close. "I didn't want to make you uncomfortable," he said. "You're still afraid of men, Ida. Even me."

She ground her teeth together. How had he known that? "I'm trying," she said after a minute.

He drew back and tilted her face up to his. Her blue, blue eyes were full of consternation, turmoil. "Don't worry about it," he said quietly. "You don't really know me. But you'll have all the time in the world. You don't see people as they really are until you live together. You'll find out that I'm messy, ill-tempered from time to time, unreasonable and bullheaded and impatient."

"I'm messy, too, and I have a quick temper, but it's mostly flash fire. I get mad and I'm over it." She paused. "I can be unreasonable and bad-tempered, too. But I'll try not to be."

He chuckled. "We'll both try not to be." He looked down at her with faint affection. "We like the same things. We have a lot in common. Marriages have succeeded on far less. And infatuation is no reason to marry, because it quickly becomes disinterest."

"I guess so," she replied, and she thought of Mina, whom he loved. That had been no infatuation, and months after Mina had married the Texas cattle baron, Jake was still hung up on her. She would have to be patient. Mina was a sweet woman. Ida wished she knew how to dim Jake's memory of her. She wondered belatedly if they'd even have a proper marriage, with her third husband in love with another woman. It hurt her pride, she told herself. She wasn't jealous. She sighed. Yes, she was.

"Don't worry," he said softly. "It will be all right."

She drew in a long breath. "Okay, Jake."

The sound of his name on her lips made ripples in his emotions. He ignored that and smiled. "Okay."

THEY WENT TOGETHER to see the minister, so that Ida knew who was going to marry them. Tolbert Drake was pastor of an interdenominational church in the middle of Catelow. He was tall and blond and had a live-wire personality. When Jake had asked him about marrying them, he'd responded positively at once.

"We have a very mixed congregation," he told them. "Every race and gender and political affiliation known to man." He leaned down. "And a former Mafia don, too," he added with a chuckle.

"Goodness!" Ida exclaimed.

"So marrying you two is no problem for me. I think God is a great deal more forgiving than most people realize." He glanced at Ida as he said it and she flushed.

Which made Jake feel oddly protective. "Her second husband abused her physically," he told Tolbert. "Broke her hip and her spirit and now he's making threats, because she's rich and he has gambling debts he wants her to pay."

Tolbert frowned. He hadn't heard about that.

"I gave myself a red-hot reputation to keep men at bay," Ida said in a subdued tone. "My first husband was a wonderful man. He was gay, and I didn't know." She smiled. "We were still close and loved each other, but he died. My second husband caught me at a weak moment. He seemed to be everything a man should be. And he was, until we were behind locked doors." Her blue eyes were wide with painful memory as she stared up at the minister. "So you see, I have no judgment about men. I thought the best way to keep them away from me was to pretend I was so, well, educated intimately that I'd ridicule any man brave enough to ask me out."

"You were dating the man Mina Michaels married," Tolbert recalled.

She smiled. "Yes. He was like me, rich and worried about being just a walking wallet. We played chess together. Nothing else. I..." She swallowed, hard, and averted her eyes. "I don't think I'm capable of being with a man ever again." She stopped, horrified, as she met Jake's eyes with apology in her own.

"I'll explain," Jake said gently and smiled. He addressed the minister. "It's to be a marriage of friends," he said. "We like the same things. We like each other. We have common interests. That will outlast any infatuation either of us might have felt in the past for other people."

Tolbert saw more than they realized. He smiled at Ida. "Even ministers listen to gossip," he said. "I'm sorry. I should know better than to take anybody at face value.

We show a face to the world that we don't show in private." There was something dark in his eyes as he made the remark, quickly erased. "I think your reasons for marrying are sound," he added, "and I'll be very happy to officiate at your wedding. You mentioned next Saturday?"

Jake and Ida stared at each other blankly. The actual date was something they hadn't really discussed.

"Do you have a marriage license?" the minister added.

They both stared at him.

"I'll get one today," Jake said, mentally flogging himself for having forgotten. He'd been involved in a long-distance, very tricky business deal, and the wedding had gone right out of his mind. He wasn't telling Ida that, of course.

Tolbert smiled. "Then if you get the license tomorrow, I could marry you both on this coming Saturday morning. If you like," he added. "And you won't have to wait a week."

"Well?" Jake asked Ida.

She had doubts. She had concerns. She didn't really know Jake that well. What if he was like Bailey when they were really alone?

He touched her cheek with the tips of his fingers. "I would never hurt you," he said softly, and the truth of it was in the silver eyes staring so intensely into her own.

She relaxed. She did trust him. "Saturday morning would be fine," she said after a minute.

He smiled. "Okay." He wasn't sure why he wanted to marry her. He was only sure that he did.

"I FORGOT SOMEONE. I want to invite Pam Simpson and her husband," Ida said as they sat drinking coffee at the kitchen table, while Maude pottered around cooking things for their dinner much later in the day. "And, Maude, you have to come, too," she added.

Maude was surprised. She liked Ida very much, but she felt her place in the household. She had to be browbeaten into even eating with them in the dining room. "Me?"

"Yes, of course, you," Ida replied. "You've been so kind to me. Kinder than anyone in recent years," she added softly. "You can be my matron of honor, and if you need a fancy dress, Jake and I will take you out and get you one."

Maude felt lighter than air. She smiled from ear to ear. "You'd do that, for me?" she asked with visible excitement. She flushed a little. "You see, we don't have much money for extras, although Mr. McGuire pays me a lot more than I'm worth. My husband has a disability check. His back was broken years ago, breaking horses, so I'm the only one working."

"Of course we'll get you anything you need," Jake said, beaming. "And I do mean anything. You might have noticed that we're both a little better off than most people."

"I think the Mercedes and the Jaguar emphasize that," Maude said, tongue-in-cheek.

They both laughed.

AND THEY DID take Maude shopping, all the way to Los Angeles to one of the most expensive boutiques in town.

Maude was like a little girl in a candy shop. She went from garment to garment, looking as if she'd won the lottery, while an affectionately amused couple watched her.

"She's such a sweet woman," Ida murmured to Jake when Maude took two dresses into the fitting room, either suitable for a fancy wedding.

"She is," Jake replied. "We might consider giving her a raise. She's worth rubies."

She grinned. "She is. I'd like that, too."

He slid a careful arm around her shoulders, just a sign of affection, but it sent a thrill through his tall, fit body. He hoped she didn't feel it and become afraid of him.

She did. She was feeling the same thing. Like a jolt of lightning, she told herself, but a sensual one. She was shocked that it pleased her so much, being close to him. Unconsciously, she moved closer to him, and the arm tightened, just a little. It was a shock to both of them. They looked at each other with faint surprise on their faces.

They didn't speak or move until Maude came out wearing one of the dresses, the color of faded antique pink roses. It made her plain face glow.

"That one," Jake said before Ida could. She just nodded and smiled.

Maude came up to them, smiling at the saleslady. She leaned toward Jake. "Sir, do you have any idea what this dress will cost?"

"I don't care," he said.

Ida grinned. "Me, neither," she teased. "We want you to be the most well-dressed woman there. Well, except for me," she added with a gamine smile. "But I'll be in white. You look very nice, Maude. The color truly suits you."

"Thank you," Maude said. "And for the dress. I've never had anything so pretty." Her eyes were very bright. She turned away and went back to the saleslady.

Ida shifted so that she could put her cheek against Jake's broad chest. "You really are a kind man," she said gently.

His big, lean hand smoothed over her back. "Maude's

a treasure. I'm sorry I didn't think about this sooner. I know what it is to be poor. So do you. There were never any extras in our household. I went to school with holes in my pants that weren't made deliberately as a fashion statement, and boots that often had holes in the soles."

"We had plenty to eat, because we lived on a ranch and we grew our own vegetables and beef and pork. But shoes were always a problem because my feet grew so fast."

He looked down and smiled. Her feet were encased in neat pink sneakers that matched the silk blouse under her long leather coat. "Cute little feet," he remarked.

She looked down and chuckled. "I'll bet you have to wear the shoeboxes," she whispered.

"Big feet, big heart," he retorted with mock haughtiness.

She laughed.

"While we're here, you need to look at wedding gowns, Ida," he added.

She was hesitant. "Are you sure?" she asked, worried. "I'm not a young girl and it's not a first wedding. Besides, it's just going to be a small wedding..."

"We've already had this discussion," he reminded her. "Warm winter white. Something flattering. And with a veil."

She remembered that he'd insisted on that. Neither of her other two husbands had wanted anything resembling a proper ceremony. She looked up into Jake's soft eyes and gave in. "Okay," she said. "White it is. And a veil."

She left Jake sitting while Maude searched for other necessities to go with her bridesmaid's gown, and she went to the couture wedding department, her eyes full of stars.

She looked through what felt like oceans of white, until

she was almost blinded by the choices. But one particular gown caught her eye. It had a keyhole neck, trimmed with antique lace, tight in the bosom and the waist, flaring out into a wide, ankle-length skirt, and with a train. It was satin with a lace overlay, puffy sleeves, and intricate embroidery on just the bottom of the skirt, around the hem, in pastel colors. Those were echoed in trim around the band of the sleeves, and the neckline. The veil was antique lace, and its hem had the same fine, pastel embroidery. It was like something out of a fairy tale, Ida thought as she studied herself in the three mirrors in the fitting room.

She sighed, worrying that she was too old for a gown like this and should choose something simpler.

But the saleslady came in and saw her in the dress and caught her breath. "Ma'am," she said softly, "I've never seen a bride look so lovely in a gown. That's by a new designer, too, and he has some of the prettiest gowns you'd ever want to wear."

Ida let out the breath she'd been holding. She laughed. "I was worried that I'm too old for it," she said. "I've been married twice, you see…"

"Nobody is too old for a beautiful wedding gown like that," she replied, and she smiled.

Ida took one more look in the mirror and had to agree. She smiled from ear to ear. "I'll take it," she said.

MAUDE WAS LET out at her house, so that she could put up her dress after showing it and her other purchases to her husband.

Jake and Ida, sitting in the back of the limousine, waited for her patiently, exchanging idle conversation while Fred, the driver, kept glancing in the rearview mirror, as if he was impatient to go.

"Getting jumpy, Fred?" Jake teased. "We're not robbing a bank, you know. Although, the way you drive sometimes, you remind me of a wheel guy," he chuckled.

Fred smiled, but in an odd way. "I guess those guys have to be pretty good at the wheel," he said.

"Very good, I should think," Jake agreed, nodding. Then he turned back to Ida. "How about the symphony tomorrow night? Supper before."

"We don't have a symphony in Catelow," she said blankly.

"Well, no, but there's one in Manhattan, and I happen to know that they're doing Debussy."

Her breath caught. "How did you know that's my favorite?"

"I didn't," he returned, surprised. "It's my favorite."

She laughed. "Something else in common. What restaurant?"

"The Plaza, of course," he teased. "Unless you'd rather go to the Bull and Bear." The latter was at the Waldorf Astoria.

"There's one I want to see very badly, in Manhattan, and I've only been there once. It's the Algonquin Hotel…"

"My God!" he exclaimed. "Dorothy Parker and the other literary lights of the day!"

Her blue eyes widened and softened with delight. "Yes!"

He just shook his head. "Ida, we're going to be the greatest marital success story in the history of Catelow," he mused softly.

She grinned at him. "We just might be."

She was over the moon. She wasn't even impatient

waiting for Maude. Her heart felt so full it was almost to bursting. What she'd dreaded at first was turning into one of the best decisions she'd ever made. Gone was the fear of Bailey and his thugs. Gone was her uneasiness about marrying Jake. She was suddenly positive that they really were going to make a wonderful marriage.

It was a long way to Manhattan, a tiring trip. But she wanted to go very much. An evening with Jake would be out of this world. She thought about travel with him after they were married. There were worlds of places to go and see. And just being married to him would be very nice.

The only thing was, she wanted a child. She'd spoken to Dr. Menzer about it, without Jake's knowledge, because she had to know, just in case, if she could carry a child with her health issues.

He'd assured her that she could. It might put more stress on her bad hip, but there were ways of coping with that. He'd grinned and teased her about her so-called platonic marriage to the most eligible bachelor in town. She was quick to mention that she and Jake had agreed that it would be a marriage of friends. The doctor, however, was certain that it wouldn't remain that way for long. Not if she was asking about her chances of carrying a baby to term. But he didn't say that.

She glanced at Jake, wondering what a child of his would look like. He had silver eyes and hers were blue. They were both tall and musically inclined. Their child might be a prodigy, who could say? She allowed herself a brief daydream, of her holding a baby in her arms and Jake bending over her with joy in his face, his eyes. Truly a pipe dream, she thought after a minute. An impossible dream.

MAUDE WAS BACK by the time Fred got really twitchy. He was tapping in rhythm on the steering wheel and looking all around him, as if he expected the police any minute. It amused Ida, who had no idea why he was so nervous. She'd mention it to Jake later, if there was time.

Fred took them back to the house, and Maude, after a minute of heartfelt gratitude to them both, went to the kitchen to cook something magnificent for supper.

"You need to rest for a while," Jake told Ida. "You've been on your feet too long." He felt the weight of the dress she'd purchased, in its neat bag that he couldn't see through. "Going to show it to me later?" he asked with a wicked grin.

"Not until the wedding," she said firmly.

"Does it come with a veil?"

She laughed. "Yes. It comes with a veil."

He moved closer, one lean hand going to her cheek as his silver eyes looked intently into hers. "I'll lift the veil when we're married, and be the first to see you as a married woman," he whispered.

Her heart ran away with her. Her breath caught in her throat as she stared at him with fascination. She'd never known anybody like him, and she'd have bet her life that he'd never raise a hand to her or shout at her as Bailey had.

"Mrs. Jake McGuire," he added in a husky whisper, his eyes all over her beautiful face as he studied her.

She just stared at him helplessly. "Yes," she managed.

He bent his head and brushed his mouth softly, tenderly, against her own, briefly, so that he didn't upset her or make her feel threatened.

He drew back. She tasted like honey. He smiled. "Don't

panic," he teased. "I'm just practicing for when Tolbert marries us."

She laughed very softly and her eyes were full of her own delight. "Okay." She hesitated. "Are you sure we don't need just a little...more practice?" she faltered, uncertain of him.

But he smiled. "We might," he murmured.

He bent again, but this time the kiss lingered, slowly building to an intensity that brought her closer as the arm that wasn't holding the dress went around her shoulders and pressed her to him. His mouth was warm and gentle, even though his heart was racing and he felt himself going very taut at even that contact. But he mustn't frighten her, he told himself. He had to be gentle for a while, and not give way to the desire that had unexpectedly bubbled up in him.

He drew back far too soon, his breath going into her mouth as he lifted it. She looked—he wasn't certain—dazed, perhaps. Fascinated. He smiled. He liked the way she looked very much. He started to bend his head again, afraid that this time it wouldn't be gentle or brief, because he was rapidly losing his self-control. He was in over his head. He couldn't stop. But he had to. His lips were almost touching hers when the kitchen door opened suddenly and they broke apart.

CHAPTER TWELVE

MAUDE HID A smile as she told them that dinner would be served momentarily. They looked flushed and disoriented. Good, she thought. This might be a better marriage than they'd planned. Especially, she added to herself, since the boss lady was knitting a baby blanket. She'd said it was for the child of a friend, but the way she looked as she worked gave away her own hunger for a child. She wondered if the boss knew it.

He didn't. He was too concerned with wedding preparations and faint doubts. He liked Ida, a lot. He was comfortable with her. But he had memories he couldn't share with her, memories that brought him awake shouting in the dark. Flashbacks of horror, gore, war. He lived alone, so nobody knew about them.

He did recall Cindy mentioning that Ida had woken her screaming one night, and she'd called the sheriff, thinking the poor woman was being attacked. It was bad memories there, too.

Jake sighed. If Ida had nightmares, too, they might get along well. But he also had battle scars that he'd never shared. He didn't go shirtless in the summer, even on the hottest days when he was helping the men out on the ranch, here and in Australia. It brought comment, which had quickly been squelched by foremen who knew about him.

He wondered if Ida had cold feet, too. He'd given his word, promised to marry her, bought her a ring. It was too late to back out. He'd have to go through with it. Some small part of him wanted to marry her. He was lonely. He missed the wonderful days he'd had with Mina when he hoped to make her love him. Those days were only memories. They comforted him when he was sad. He thought about her with the baby boy she shared with her husband, Cort, and recalled how much he'd wished it was his child.

He didn't think Ida would want children, not in her physical condition. He wasn't certain that she could carry a child in her body with all the damage it had sustained. But he remembered her knitting the baby blanket. It gave him an unexpected jolt of pleasure.

He went back to talk to Tolbert, because he was concerned. The wedding was tomorrow. He couldn't back out now. The marriage had been announced in all the surrounding counties' newspapers. Jake was well-known in cattlemen's circles, in sophisticated circles in cities, as well. There would be coverage of the wedding. He hadn't told Ida. It would be impossible to keep the newsmen away, even if they could be barred from the church during the brief ceremony. It was just one more worry to address.

"You're concerned," Tolbert guessed when they were sitting in his office at the church.

"Yes," Jake confessed. He was perched on the edge of the chair, his elbows resting on his knees as he leaned forward. "I guess most bachelors get cold feet just before the ceremony."

"Every one," Tolbert said with a smile. "Women, too. I expect your Ida is pacing the floor herself."

He hadn't thought of that. But it made sense.

"Listen," Tolbert said gently, "you and Ida are very suited. She's beautiful and rich and talented. Yes, she has physical problems, but she can afford any rehab she needs to keep going. Women with hip replacements can have kids, you know," he added and noted Jake's surprise. "We have two women in our congregation who had babies, and they had complaints at least as bad as Ida's."

"Well!" Jake said, brightening. He sobered. "But it's not going to be that sort of marriage," he added quickly. "Just friends."

"Certainly," Tolbert agreed easily. "Just friends." But he was hiding a smile.

IDA JUMPED WHEN Jake tapped on her bedroom door. She opened it, looking as harassed and worried as he'd felt before he had the talk with the minister.

"Come out and drink coffee and we'll talk about cold feet and the future," he said with pursed lips and an amused smile.

She burst out laughing. "Look who reads minds," she teased, her blue eyes sparkling with humor.

She was incredibly beautiful, he thought, staring down at her. He smiled, hiding his reaction to her. He didn't want her any more nervous than she already was.

She walked beside him, without her cane.

"Feeling okay today?"

She nodded. "I'm taking the ibuprofen. I can take it until Sunday." She made a face. "Then it's off for ten days." She looked up at him. "I'll never be the same again as I was," she said. "Is it all right? I may not be able to keep up with you if the weather's bad and the joint gets inflamed…"

"If you can't keep up with me, I'll carry you," he said softly.

She went red as a beet. It was the last thing she'd expected him to say. "Oh."

He chuckled. He liked her reactions to him. She had little conventional knowledge of men. Both her marriages had been out of the mainstream, and the second one had turned her into a broken version of herself. But broken people could be fixed, he assured himself. He was going to make sure that Ida had a good life, that she was safe from her maniacal ex-husband, whatever it took. If he had to, he'd borrow Mina's band of mercs and set them up around the house. Let Trent and his thugs try anything then! He smiled to himself.

"You look smug," she pointed out, wondering why.

He chuckled. "I was thinking about Mina's group of mercenaries."

She lowered her eyes and felt her heart sink. "I see." He was still tied to Mina. He loved her in a way he'd never be able to love another woman. Why did that thought hurt so much?

"Your ex-husband and his thugs would think they'd hit a brick wall if he ran into them," he pointed out.

Her lips parted on a quick breath. He was being protective. Maybe he cared, just a little. He had to care, she told herself. He'd taken her in, protected her, saved her cat, done everything in his power to ease her worries. If that didn't add up to at least affection, nothing would. She felt better. There was a little warm glow inside her that grew as she looked up and smiled at him.

He felt that smile to the soles of his feet. Her eyes were soft and curious, almost…loving. He felt his breath catch as he looked down at her. The tension grew exponentially. He moved a step closer and his big hand went to lie against her soft cheek.

"Tomorrow," he said softly, "we'll be married."

"Yes," she replied.

"No more cold feet."

She smiled. "Okay."

He smiled back. The tension was making him very uncomfortable. He turned away. "How about some coffee and pie? I'll bet Maude's concealing both in the kitchen."

"Concealing them?" she asked and laughed.

He shrugged. His pale silver eyes twinkled. "Bad choice of words."

"And here I was thinking it was unique!"

He held out his hand. She slid hers into it. The contact felt wonderful, she thought, and wondered why her feet didn't feel as if they were touching the floor.

"I FOUND A way to get Cindy a dress without hurting her pride," Jake said while they drank coffee.

"You did? How?"

"Her husband does odd jobs for me when he isn't working at his full-time job. I told him it was an early holiday bonus, but he had to use part of it to buy Cindy a bridesmaid's dress and outfit her. I also mentioned that Maude was wearing a color like pale roses." He cocked his head. "Did I do all right?"

She let out a long sigh. "Oh, yes. It broke my heart to think that she wouldn't come. She's been such a good friend. I didn't know how to work it out. Thank you."

"My pleasure," he replied. "I like Cindy, too. She'll

probably call you later. Her husband was going to take her shopping this morning."

"Lovely!"

He looked at her bright, happy face over his coffee cup. "This time tomorrow, we'll be married."

Her heart jumped up into her throat. She was sure that he wasn't anything like Bailey. And there was no chance that he didn't like women. The only thing that worried her was Mina. He'd never gotten over her. What if he never did?

"No more cold feet," he said, reading the worried expression on her face without understanding why it was there. "We're going to make a good marriage."

She searched his eyes for a long time, feeling the electricity jump all over her body at the intensity of the look they were suddenly exchanging.

"You were knitting a baby blanket," he said, his voice sounding oddly husky. "You like kids."

"Oh, yes," she said softly.

He looked down into his coffee cup. He wasn't going to mention what he and the minister had talked about. Still…

"The minister mentioned that he had a couple of women in his congregation with injuries similar to yours. Both of them had kids."

Her heart ran wild in her chest. Her lips parted on a stunned breath. "Really?" she asked, without confessing that she'd consulted her orthopedic surgeon about it.

"Not that we're going to have that sort of a marriage," he said quickly, misreading the look on her face. He averted his eyes. "Children take a lot of work."

"Yes." She had to hide her disappointment. She forced a smile. "We'll have several people at the wedding."

"A nice little bunch, without overcrowding," he said, pleased to let the subject of children pass by. It disturbed him, how much he wanted a child. Ida was beautiful. He wondered if a child of theirs would have her blue eyes or his silver ones. He thought about a miniature version of himself, in little cowboy boots, following him around the ranch. He smiled to himself and then wiped the smile clean. Impossible dreams were a waste of time.

"Well, I've got a few phone calls to make. People get married, but business goes on forever," he teased. "I'll see you later."

"Okay."

SHE SAT WITH MAUDE, discussing little details about the ceremony. The phone rang and it was Cindy.

"My husband got a very early vacation bonus," she said excitedly. "And he said we were going to spend it on a bridesmaid dress. He said Maude had a pale rose-colored dress, so I got one, too… Am I invited?"

"Are you kidding? Of course you're invited! Oh, Cindy, I wanted you to come so badly, but I knew you'd never let me outfit you…"

"No, I wouldn't," Cindy replied, but there was a smile in her voice. "I'm so happy that I get to come."

"Me, too. We've been friends for a long time. In a way, I owe our marriage to you. If you hadn't been so thoughtful when my car broke down, Jake and I might never have gotten together at all."

"Oh, I doubt that," Cindy teased. "He used to stare at you when you were both in the café," she added.

Ida's heart jumped. "He did?" she asked breathlessly.

"He did. I'm not sure he realizes what he feels, you know," she said very softly. "But he does feel something."

"Thanks," Ida said, her voice quiet, hopeful. "He's been very kind to me. I was afraid that it was, well, pity."

"He wouldn't marry anybody just because he felt sorry for her," Cindy said. "Oops, customers piling in. I have to go. I'll see you at the church tomorrow. Did you get a pretty dress?"

"I did. Something white, because Jake insisted."

There was a quick laugh. "Well, honestly, you haven't really had a conventional marriage until now, so white seems very appropriate."

"I just hope nobody comments on it. There are a lot of people who think it should be scarlet instead of white. I haven't done myself any favors, trying to discourage men."

"You'd be surprised what people are saying about you lately... Gotta go! See you tomorrow!" And she hung up.

Ida put down her phone, her expression quiet and curious. "Cindy said people were saying things about me lately," she said to Maude.

"Yes, about your disgusting ex-husband and what you did to keep men from bothering you," Maude said with a smug look. "Cindy and I started some gossip of our own." She looked guilty. "I hope you don't mind. I felt so bad about the way I treated you when Mr. McGuire first brought you home with him. Cindy wasn't happy about the gossip, either, so we put our heads together and talked to some people."

Ida smiled. "Thanks, Maude," she said. "Thanks a lot."

"Wasn't much. I'm glad it helped." She smiled. "Why don't you lie down for a while and rest? Big day tomorrow!"

"Oh, yes."

IDA STRETCHED OUT on the cover of her bed with a sigh. She'd already had her morning dose of ibuprofen, which was helping a lot, but she still had some pain. She closed her eyes, just to rest them, but she dozed off.

She was running from Bailey. He was chasing her with a club and yelling curses at her. She was almost to a safe place when she tripped and fell. Bailey caught her with one hand and raised the club in the other.

"I'll make you pay for putting me in jail!" he was yelling.

The first blow came against her shoulder. She cried out. The next hit her lower back, the next her injured hip. She felt the blows as if they were actually happening; she was crying, screaming for help...

"Ida," came a soft voice in her ear.

She felt herself lifted, turned, held close to a broad chest that smelled of soap and expensive cologne and leather.

"Ida," the deep, slow voice came again. "Wake up, honey. Wake up. You're safe. It's just a bad dream. You're safe."

She was shivering. Her blue eyes opened, full of fear and pain and tears. "Jake?" she whispered, her voice breaking on his name. "Oh, Jake!" She curled into his body and clung to him, still shivering.

Maude was hovering in the doorway, her face drawn and worried.

"There are two liquor bottles in the cabinet in my office that I keep for visitors. Pour me a shot glass of brandy and bring it here, please," Jake said.

"Right away, Mr. McGuire."

Jake's arms tightened as Maude went to the liquor cabinet in the den.

"He was chasing me, with a bat," Ida murmured into his shirt. "He hit me, over and over!"

"He's not here. He'll never get to you again, I promise!"

She swallowed. "I was so…afraid."

His big hand smoothed over her sleek hair. He kissed her forehead. "I won't let him hurt you. I won't let anything hurt you, ever again."

She closed her eyes with a ragged sigh.

Maude was back, with a tiny glass of brandy. "I hope this was the right bottle. I don't know much about spirits," she said apologetically.

He chuckled. "You haven't had to, up until now," he pointed out. He took a whiff of the liquid. "Well, it's not brandy, it's whiskey, but what the hell, it'll do."

He placed it at Ida's lips. "I know you don't like liquor. But you need it. Come on. Open up."

She put her hand over his on the little glass and sipped it and made a terrible face. "It tastes like gasoline," she complained.

"Mostly liquor does, to me, too," he confided. "But drink it anyway." He hesitated, smiling. "All at once is best."

She drew in a resigned breath and tossed it down. "Oooh!" she groaned. "It's horrible going down!"

"Give it a minute." He handed the jigger back to Maude, who was hiding a grin.

"None of us would ever qualify for rehab," he pointed out.

"Why do you keep a liquor cabinet if you don't drink?" Ida asked when she could get her breath.

"Because I have business dinners, and a lot of business-men do drink." He shrugged. "When in Rome."

"Business dinners?" she asked, worried.

"You'll be the perfect hostess," he promised. "You're beautiful and cultured and you don't slurp your coffee."

Maude lost it. "I'll just wash this out," she choked and made for the door.

Ida burst out laughing, too. "I don't slurp my coffee?"

"Well, it's an admirable trait to me," he pointed out as Maude closed the door behind her.

She just smiled up at him, the bad dream forgotten, soft and pliable in his strong arms. Her fingers smoothed over the center of his chest and onto where his heart would be and stopped, dead.

There was a thick, wide ridge of tissue. Her eyes lifted to his and saw the unrest there. But she didn't lift her fingers. They smoothed over the scar tissue. "Does it still hurt you?" she asked.

It was the last question he expected. "No."

"Are there more?" she asked softly.

His face was taut, hard as stone. He moved her fingers down to his rib cage. There was another scar, almost as bad as the one higher up. He moved her fingers to the other side of his stomach, where there was a smaller scar.

"Oh, Jake," she said gently, frowning. "You must have been in agony when it happened!"

The discomfort in his expression eased a little. "They aren't repulsive?"

"Don't be silly," she replied, her hand lifting back to the thick one. "Can I see?" she asked, her blue eyes searching his silver ones.

He was hesitating when Maude came to the doorway.

"I'm out of eggs and I want to make a wedding cake. I'll run to the store. Do you need anything while I'm out?"

"Nothing at all, Maude. Thank you," Ida said.

Maude smiled at her. "No problem. Oh, and I fed Butler and Wolf. They're in the kitchen. I'll make sure I close the back door before I go out." She hesitated. "Feeling better now?"

Ida nodded and smiled back.

"Okay, then. Won't be long."

Her footsteps died as they went down the hall. A minute later the back door opened and closed.

Ida was still looking up at Jake, the question in her eyes.

He'd been self-conscious about the scars for a long time. Even with Mina, whom he loved, he was reticent about speaking of them, much less displaying them. But Ida wasn't repulsed.

He shrugged and unsnapped the chambray shirt.

When he pulled it aside, Ida's soft blue eyes winced. The scars were deep, buried now under thick, curling black hair. His chest was broad and muscular, but the scars didn't distract at all or make him look less sensuous. Ida was surprised at how much she liked looking at him, touching him as she traced the biggest of the scars.

"How?" she asked, looking up to surprise an odd expression on his hard face.

"IED," he replied. "We were in a convoy. I remember a jolt and a loud noise, as if the world had exploded. I woke up in a hospital in Germany. They said I was out for the better part of a day while they airlifted me from the field hospital."

"It's a miracle that you lived, considering where this

scar is," she noted and thought what a loss it would have
been to her if he'd died. The thought was painful.

"They had to dig out a lot of shrapnel," he agreed.
"Some of it is still in there, but not close enough to en-
danger my heart or lungs." His big hand smoothed over
the backs of her long fingers. "I've never let a woman see
these," he confessed tautly.

He'd had women. Of course he had. In the dark, so the
scars wouldn't show, because the sort of women he was
used to wouldn't like any physical imperfection.

She drew her fingers away, disturbed by the thoughts
filtering through her mind.

"Sorry," he said curtly. "I keep forgetting how naive
you are."

She looked up at him, her head tilted to one side. "I've
been married twice," she began.

"And you don't know the first thing about men," he replied, his eyes kind and soft. "I like it," he added quietly.

She flushed a little. "Why?"

He shrugged. "I'm not used to innocents," he said simply. "I preferred a different sort of companion, when I was
going out and about."

"Let me guess," she mused. "Showgirls and jet-setters."

He chuckled. "More or less."

She sighed. "Sophisticated, experienced women," she
murmured.

"Exactly. Women who knew how not to get pregnant."

The flush grew to a wild rose.

He laughed softly. "What an expression." He moved

her fingers back onto his chest, not minding the scars anymore. His cheek nuzzled her dark hair.

"I knew how not to get pregnant, too," she said, with painful memory.

"Good thing," he said.

"Yes. Bailey said he didn't want children, but I was afraid that he might try to get me pregnant. It would have given him a weapon to use against me. I'd have done anything he wanted, to save my child."

His big hand smoothed her face against him while he tried to ignore the exquisite feel of her soft skin against his bare chest.

"Did you ever enjoy him?" he asked quietly.

"No." She shivered. "He was so brutal. The first time, it hurt so bad… I screamed and he laughed. He always laughed…"

His arms contracted. "My God!" His lips were tender in her hair.

"I'll bet you've never hurt a woman in your life," she murmured.

"Never," he replied.

"I'm so afraid of it," she confessed in a whisper.

"No wonder." His chest rose and fell against her while he silently cursed her ex-husband for all he was worth. "I don't suppose it's any use telling you that most men don't get pleasure from hurting a partner."

"I've led an odd life," she replied. Her eyes were open, looking across his hair-roughened chest to the window beyond.

"You truly have," he said. "You never missed intimacy

when you were married to your first husband?" he added, curious. "You were married for five years."

"I read about it in a book," she said. "If you've never been intimate with anyone, you don't miss it, because you have no experience of it."

"I suppose that makes sense."

"I was curious, you know," she added. "I tried all the things I read in magazines to get him interested. Slinky negligees, perfume, the works. He hugged me and said I looked beautiful and why didn't I go shopping and buy a lot more negligees to delight him with." She sighed. "So I bought a closetful. Then he sent me to MIT."

"No men there, honestly?"

"I was married, Jake," she reminded him, because they'd had this conversation before. "I'd never have cheated on him."

His heart jumped, because he knew she'd apply that same logic to their marriage. No matter what, she'd never cheat on him.

"Why were you so self-conscious about these?" she asked, sliding her fingers gently over the big scar on his chest.

His hand covered hers. His eyes were on the wall, not on her. "A few months after I came home, one of my cowboys brought his girlfriend over for roundup. I had my shirt off. The scars weren't healed, and they were still fresh and red. She told her boyfriend that she couldn't stay out there where I was. She told him that she was sure I'd never get a girlfriend who could stand to look at me."

"What a stupid woman," she muttered.

He looked down at her, surprised and delighted by the expression on her face. She was outraged.

She felt his eyes on her and lifted her face. "And what sort of a man would even date a woman who had no heart?"

He laughed softly. "As a matter of fact, he was pretty outraged himself. He dropped her like a hot rock after that day."

"Good!"

He shrugged. "All the same, I kept my shirt on afterward." He made a face. "And when I was with women, I made sure the lights were out. Still, one of them felt the scars and said she was sorry, but she couldn't go through with it. She got up and dressed and left. I got drunk."

Her face contorted. She hadn't known any of this about him. She was certain that nobody else knew it, either. It flattered her that he could share something so very intimate with her. Not that she liked the references about what he did with other women.

He was studying her. His pale silver eyes narrowed. "What an expression," he mused. "Have I embarrassed you?"

"Yes," she said flatly, trying not to blush. She failed.

His lean fingers touched her face with its exquisite complexion. "It was a long time ago," he said gently. "I'm not a playboy now."

She looked worried.

"Now what's wrong?" he teased gently.

"It's just that, well, you're used to being intimate with women," she said. "And I'm…broken."

"And you think I'll howl at the moon because I can't sleep with you?" he asked, his eyes twinkling.

"You're too honorable to cheat, and I'm terrified of men when the lights go out," she pointed out. "Oh, Jake, what will we do if…?"

She stopped because his mouth settled slowly, tenderly, on her parted lips. She forgot what she'd started to say. Her eyes closed. He was gentle, not demanding anything. The sudden stiffness went out of her body and she sank against his strength, not protesting. Her fingers on his bare chest were like ice, but she didn't pull them away.

"You can tell me what you want, when you want it," he whispered against her lips. "If you don't want anything, you can tell me that, as well."

He lifted his mouth from hers and just looked down at her.

She felt her heart running wild, just from the slow, soft pressure of his mouth on hers. She looked oddly like a child on Christmas morning, faced with a lapful of presents.

He smiled.

She smiled back, fascinated.

"You understand what I mean?" he asked.

She nodded slowly. She looked at the broad expanse of his chest under her hand, at the powerful build of him, the rugged, handsome face, the thick black hair. She loved the way he looked. She loved the way he felt, so close against her. She wasn't at all afraid of him.

He knew that. He could see it, in the relaxed softness of her body, in the quiet warmth of her blue, blue eyes.

"I'll…try," she said after a few seconds, her voice so low that it was almost imperceptible. "If you'll be patient."

He smiled. "I'm always patient."

She smiled back. What had started as a businesslike proposition was taking on a different form altogether. She was afraid and excited and hopeful and full of wonder.

Jake saw that in her eyes and felt optimistic about the future.

CHAPTER THIRTEEN

THE CHURCH WAS full of flowers of every description, and Jake had ordered a bouquet of orchids for Ida's wedding bouquet.

He'd gone to the church with Ren Colter, his best man, and Maude was to bring Ida with her. Ida had worried about having someone to give her away, and she was sad that her father had died so many years ago, that he and her mother wouldn't see her wed. But maybe they were watching from some distant, happy place where they were together.

"You don't have anyone to give you away, do you?" Maude asked as they reached the church.

"No," Ida said softly, straightening her veil in the lit mirror in the ranch car. She smiled at her companion. "But it's okay. I just wish my parents were here."

"They know," Maude said comfortingly.

Ida smiled. "That's what I think, too."

THEY STOOD AT the doorway. Ida signaled to the minister. The organist began to play the "Wedding March" and all eyes turned toward the lovely bride, in her elegant white gown, as she walked slowly down the aisle with Cindy and Maude already having taken their place at the altar, with tall, handsome Ren Colter.

Just as she reached Jake, he turned and looked down at her. His expression was impossible to read. He looked surprised, delighted, absolutely without words. He caught his breath and reached down to link his fingers with hers.

The minister smiled at them and began to read the words of the wedding ceremony. Ida had hardly listened to them before. She'd been very nervous and excited when she married Charles, and painfully in love when she married Bailey. She hadn't heard what the minister said. But this time she heard every word. When he reached the part about "in sickness and in health," she was remembering how kind Jake had been when she was hurting from her injury, when her horses had been beaten, when her cat had almost died. She looked up at him and loved him so much, so deeply, that she could hardly contain it. But he only thought of her as a friend.

The pain of knowing that drained the blood from her face. Fortunately, with her veil in place, it didn't show. But her fingers, so closely linked in Jake's, were unsteady and suddenly cold. His contracted, as if in comfort.

Jake fumbled in his pocket for the wedding bands they'd chosen and let out a faint, almost inaudible sigh when he found them. He slid hers gently into place and then waited while she slid its counterpart, silently pressed into her palm, onto his finger.

The minister pronounced them man and wife, a poignant and mystifying thing that made her heart race with joy. Jake turned to her and slowly lifted the veil away from her beautiful face. He'd never seen her look so lovely. He just stared at her for a few seconds, his eyes full of delight, before he bent his head and kissed her with a tenderness that made her shiver with pleasure. He lifted his head quickly, because he felt the shiver, and he frowned. But she was smiling with her whole heart in her eyes and he relaxed. He smiled, too.

They walked down the aisle to congratulations and, outside the church, confetti that covered them lightly as they made their way to the fellowship hall right next door. The crowd followed them.

Jake chuckled as he and Ida brushed each other off at the door.

"Sorry," Maude and Cindy murmured together as they joined them. "We couldn't resist it."

"Not a problem, and the rain will melt the paper and not cause an environmental disaster," Sheriff Cody Banks drawled. "I crashed the wedding," he teased.

They both turned and burst out laughing. "Nobody minds," Jake assured him.

"Absolutely nobody," Ida agreed.

He shook hands with both of them, to Ida's relief, because she was nervous even of nice men. She'd wanted Jake to kiss her—but no other man.

They ate cake and shared punch and socialized with all the people who came to share the special day with them. Only a few had been invited, but it was as if half of Catelow showed up at the wedding.

"I'm so happy for you," Pam Simpson told Ida. She was beaming. "I feel like I helped this along, in my own small way."

Ida was remembering dinner at Pam's when Jake hadn't liked her very much. She smiled from ear to ear. "You did, and I'll never forget it. Thanks." She hugged the older woman.

THEY WENT BACK HOME. Jake lifted her out of the car with Fred at the wheel and carried her into the house.

He paused at the front door to kiss her, very gently. "Mrs. McGuire," he teased softly.

She smiled back and tucked her face under his chin. "You smell nice," she murmured as he carried her back to her bedroom.

"So do you, angel." He put her gently down onto the cover. "Maude left us cold cuts for later. I'm so full of cake I could barely drink coffee, but I'll make some if you'll drink it with me," he added.

"I'd love some," she said.

Wolf came in the door, panting a little because the heat had been turned up. Butler trotted along behind him and bounced up onto the bed to butt his head against Ida. She petted him absently and then smoothed her hand over Wolf's head. "Thanks for letting Butler sleep inside," she murmured.

"He's a member of the family, just like Wolf. Wolf lives inside, too, you know," he added. His eyes went over her slowly, like caressing fingers. "You were the most beautiful bride. I suppose the photographers got enough shots to last them for a month. One even said he'd thought about luring you out of the church with chocolates and flying you off to someplace exotic before the ceremony."

She flushed and laughed. "My goodness." She sighed. "I didn't realize there would be so many reporters there," she added. Her blue eyes twinkled. "But I noticed that they didn't even get as far as the fellowship hall, thanks to our sheriff."

"Cody had his deputies make a cordon around the church," he confessed, chuckling. "Nobody got through it."

"That was nice." She cocked her head and smiled up at him. "Coffee?"

"Coming right up. Maybe we should change first." His eyes swept over the wedding gown. "I've never seen a dress that pretty. It would be an heirloom..." He stopped short, turned and walked out the door.

Ida knew what he was thinking. The gown should be handed down, to a loved daughter. But their marriage wasn't like that. There would be no children. She fought tears as she changed from her finery into jeans and a pink pullover sweater.

She went into the kitchen and sat down at the table, wincing a little. She'd been on her feet for a long time.

"Hip hurting?" he asked, not missing a thing.

"Just a few twinges," she said and smiled to stop him from worrying.

He poured freshly perked coffee into two mugs and sat down at the table with her. "It's been a long day," he mused.

She nodded, blowing on her coffee before she tried a sip. Too hot. She put the mug back down. "But a nice one."

"We'll have a honeymoon later on," he promised. "Any-where you want to go."

"Decisions, decisions," she teased.

"Today, though, you rest. I've got some phone calls to make and I need to check on the livestock. Especially your horses."

He'd brought the horses back from Ren Colter's ranch a few days earlier, and he had two men, armed men, watch-ing them.

"Bailey won't try anything, will he?" she worried. "He hasn't called me since his thug ran for the hills."

"We can hope. But if he does, I'll handle it," he said firmly. "You're safe here."

She smiled. Her heart was running wild as she looked at him. "I know that, Jake."

He finished his coffee. "I'd better get to work," he said. He didn't want to leave her, but he was having some issues. She was beautiful and every day his passion for her grew. He couldn't afford to let the aching need get loose. She needed patience. Lots of patience. He smiled and left her at the table.

FOR SEVERAL DAYS he worked himself half to death on the ranch, doing jobs he could easily have delegated. Ida was beautiful. She worried about him, and that hurt, too. He'd been so cold to her at the beginning. He'd said things he wished he could take back. She made him hungry, and the ache just grew by the day. He didn't know how to handle it. He was backing away and he could see the wounded look on her face when he did. He didn't want to hurt her, but he couldn't let himself get close. If he lost control, he'd do even more damage to her than her idiot ex-husband had.

Bailey hadn't been in touch, but late one evening when Jake was in his office making business calls, Ida's phone rang.

She answered it without thinking.

"Think you're safe, don't you, Mrs. McGuire?" Bailey's angry voice chided in her ear. "I've got plans for you. Big plans. You'd better change your mind about that money. If you want to live, that is."

He hung up. She was shivering with fear. Bailey had that effect on her. She wanted to run and tell Jake, but what good would it do? They already had protection all around the ranch. Jake was doing everything he could to keep her safe.

She kept her fears to herself and dressed for bed, in a pale yellow silk gown with lace appliqués and spaghetti straps. She looked fragile and beautiful in it. But of course, she reminded herself, nobody would see it but herself.

She slept. She was running again, from Bailey, sobbing and terrified. He was chasing her again, but this time with a gun. She ran toward safety, toward Jake, who was standing in the distance with his arms open, calling to her. She ran and ran, and then she heard the gunshot. But it wasn't for her. It hit Jake. He doubled over and fell, and she screamed and screamed…

"Wake up!"

She felt herself held close to comforting strength as her eyes flew open. She looked up at Jake. He was wearing just pajama bottoms. His hair was mussed. He looked very sexy. She was coming out of the terror, her mind still almost in limbo.

"He shot you!" she choked, her eyes on his face. "He shot you! He was chasing me. It should have been me!" She wrapped her arms around his neck and pressed close, clinging with all her might. "I thought he'd killed you! I'd have died, too. I'd have died if I lost you!"

His heart ran wild. She…cared. He hadn't realized it before. His arms contracted hungrily and his mouth slid down to her soft throat. His big hands smoothed up and down her back against the warm silk. He could feel her breasts pressed hard against his chest, feel their hard tips as she strained even closer.

"Ida," he choked, trying to pull away.

"Jake," she whispered, shivering a little. "Jake…would you…touch me?"

His breath caught in his throat as she turned just a little and arched toward him, her eyes misty with hunger, her full lips parted.

"Where?" he asked huskily.

She caught his fingers and drew them very slowly to her breasts. It was like part of the nightmare but turning into the sweetest dream she'd ever had. Half-awake, she had no fear of him at all.

She arched as his hand slid under the strap of the gown, against soft, hot skin that felt like silk.

"Oh, God," he whispered reverently, because he knew he didn't want to stop. He did try. "Ida…" he began, trying to lift away.

"Please don't go," she whispered and reached up to kiss him.

As if he could, after that! He followed her down onto the bed. And despite the fact that it had been months since he'd been with a woman, he was slow and patient and tender.

He eased her out of the gown, his lips following its path down her trembling body. He kissed his way back up again, his hand making magic on her inner thighs as it suddenly found her in a way she'd never been touched.

She gasped, embarrassed, because all the lights were on.

He only smiled. "This is part of it," he whispered. "I won't hurt you."

She shivered. "It feels…good," she choked, surprised, lost in his silver eyes, the only things alive in that hard, set face.

"It's supposed to feel good." His mouth slid down to her bare breast and took one inside his mouth to tease the nipple with his tongue as he began to suckle her.

The reaction he got was surprising. She lifted right off the bed, arching up to his mouth, and the strangest little cry shot out of her throat.

"You like that," he whispered and did it again.

She went from plateau to plateau, no longer worried about whether or not he'd hurt her, because she'd never dreamed that lovemaking could be so sweet. She ached for him, burned for him, followed his whispered commands hungrily and then, suddenly, felt him inside her body, all the way inside, as he moved onto her, one long, hair-feathered leg inserting itself between both of hers.

"Look at me," he whispered unsteadily.

She met his eyes, her own wild with hunger, faintly embarrassed, as the pleasure built to insane levels. "Jake!" she cried out, surprised at the fever he'd kindled in her, blazing with pleasure that she thought might kill her. She whispered that to him, her eyes locked with his as they went into the fire together.

She felt one lean hand under her hips as his mouth covered hers in the last few seconds before they shuddered and shuddered, perfectly attuned as passion bit into them so deeply that they both cried out.

Tears rolled down her cheeks, but she was clinging to him, not trying to get away. She kissed his hot, damp throat, her nails biting into his broad shoulders as she moved helplessly under him, unable to stop as little jolts of pleasure went on and on, echoing the satisfaction he'd given her.

"I didn't...know," she whispered shakily.

His chest rose and fell over her damp breasts. "I didn't know, either," he whispered, kissing her tenderly. "Never like that, Ida. Never in my life, with anyone."

Her arms contracted. She loved him so much. More than anything, anyone. She wanted to tell him, but he hadn't spoken of love. It might wound him, if he didn't feel the same way. So she kept her silence, savoring a closeness she'd never experienced.

Finally, he rolled away, breathing heavily, sweat beaded on the thick hair that covered the hard muscles of his chest.

Ida sat up, no longer embarrassed about her nudity, and looked at him boldly. There were more scars, some on his upper, muscular thighs. She only smiled. "Marks of honor," she whispered.

He smiled, surprised at the comment. She didn't seem to mind the scars at all. He brought her down to him and turned her, so that he could see the scars on her hip, where the surgery had been performed.

"It's ugly," she said.

"It's not," he replied. He pulled her close and curved her into his body. "I don't want a platonic marriage."

"Neither do I," she whispered. She moved even closer. "Jake…"

"What?" he asked, his big hand smoothing over her hair.

"I want a baby," she whispered unsteadily.

His arms contracted suddenly as the words washed over him like fire. "So do I," he said, his voice deep and rough with hunger. The words kindled a sudden, unexpected reaction in his body.

She felt it with wonder. She rolled onto her back and

looked up at him. She moved sinuously, her hips arch-ing, as if he'd asked a question and she was answering it, without words.

He moved onto her, his silver eyes holding hers as he roused her all over again. It was the most poignant few minutes of his life, even more intense than their first in-timacy, because he was thinking about a child, and so was she.

At last, he cried out from the pleasure, biting into him like nails. She sobbed, her own body contorted with the force of sensual fulfillment. They clung to each other in the aftermath, comforting each other.

"In all my life," he said at her ear, "I've never tried to make a woman pregnant."

She laughed softly. "Until just now."

He lifted his head and looked into her soft, drowning blue eyes. "Until just now." He smiled.

She reached up and drew her fingers over his hand-some face. "I was afraid, just at first."

"But not anymore?" he asked tenderly.

"Never anymore," she replied solemnly. "I…" She hesi-tated and tried again. "Jake, I…"

But before she could get the words out, the phone rang noisily, the base phone in the living room.

"Oh, damn," he muttered. "I cut off my cell phone…"

He got up, slid on his pajama bottoms and, with a gentle smile, went to see who was on the other end of the line.

Ida, content as a cat after a saucer of cream, stretched and reluctantly got back into her yellow gown. She'd never dreamed that she could feel passion after Bailey. But Jake had been everything she'd ever dreamed of, tender and patient. She was aware that he'd been a long time without a woman, but she hoped that his reaction to her wasn't just that.

He said that he wanted a baby, too. She sighed and closed her eyes, imagining a baby in her arms and Jake at her side, looking down at her with loving eyes. Well, affectionate eyes, she amended silently. He might never love her, but he wanted her. That would have to do for now. Perhaps if she worked at it, very hard, he might come to love her back one day.

He paused at the bedroom doorway, his chiseled mouth pulled to one side. "A deal's about to go awry because the prospective partner has decided that he only wants to do business face-to-face."

She sat up, her blue eyes curious. "Where is he?"

He made a face. "Texas."

Her heart jumped. It was a long way away. Her face reflected the sadness she felt.

He sat down beside her, his hand smoothing back her disheveled black hair. "I don't want to go," he confessed. "But I'll have to."

She almost asked to go with him, but there was something odd in his expression, something that hinted of confused emotions and doubts. She didn't dare push.

"Okay," she said softly. Her blue eyes twinkled. "Make sure your pilot is sober," she said in a stage whisper.

He burst out laughing. It was the last reaction he'd expected. They were newlyweds. She might have felt justified in resentment, because he hadn't asked her to go with him. But he was uneasy about their suddenly changed relationship and he needed to step back and take a good look at things.

"I won't be gone longer than a few days," he said.

"That's okay," she replied. "I'll get out my clay and my tools and make exotic statues or something."

"Erotic?" His deep voice was amused.

She stared at him and almost saw the wicked thoughts in his mind. "Models of birds and lizards," she exclaimed and actually flushed. "Exotic wildlife! Not…that!"

He was laughing. She loved the way his silver eyes glittered with humor as he looked down at her.

"You are a bad man," she said curtly.

He leaned down and kissed her, but on the forehead. "Yes, I am, from time to time," he confessed. He sighed. "Ah, well, so much for my hopes of having something from the *Kama Sutra* to put in my office."

The flush got much, much deeper. He studied it with true fascination. Two marriages behind her, and she was still, in some ways, quite innocent. He smiled at her, and she smiled back.

"Well, I'll drag out my pilot and be off. Maude will be here in the morning." He frowned. "Will you be all right, alone, tonight?"

"Of course," she replied. "The house is wired like a bomb and there are full-time cowboys who live just down the road. I have my phone, and if I call 911, Cody Banks will have somebody out here like a shot. Don't worry," she added, confused and pleased that he was concerned about her.

He smoothed her hair again. He scowled. He was worried. He hadn't realized how much. Her crazy ex-husband was gunning for her, and she could be in danger.

"I'll be all right," she emphasized. "Honest."

He sighed as he got to his feet. "I'll phone you every night."

"I'll keep my cell phone with me. But if I'm sculpting, you'll have to be patient. I can't answer the phone with clay all over my fingers," she added impishly.

He pursed his lips and his silver eyes twinkled. "Why don't you do a bust of me?" he asked. "Immortalize me in baked clay."

She laughed. "I don't do people well," she replied. "Animals, yes, even flowers. But not people. We all have our strengths and weaknesses."

"So we do." He looked down at her and thought without wanting to that she was rapidly becoming one of his own weaknesses. Ridiculous, of course. He was fond of her. He wouldn't mind having a child with her. She was beautiful. A little girl, he was thinking, with that same black hair and light blue or silver eyes...

"I'd better get dressed," he said, bringing him back to cold reality.

She watched him go, confused. He'd looked at her as if he resented her. Perhaps he did. If he was still besotted with Mina Michaels Grier, then it was understandable. He wanted a child, but he'd wanted that with Mina. Was he only making do with second best? It was a worry that would haunt her.

SHE GOT UP and dressed, too, so that she could see him off. They paused in the doorway. Fred sat outside at the wheel of the limousine, waiting, looking all around and tapping his fingers on the steering wheel.

"He always looks like he's waiting for the police," Ida whispered to Jake and laughed softly.

He laughed with her. "I checked him out," he replied.

"He's clean. Maybe he has dreams of being a wheelman for a robbery ring, though."

"He drives like he'd be a good one." She looked up at him, trying to hide her sadness. "You'll phone when you get there? So I know you made it okay?"

His heart jumped. "I will. You take care of yourself. Don't overdo."

She smiled gently. "Of course not. You be careful, too."

He sighed. "This isn't working out the way I expected," he said nebulously. He bent, and for a few seconds, she thought he was going to kiss her. He did, but on the cheek.

"I'll see you in a few days," he said in a stilted tone and walked out to the car. He didn't look back. Not once.

IDA DID BREAK out her clay and start sculpting. Maude hesitated at the door to the guest room she'd taken over for her art. There was a tarp on the floor under the table Ida used, because sculpting with clay involved water and wet cloths, and there was a pristine carpet under the tarp. She knew that Jake could afford to replace the carpet, but it seemed wiser not to put it at risk in the first place.

"Oh, my goodness," Maude exclaimed when she saw what Ida was doing. "What a sweet little fawn!"

Ida laughed. "Thanks. I do animals better than people. Jake wanted me to do him, but I'd never be able to capture him in clay. He's too complicated."

Maude sighed. "That little deer looks as if it could walk off the table and into the woods," she added. "You really are talented."

"Thanks."

"Mrs. McGuire," Maude began.

"Wow," Ida said, stopping her in midthought. She

laughed. "Sorry. I just like the sound of my married name." She flushed a little. "What were you going to say?"

Maude sighed. "I was going to ask you about Fred."

Ida turned to her, her hands gray with clay, wiping them on a cloth. "What do you mean?"

"He went off by himself last night," she said. "I saw the limo going down the road toward Catelow."

"He was probably going to get gas," Ida said easily. "He takes very good care of the car."

"Yes, he does. He acts like a getaway man," Maude blurted out.

Ida burst out laughing.

"Well, he does," Maude persisted, a little embarrassed.

"Jake and I talked about that," came the amused reply. "We think he's just nervous. Jake said that he had Fred checked out and that there was nothing in his past to worry anybody."

"I suppose so." She studied the younger woman. "But you know, a lot of people commit crimes and get away with them and never get caught. Somebody like that wouldn't have a criminal record, would he?"

Ida hadn't considered that. But she dismissed it. "If he had evil intent, he's had lots of time to do something, though." She hesitated. "Bailey made another threat. I didn't tell Jake. He had enough on his mind, about this merger that was about to fall through."

"You should have told him," Maude said gently. "He's your husband."

Ida nodded absently. "I've been so much trouble already that I thought I'd just let this threat slide by, you know? Bailey's inside man left skid marks behind him trying to get away just after he hurt Butler."

"He was brutal to your animals," Maude agreed. "And he might have worried that he was about to be caught. I worry," she added with a shrug.

Ida smiled at her. "Thanks, Maude," she said. "I don't know what Jake and I would do without you, and that's the truth. But Fred's just the chauffeur, and he's never said or done a thing out of line. Besides," she added, "he's not Bailey's sort of henchman." Her face hardened. "Bailey was always hanging out with men who looked like they belonged to some secret, evil organization with ties to crime bosses. He wouldn't go near somebody as clean-cut and conventional as Fred." She laughed. "Fred doesn't even look like a man who'd break the law, now, does he?"

Recalling the little man's smile and good manners, Maude had to admit that he didn't seem the type.

"Just do be careful, if you have him drive you any-place," Maude persisted.

"I will. But I can't imagine I'll need to go anywhere before Jake gets back."

"How long is he going to be away?"

"He said three or four days," Ida replied and tried not to think about it. She missed him already. She wondered if he was missing her.

HE WAS SITTING in a hotel room in El Paso, Texas, after a successful meeting with a new prospective partner. The deal was accomplished. He could go back home when-ever he felt like it. But he was restless.

He picked up his cell phone and called the Griers. They were home from Jacobsville, where they'd been visiting, and he was invited to supper by Cort and Mina alike.

"You have to see your godson," Mina gushed as she

and Cort met him at the door. "He looks more like his dad every day!"

Jake chuckled. "Poor little kid."

"Stop that," Mina teased. She cocked her head and looked up at him. "You got married, to Ida Merridan."

"Yes." His face tautened. "Her ex-husband is still after her. He put her in the hospital before she divorced him. He's out of jail and determined to make her life hell for putting him there. He owes gambling debts and he's trying to force her to bail him out." His eyes glittered. "He had one of his minions go after her horses and even her cat!"

Mina's breath caught. "Good Lord!"

"He put her in the hospital. Threw her over the wall of a parking garage and broke her hip and one of the long bones in her thigh."

"I had no idea," Mina said, recalling how angry she'd been at Ida.

"Nobody did. She's living in fear of her life. Poor kid. Married to a man who didn't want her for five years, then abused by her second husband. She was scared to death of men, so she reinvented herself as a seductress and talked about the men who'd disappointed her." He shook his head. "Some reputation, when she can hardly walk when it rains or she does too much."

Mina and Cort exchanged amused glances. Jake had been vocal about Ida's reputation, and now he was married to her and, apparently, very worried about her.

"I knew all about that," Cort said quietly. "I felt very sorry for her. She wasn't at all what people thought she was."

Mina moved closer to him, resting her cheek on his shoulder as his arm curved around her. "And I was so jealous I could barely manage two words to her. I'm sorry for that now."

"She doesn't hold grudges," Jake said. He smiled. "She's at home, sculpting animals."

"What about her ex-husband?" Mina asked.

"I have good people working for me," Jake said easily and laughed. "Nobody can touch her on my ranch. She's very safe. Now. Where's my godson?" he added with a grin.

CHAPTER FOURTEEN

BUT IDA WASN'T at home sculpting. She'd had an invitation from Pam Simpson to come to lunch. She was bored and miserable. Jake had phoned to see about her, idly mentioning that he was going to spend a couple of days with Cort and Mina and his godson.

The news had taken the wind out of Ida's sails. She hadn't expected that. She wondered how Cort felt, having his wife's former suitor under his roof. Jake was still crazy about Mina. That was never going to change. He might want Ida physically, even be fond of her. But Mina still had his heart. Ida had never felt so depressed.

"Maude, Pam Simpson asked me over for lunch. You haven't started cooking yet, have you?" Ida asked at the kitchen doorway.

"No, not yet," Maude replied with a smile. "Will you be back for supper?"

"Yes. But let's have something light," she added with a sigh. "I'm feeling a little queasy."

Maude, who had no idea that her employers were more than good friends, just nodded. "It may be that stomach virus that's going around. You come home if you don't feel better, okay?"

"Okay." She smiled. "I won't stay long. I just need to get out for a while."

"Mr. McGuire isn't coming back today?" Maude asked, because he'd said a couple of days, and this was the third day of his absence.

"He's in El Paso. Near El Paso. He's staying with Mina and Cort Grier," she added reluctantly and was unaware that the deep sadness in her face was visible to the older woman.

"Oh. Probably went to see that little boy," Maude replied, trying to be comforting, because she knew even better than Ida how much in love Jake had been with Mina. After Mina's marriage, he'd stayed drunk for three days. Nobody knew about that. Just Maude.

"I guess so," Ida said.

Maude almost said that the two of them ought to be thinking about a family of their own, but she didn't dare. The boss was tight-lipped and so was Ida. It wasn't worth her nice job to make such suggestions.

"Well, you have a good lunch at Mrs. Simpson's house," Maude said. "I'll feed Butler for you," she added.

Ida smiled. The cat slept with her. So did Wolf, in fact. It had shocked her when the big German shepherd jumped up on the foot of the bed and curled up with Butler. It had given her a feeling of security, as well. She loved both animals.

"We need to get somebody to take Wolf out for a run," she added. "I'd try, but…"

"We'll get one of the cowboys to do it," Maude interrupted. "Don't you worry. I'll get Johnny to do it. He loves Wolf and he'll make sure not to let him get hurt. Okay?"

"Okay. Thanks, Maude. I'll be back in a couple of hours."

"I'll see you then."

IDA WALKED OUT and got into the back of the limo. Fred held the door open for her, smiled politely and closed it.

Ida sank into the soft leather of the back seat and closed her eyes. "You know where to go, right, Fred?" she asked.

"Mrs. Simpson's. Yes, ma'am."

"Okay."

SHE WAS DROWSY. She hadn't slept well and her stomach was still queasy. It must have been something she ate, she thought, but she hadn't had anything out of the ordinary. Still…

Her eyes went to the landscape and she frowned. "Fred, are we going the right way?" she asked.

"It's closer this way, ma'am," he assured her. "I hope you don't mind."

"Of course not." She smiled. "You're a nice man, Fred. We're lucky to have you to drive us."

There was a stunned hesitation. "Well…well, thank you, Mrs. Merr… I mean, Mrs. McGuire," he stammered.

She leaned back against the seat and closed her eyes again, feeling sleepy.

JAKE WAS SITTING down to dinner with Mina and Cort, after spending a wonderful half hour with his godson on the floor with a massive amount of plastic toys. He was in a good mood. He thought about a child of his own, with Ida.

"She talked to her doctor about having a child," he mentioned to his shocked fellow diners. "She's had a partial hip replacement, and it's hard for her to get around sometimes."

"One of my sisters-in-law had a bad heart valve when she got pregnant," Cort said. "She came through in spite of it. She and Garon have a son and she's expecting again, artificial valve and all." He chuckled. "Theirs was a turbulent relationship. He thought she was an old-fashioned woman with no skills, and she turned out to be a member of Mensa. Shocked him speechless when she started spouting Arabic to a witness in his office. He's SAC at the Jacobsville satellite FBI office," he added.

"Well, if a woman with that bad a condition can get pregnant, there's no reason Ida couldn't," Mina mused.

Jake actually blushed, but then he grinned. "Absolutely," he agreed.

Mina and Cort hid smiles.

But a few minutes later nobody was smiling. Jake got a call from home, from Maude.

"I'm sorry to bother you, Mr. McGuire," Maude said, "but Ida left over three hours ago to have lunch with Mrs. Simpson. I got worried and called over there to see if she'd got talking or something, and Mrs. Simpson said she never showed up…"

There was a skirl of harsh language. Jake had gotten out of his chair and he was cussing mad. "Is she with Fred?" he asked abruptly.

"Yes, sir. He drove her."

"Call Cody Banks and tell him what you just told me. I'm on my way to the airport. I'll be there as quick as I can. If you hear anything, anything at all, you call me!"

"Yes, sir."

He hung up and called his pilot and his driver. Afterward, while he waited for his ride, he turned a pale, worried face to Cort and Mina. "Ida's missing. Her exhusband's made a lot of threats. I have to go."

"If we can do anything, we will," Mina said, Cort nodding beside her.

"Thanks." He rushed out the door when the limo showed up. "Can you send my bag on to Catelow?" he called over his shoulder.

"First thing," Mina called after him.

He threw up a hand, climbed into the car, and it sped away.

Mina peered up at Cort with a smug little smile. "I told you."

He chuckled, pulling her close. "You did."

"I hope she'll be all right," she added quietly. "What a terrible thing to have happen."

"Jake will get to her in time," he assured his wife. "He's not a bad man, now that he's not trying to talk you into marriage," he added.

She laughed. "He just had his priorities mixed up. I guarantee, they're not mixed up anymore. He'll be sitting beside his pilot, trying to make the plane go faster." She shook her head. "I'll bet he didn't even realize that he loved her."

THAT WOULD HAVE been a safe bet. Terrified of what he might find when he went home, Jake could have kicked himself for not realizing it sooner. He was crazy about Ida. Maybe he always had been. But certainly, from the time he'd driven her to her doctor's office, that first day, she'd never been far out of his mind. He'd taken care of her, worried about her, married her to keep her safe. And even after all that, he hadn't realized how he felt about her.

He certainly realized it now. He just hoped that it wasn't too late. He ground his teeth in anguish.

MEANWHILE, IDA WAS sitting in the back of the limousine drinking a cup of coffee that Fred had bought for both of them at a coffee shop in Billings. It had been a long drive. Fred had been quiet and miserable, especially when Ida realized that they weren't headed toward Pam Simpson's house.

"Where are we going, Fred?" she asked, leaning forward, her beautiful face drawn with fear. "Please tell me you're not mixed up with Bailey. Please tell me that!"

The terror he saw in her face, added to his own guilty conscience, had slowed the car. He pulled into a grocery store parking lot and let down the glass between the front seat and the back and switched off the engine.

"Mrs. McGuire, I've never hurt a human being in my life," he said miserably. "But he's got my mother..." He stopped, almost choking on the fear.

"Oh, Fred," she said softly and winced. "I'm so sorry!"

"No. I'm sorry. He promised he'd let her go. All I had to do was bring you to a house he was staying at, over near Powell, Wyoming." He averted his eyes. "It didn't sound so bad. I mean, I didn't think he'd hurt you." He looked back at her. "I didn't know what he'd done to you. I was unhappy about him hurting your cat. I have a cat. She's twenty years old. I love her."

"I love Butler, too," she said.

"I don't know what to do," Fred said heavily. "See, I worked as a wheelman for a robbery ring in Denver, years ago. Bailey knew. He sent me to apply for that chauffeur job with Mr. McGuire, once he found out that Mr. McGuire was taking you out. I thought he was helping me. You know, giving me a second chance because I'd just got out of jail and there aren't a lot of people who'll hire an ex-con. He said he'd make sure my background looked real clean." His eyes closed. "I didn't want to do this." He looked back at her. His face was torn with discomfort. "I don't want to let him hurt you. But he's got my mom, and she's all I have in the world. She stood by me when I got arrested, in spite of always warning me to stay away from bad people. She came to see me every week when I was behind bars. I don't know what to do!"

"Fred, will you trust me?" she asked softly.

"I would. But you shouldn't trust me. I'm an evil man!"

"You aren't," she said, her voice quiet and soft. "I'm going to call my attorneys in Denver. They sent Bailey to prison in the first place. I want to tell them that you'll testify against Bailey. Will you let me do that?"

"My mom…!"

"They have a first-rate investigator. He was a mercenary before he took on the job." She smiled. "He's got contacts that you wouldn't believe."

"As long as my mom doesn't get hurt…"

"I can promise you that she won't."

He hesitated, but only for a few seconds. "Okay."

The parking lot was well lit. They were waiting for the investigator. He'd been with them for years, all through Ida's turbulent second marriage and its aftermath. He was in his midthirties now, but still as dangerous a man as she'd ever known.

He parked next to the limousine, giving Ida and Fred a few anxious seconds until he climbed out of the dark sedan and opened the back door of the limo.

He didn't waste words. "Where is Trent?" he asked Fred.

Fred told him. "He's got my mom," he added.

Hunt Garrison just smiled. "No, he doesn't."

Fred almost gasped. "He doesn't?"

"She's safe and sound in a motel outside Catelow, with one of Mr. McGuire's men guarding her like a hawk."

"Oh, thank God!" Fred said reverently. "Thank you! I don't deserve it, but thank you!"

"You'll testify?" Garrison asked Fred.

The little man looked at Ida with regret and sorrow. "You bet I will," he said. "Even if it means going back to jail. I'm an ex-con…"

Garrison waved a hand. "We know all that. Nobody's pressing charges against you. Unless…?" He looked at Ida.

"Nobody's pressing charges against him," Ida replied, and she smiled at a shocked Fred. "It's hard to find a really good driver."

They all laughed, breaking the tension.

Just then, her phone rang.

She answered it, still buoyed up by her delight at not having to face a furious Bailey. "Hello?"

"Where the hell are you? Are you all right? If that weasel has hurt a hair on your head, I'll beat him to a bloody pulp and feed him to Wolf…!"

That was her husband, and he was raving mad. "It's okay, Jake," she said softly. "I'm here with Fred and Mr. Garrison, from my attorney's office. Fred's going to testify against Bailey. Bailey had his mother," she added quickly. "But he couldn't go through with taking me to Bailey." There was a pregnant silence. "He's the best driver we'll ever get," she added, a faint plea in her voice.

"Where are you?" he repeated.

She looked around. "Where are we?" she asked the two men.

Garrison told her with an amused smile. She told Jake.

"I'm in the air. We'll land at the Rimrocks. Can you meet me there?" He gave her the ETA.

She gave it, in turn, to the men and asked if they could get her to the airport.

"We'll get you there…" He paused, because his own phone was ringing. He got out of the car to answer it.

"If anything had happened to you," Jake began through his teeth.

Elation filled her like cake. "I'm fine. Really."

He relaxed. "Okay. I'll see you soon."

She hung up. "It's okay," she assured Fred, who was still tormented.

Garrison got back into the car. "That was your sheriff, Cody Banks. He's been in touch with the Denver authorities. They sent a US marshal to pick up your ex-husband. He's in custody."

Ida and Fred both let out sighs of relief.

"We're safe, Fred," Ida told the driver.

He laughed. Then he grimaced. "Well, until your husband gets here, at least," he said sheepishly.

"I wouldn't worry," Garrison chuckled. "I expect he'll be too relieved that his wife is safe to go looking for a big bat."

Ida hoped that was the case.

JAKE'S FACE WAS drawn and pale, and he strode toward her so quickly that before she could even say hello, he had her up in his arms off the ground, and he was kissing her, blind and deaf to the comings and goings of amused travelers around them.

"My sweetheart," he groaned into her ear as his arms

tightened. "I thought the plane would never get here! Are you sure you're all right?" he added, putting her down gently.

"I am, thanks to Fred and Mr. Garrison," she added, indicating the two men.

Fred moved forward, hunched and miserable. "I'm so sorry, Mr. McGuire. I've got a record. I was a wheelman for the mob and I've served time. Mr. Trent had my mom. She's all I've got. He said he'd kill her if I didn't do what he said." He looked up at Jake. "I won't mind going back to jail. My mom's safe…"

"Your mom and you," Jake said quietly. "I can't thank you enough for what you did. It took guts."

"How do you know?" Fred asked.

Jake indicated Garrison, who was grinning. "He phoned me."

"Oh." Fred looked up at him. "I'm not fired?"

"Good drivers are hard to find, Fred," Jake murmured, smiling.

Fred averted his face to hide his very bright eyes. "Thanks," he choked. "I'll be the best driver you ever had, and I'll never let anything happen to Mrs. McGuire. I swear it!"

"I'd better get back," Garrison said. He'd driven his own car to the Rimrocks to meet the plane. "We'll be in touch with Fred after the bail hearing, or at least the district attorney will be. And we'll make sure that bail is set high enough that Mr. Trent won't be getting out anytime soon."

"Thanks, Mr. Garrison," Ida said, shaking hands.

"That goes double for me," Jake added, doing the same.

"All in a day's work." Garrison patted Fred on the

shoulder. "You should call your mom. She's got her cell phone. She was worried about you."

Fred chuckled. "Yeah. I was worried about her, too. Thanks."

The other man shrugged, waved and went toward the parking lot.

"Fred, you'll have to drive the car back to Catelow," Jake said. "I'm taking Ida on the jet."

"No problem, Mr. McGuire." He pursed his lips. "Want to bet on who gets there first?"

Jake gave him a cold stare.

Fred held up both hands. "Just kidding. Honest."

Jake burst out laughing.

JAKE HAD IDA in his lap all the way back, kissing her softly from time to time as they discussed a lot of things, mostly her almost-kidnapping and Fred's surprising turnaround.

"Were you scared?" he asked.

"Only at first. Poor Fred. He loves his mother. He loves animals, too. He was furious about what Bailey had done to my horses and Butler, but he was afraid for his mother's life. I still don't know how Mr. Garrison managed to find her and rescue her."

"I believe he had a little help."

Ida's arms contracted around his neck. "What sort of help?"

"Mina called her guys," he said, and his eyes were soft on her face.

"Oh." Mina again. She sighed without realizing it.

He tilted her face back up to his. "I was infatuated with Mina. You know that." His silver eyes narrowed. "But I love you."

Her whole face went red. She couldn't manage a single word. It was like having every sweet dream of her life come true, all at once.

"Not bad news, I expect?" he teased gently.

She buried her face in his throat. "I love you, too," she whispered brokenly. "But I thought you just wanted us to be friends."

He laughed softly and kissed her hair. "I want us to be everything to each other, all the time. My God, I didn't even realize how I felt, until I knew what danger you were in." His arms tightened. "I went crazy."

She smiled at his throat. "I'm sorry you worried. But I'm glad that it's not Mina anymore, if you see what I mean."

He bent and kissed her tenderly. "It was you from the day you had the flat tire," he said simply. "It just took me a while to realize it."

"Me, too." She nuzzled her face against his broad chest. "It was when we were getting married. I looked up at you in the church and I knew, right then. It was like…like…"

"Like a bolt of electricity," he finished for her. "Yes."

She leaned back in his arms and studied his lean, handsome face. "I hope we have a son who looks like you."

"I hope we have a daughter who looks like you."

They smiled at each other. She didn't tell him about the queasiness. She didn't quite connect it. Until a week after they were back home.

SHE WENT TO the doctor two weeks after that, when she was more certain of her symptoms, and was told what she'd wanted so badly to hear.

Fred broke speed limits getting her back home, because he'd already guessed what was going on.

She ran into the house, into the den where Jake was on the phone. Her expression caused him to end the phone call at once and go to her.

"What is it?" he asked worriedly. "Are you all right?"

"I'm pregnant!" she blurted out.

His face went white. Then red. Then he burst out laughing and whirled her around and around. "Pregnant," he said, his voice breathlessly tender. "Well, there goes that business meeting I planned for tomorrow. We have to talk about colleges!"

"Jake, that's years away!" she protested, laughing.

"The years will fly by. You'll see. But not too quickly, I hope," he added, kissing her tenderly. "I want to savor every minute of every hour of every day. Especially now."

She sighed and kissed him back. "So do I. Especially now."

Fred and Maude were standing in the kitchen, both having guessed what was going on. They grinned at each other.

"Job security," Fred whispered.

Maude nodded fiercely.

BY THE TIME their newborn daughter was six months old, and their son was two, the court case had ended, and Bailey Trent was back in prison on charges of attempted kidnapping and conspiracy to commit extortion. Sadly for him, he ran afoul of a gang leader in prison and ended up in the morgue. Ida felt sorry for him, in a way, but his demise left her with fewer worries about the future now that she and Jake were parents.

"You know," Jake mused as they watched their little boy putting together a colorful giant puzzle on the floor, "of all the things I've ever done in my life, I think being a family man is far and away the best." He drew her close and kissed her, then dropped his head to put a kiss on the head of his little daughter, who was nursing.

"I never dreamed I'd ever be so happy," Ida confessed. "And it's nice to have Fred back," she added with a smile. "Even nicer of the governor to grant him a full pardon."

He pursed his lips. "I did make a few phone calls."

"You devil," she teased.

"Well, he's a great driver. And he does have some great stories about his former profession," he added with a twinkle in his silver eyes.

"I think we might not let the kids hear those stories right away," she replied with a laugh. "At least, not until they're teenagers."

"One day at a time, sweetheart."

She pressed close to him, watching her daughter nurse. "One day at a time," she whispered and sighed. The face she lifted to her husband's was almost luminous with joy.

* * * * *

Eager to escape her family, heiress Gaby Dupont finds a career for herself working for powerful lawyer Nicholas Chandler. But soon, she butts heads with her sexy boss. Ultimately, it will be up to Nicholas to save Gaby's life—and both of their hearts...

Read on for a sneak preview of Notorious, *part of the Long, Tall Texans series from* New York Times *bestselling author Diana Palmer.*

CHAPTER ONE

GABY DUPONT GLANCED again at the paper in her hand. She hesitated to do this, but her grandmother had pleaded with her. They needed to know something about this noted Chicago criminal attorney, Nicholas Chandler, and his very famous law firm, Chandler, Morse and Souillard. Gaby was the only one of the family who lived permanently in Chicago, where he did. If her grandmother hadn't been so upset, and so insistent, perhaps Gaby could have found another solution. But this might be her best option.

She pushed the doorbell and stood nervously waiting for someone to open the door. This apartment was in a swanky area of Chicago, overlooking the lake. It was as expensive as the place where Gaby lived. She knew this man by reputation, and also because the law firm he headed had represented her grandfather in a criminal action that still made her sick to her stomach to remember. There was an appeal being threatened in the case, and Gaby's grandmother wanted to know if this attorney was going to consider representing her ex-husband again. She needed to know. So did Gaby.

Gaby had done masquerades before, mostly in an attempt to avoid a greedy cousin who was stalking her relentlessly for some property willed to her by a mutual great-aunt, which she wasn't willing to give him. She'd never understood the passion some people had for the almighty dollar. Gaby would have been happy poor. It was attitude, she considered, more than what happened to you. But poverty was something she'd never known.

Gaby was twenty-four and she didn't want to get married. Her grandfather, Charles Dupont, had sold her like a prize mare without her knowledge when she was sixteen. Her innocence had a monetary value, and without Gaby's knowledge—or his wife's—he'd arranged a private party and left Gaby alone with a foreign businessman to whom he owed a lot of money, and three of the businessman's friends. Gaby was to be his payoff, since Madame Dupont had refused to pay his gambling debts.

But Gaby's screams had brought her grandmother running. Two men at the party, Madame's chauffeur and bodyguard, had busted the lock on the door and saved the teenager from assault at the hands of her grandfather's colleague. One of the men had taken photos with his cell phone just as Madame Dupont went in the door and saw the horror. The photos were used in a criminal complaint. There were a few assorted bruises and lacerations before the assaulting parties had managed to escape before the police arrived.

Gaby had been transported to the hospital, her grandfather to jail. Gaby's grandmother had filed for divorce the very next day, leaving her immoral husband penniless and furious at his changed circumstances. Sadly, Gaby's assailant was a foreign diplomat, and he used his diplomatic immunity to escape any charges. His three friends vanished like smoke. Gaby's grandmother had been furious, but her attorney had been forced to relinquish the criminal charges against the diplomat. Gaby's grandfather, however, had been arrested and tried and convicted. Thanks to a friend, an influential and rather shady judge, his sentence had been lessened and the penalty also reduced. Now a mutual acquaintance had told Madame that Charles Dupont was planning to demand a retrial due to new evidence. What it was, the acquaintance didn't know. It was enough to panic Gaby's grandmother, nevertheless.

Her grandfather's nephew, Robert Mercer, a business colleague, had also been left out in the cold financially as a consequence of his uncle's arrest. He was claiming that property given to Gaby in a will from their mutual great-aunt was actually his and he was planning legal action. The property was Gaby's only real means of support. Well, her grandmother would never have let her starve, of course, but the property was rented to a large corporation, which established an agricultural operation on it, and the profits were enormous.

So the two of them, Gaby's grandfather and her cousin, posed a danger to Gaby and her grandmother. In fact, Madame Dupont had hired a new bodyguard, a former mercenary named Tanner Everett, just for Gaby. She was that afraid for her. Gaby had insisted that her bodyguard be invisible, especially when she went to see the attorney. She had more trouble than she could handle already. He agreed, but he had that amused smirk that made her want to hit him.

She'd never really liked her grandfather, whose obsession with material things had left her nauseated. Her grandmother, Melissandra Lafitte Dupont, came from titled French aristocrats, although she'd lived in Chicago since she was a girl. When Gaby's adventurous parents,

Jean Dupont and Nicole Dupont, had died while on an archaeological dig in Africa, Gaby had come to live with her grandparents at the age of thirteen. She'd always loved her grandmother. But her grandfather had been a different story. She had more to fear from him now. He was asking for a retrial, charging that the evidence was sketchy at best, and that some of it had been manufactured to convict him. He had an attorney, a small-time one who was just starting out in the business and, therefore, less expensive. But gossip was that he was going to ask Nicholas Chandler's firm to represent him once more. Since Chandler was the best criminal attorney in the city, Gaby had a great deal to lose if he took the case. But he wasn't, from reputation, the sort of man who could be approached about a potential client. He was incorruptible, arrogant and afraid of nothing on earth. So Gaby was going to try a soft approach. Perhaps he could be reasoned with by the victim of a client he might be considering.

GABY WAITED OUTSIDE the apartment after she rang the bell. She hoped that she could get Mr. Chandler to speak to her about his firm's involvement in her grandfather's case. She wanted a private chat, hence her trip to his apartment rather than to his office. It took a long time before the door finally opened.

A girl of about fifteen with spiky, purple-dyed hair and piercings everywhere, dressed in a short skirt and slinky blouse with overdone mascara and popping bubble gum, just stared at her.

"Well, what do you want?" the girl asked insolently. She gave Gaby's gray pantsuit with its pink camisole and her unmade-up face in its frame of upswept thick, red-highlighted brown hair an insulting scrutiny.

Gaby's pale blue eyes twinkled. "My goodness, I thought an attorney lived here," she said. "Is it an agency? You know, for call girls?" She added a speaking glance of her own at the girl's attire.

The younger woman's eyes almost popped.

"Who's at the door, Jackie?" a deep, curt voice called.

"I have no idea!" the girl said, dripping sarcasm. "Maybe she's selling magazines or something."

"Not likely. I don't read those sorts of magazines," Gaby returned pleasantly.

The girl's indrawn breath was interrupted by the arrival of a big, husky man. He looked like a wrestler. He had wavy black hair with a few threads of silver, a leonine face with deep-set, dark eyes and a sexy, chiseled mouth. He was wearing slacks and a designer shirt in a shade of beige that emphasized his olive complexion.

"You're late," he said abruptly and looked at his watch. "I specifically told the agency no later than one p.m." He glared at her. "Do you want this job or not?"

She was at a loss for words. She'd come to ask him a delicate question and he was apparently offering her a job. Her heart jumped at the unexpected opportunity.

"I thought it was for one thirty," she improvised.

"One," he returned curtly.

She almost gasped. "You are a very rude man," she said.

His eyebrows arched. "And you are one step away from the unemployment line," he shot back. "I need someone to organize my library and catalog my books again." He gave the young girl an angry glance as he spoke.

"I just knocked over a bookcase or two," the girl muttered.

"On purpose and with help." He took a breath. "Well?" he shot at Gaby. "Can you do it?"

Her degree was in anthropology, but probably it wouldn't take a scientist to rearrange books. "Of course I can," she said confidently. "I minored in library science." It wasn't quite the truth, but she didn't expect that he'd go that deep with a background check.

He gave her a brief scrutiny, obviously saw nothing that interested him and opened the door wider. "Do you have references?"

"Pages of them," she replied and offered up a silent prayer of thanks that she actually did have them in her purse, because she'd just come from an interview for a job she didn't get at a local museum.

"Don't hire her, Uncle Nick," the wild girl said angrily. "She's got a mean mouth!"

"Look who's talking," Gaby returned. "And at least I'm not in danger of septic infection from dozens of piercings and that colorful tattoo down your arm. How do you blow your nose with that ring in it?" she added. "And how in the world do you eat soup?"

"If you say one more word...!" the girl threatened.

"Jackie, go back to your room," the man said curtly. "Now." He never raised his voice, but the raw power in it could have backed down a mob.

Gaby would have known that he was an attorney just by the way he used his voice. He headed a prestigious law firm in Chicago, Chandler, Morse and Souillard, and he had a national reputation as a trial lawyer, famous for celebrity cases.

"Mr. Chandler?" she asked politely.

He nodded. "And you are…?"

"Gaby Dupont," she said with a polite smile. The name would mean nothing to him. There were dozens of people with her surname, no need to make up something that might come back to haunt her later.

He cocked his head. "And why do you want this job?"

"I'm starving?" she replied hopefully.

He didn't smile, but his eyes had a faint twinkle. "Come in."

He led the way back to his library. The apartment was huge, done in tasteful dark Mediterranean furniture and cream-and-brown curtains and carpets. The library had a burgundy Persian rug, an oak desk and a library that covered all three walls from floor to ceiling. The floor was full of stacked books, boxes and cartons of them.

"I've just moved in," he said, indicating the disorder. "I don't have the time or the patience to catalog and place all that, and the assistant I had decided to go back to school and study architecture," he added gruffly.

"Hence the job opening," she mused.

"Exactly. Put the books on the floor and sit down." He'd indicated the seat in front of the desk. Impressive. Burgundy leather and hand-tooled wood. Expensive. She did as he asked and sat down.

"Your qualifications?" he asked.

She handed him a sheet of paper. It outlined her college degree and her hobbies.

He looked up at her curiously. "Are you married?"

"I am not."

"Engaged? Involved? Living with someone?"

Her eyes almost popped. "Mr. Chandler, I hardly think

any of that is your business. This is a job interview, not an interrogation."

He gave her a long-suffering look. "I want to know if you have entanglements that will interfere with the work you do here," he returned. "I also need references."

"Oh. Sorry. I forgot." She handed him another sheet of paper. "And no, I'm not involved with anyone. At the moment." She smiled sweetly.

He ignored the smile and looked over the sheet. His eyebrows arched as he glanced at her. "A Roman Catholic cardinal, a police lieutenant, two nurses, the owner of a coffee shop and a Texas Ranger?" he asked incredulously.

"My grandmother is from Jacobsville, Texas," she explained. "The Texas Ranger, Colter Banks, is married to my third cousin."

"And these others?"

"People who know me locally." She smiled demurely. "The police officer wants to date me. I know him from the coffee shop. The owner..."

"Wants to date you, too," he guessed. He stared at her as if he had no idea on earth why any male would want to date her. The look was fairly insulting.

"I have hidden qualities," she mused, trying not to laugh.

"Apparently," he said. His eyes went back to the sheet. "A cardinal?" He glowered at her. "And please don't tell me that he wants to date you."

"Of course not. He's a friend of my grandmother's."

He drew in a breath. Her comments about men who wanted to date her disturbed him. He studied her in silence. He was extremely wealthy, not only from the work he did but also from an inheritance left to him by a late uncle.

"You don't want the job because I'm single?" he asked bluntly.

Now her eyebrows lifted almost to her hairline. "Mr...." She glanced at the paper in her hand. "Mr. Chandler," she continued, "I hardly think my taste would run to a man in his forties!"

His dark eyes almost exploded with anger. "I am not in my forties!"

"Oh, dear, do excuse me," she said at once. She had to contain a smile. "Honestly, you look very much younger than a man in his fifties!"

His lips made a thin line.

The smile escaped and her pale blue eyes twinkled.

He wadded up a piece of paper and threw it at her.

She just grinned.

He sat back in his chair. "Well, you can obviously deal with Jackie, which is a plus. She drives me crazy. Her mother's in Europe with her latest boyfriend and unlikely to return until her daughter's grown or married or in prison."

She laughed.

He shook his head. "And you have qualifications." His dark eyes narrowed. "You aren't connected with any foreign spy service?"

"Not unless I joined in my sleep," she assured him. "Honestly, I'm just a plain working girl."

"Working at what?" he returned with a cold smile. "You don't cite any previous job experience. How old are you?"

"Twenty-four." She thought fast. "I worked for my

grandmother as a social secretary after I got out of college."

"You don't list her on your sheet of references."

"Why would I list a relative?" she asked.

"You did list a relative. The Texas Ranger."

"Oh. Him." She sighed. "Well, a distant relation is less likely to lie for you than a close one, right?"

He laughed. "I give up. All right. We'll try it for a couple of weeks and see how you work out. You can start by cataloging the library. Can you take dictation, answer the phone, make appointments…?"

"Well, yes," she began, hesitantly.

"We'll add all that into the job description, then. You can be my private administrative assistant. It's getting harder to avoid bringing work home as the business expands, and I do need someone in that capacity. Can you handle it?"

"Of course," she said without hesitation. She'd done all that for Grandmère, after all, without pay.

He mentioned a figure that was a little surprising. It was a great deal more than most women could expect for the services he'd outlined, and her face betrayed her.

"You'll be living in. Did I forget to mention that?"

Oh, dear. Complications. However, it would be convenient. Her grandfather wouldn't know where to find her. Neither would the cousin who kept trying to force her to give up a fortune in property that he thought rightfully belonged to him—despite the concrete will that left it to Gaby. The cousin, Robert, was disturbed. Very disturbed, to her mind, but he intimidated his mother to the point that she avoided even speaking to him.

"That will be fine," she said after a minute. "Do I have

to room with the Goth Girl?" she added with raised eye-brows.

He chuckled. "No. You'll have your own room. And please don't call her that to her face," he added. "I have too many breakables in here that I'm fond of."

"I'll restrain myself," she promised.

He got up. "Well, it will be interesting, if nothing more," he said. "You'll start Monday. How's that?"

Today was Friday. That gave her the weekend to organize things. Since she owned her apartment, she had no worries about the rent going unpaid. "I'll be here first thing Monday morning," she promised.

"I leave the apartment at eight in the morning to get to the office on time. You'd better be here before then. Or you might not be able to get in," he added with pursed lips.

She took his meaning. The Goth Girl would probably lock her out once she knew Gaby was going to work here. She chuckled. "Okay. I'll be here before eight."

"Do you have other relatives besides your grand-mother?" he asked curiously.

Her face closed up. "No," she said without elaborating.

That expression made him curious. But there would be plenty of time later to dig deeper, if he wanted to. He needed an employee. Her private life was no concern of his. "Monday, then. Good day."

He let her out of the apartment and closed the door.

She was fumbling in her purse to put away the sheets of paper he'd returned to her when she heard an absolute feminine wail come through the door of the apartment she'd just left.

"She's going to work here? No!"

Gaby smiled to herself all the way to the elevator.

HER BODYGUARD WAS waiting downstairs beside a black limousine. It was a sedan, not the stretch limo he usually drove for her grandmother. Gaby had wanted to be discreet, although the last thing she'd come here for was a job. She lived with her grandmother, who was one of the wealthiest women in the country, and Gaby was her only heir. The job was an opportunity, though, and she was going to take it.

"How'd it go?" Tanner Everett asked with a smile.

She looked up, trying not to stare at the black eye patch over the blue eye that had been damaged beyond repair in some foreign country while he was plying his former trade as a mercenary.

"I got hired."

His black eyebrows arched. "Hired?"

"Well, I got cold feet about asking him questions when the Goth Girl answered the door."

He put her inside the sedan and got in under the wheel. "The Goth Girl?"

"You had to be there." She laughed and shook her head as he cranked the car and pulled cautiously out into traffic. "It seems that Mr. Chandler has a niece with enough tattoos and piercings to put her in line for a job making license plates in some big federal facility."

It took a minute for that to penetrate, and he roared. "She sounds like a handful."

"She is. I'm going to be Public Enemy Number One." She grinned. "I love the sound of that. I've led such a quiet, uneventful life with Grandmère," she added.

"You didn't get to talk to him about your grandfather, I gather."

"No. He isn't the sort of man you approach directly

with such questions. I almost made a fatal faux pas," she told him. She leaned back against the seat. "I hope my grandmother isn't going to be mad because of what I did. It was an opportunity I didn't feel I could overlook. If I get to know him, I can find out all sorts of things without having to beg for information."

"That way lies disaster," he said quietly, glancing at her in the rearview mirror. "Lies catch up with you."

"This is just a little white lie," she argued with a smile. "And nobody's going to get hurt. Honest."

"If you say so."

"I do."

HER GRANDMOTHER, SMALL and wizening and fierce for all her size, gave Gaby a severe stare when she was told about the position. She gave Everett one, too, but it just bounced off him.

"I did not tell you to get a job," she told Gaby firmly, her faint French accent coming out as she grew more angry.

"But it's the best way to find out," Gaby argued. "I won't have to stay long. Meanwhile, I can learn about him and his law practice. I can find out which attorney in his firm represented Grandfather and how he felt about what...what happened to me."

Everett made a face. "Your grandfather should have had ten years for that."

"His best friend is a judge," she said on a sigh. "Justice is largely a matter of money these days," she added cynically.

"Not always."

Madame Dupont made a gruff sound in her throat and

turned away, resplendent in a taupe silk pantsuit that took ten years off her age. "My granddaughter, working at a menial job. What is the world coming to?"

"I'll learn to catalog books as I go," Gaby replied with a wicked smile. "And I'll turn Goth Girl inside out as a personal favor to Mr. Chandler."

Madame turned, her perfect eyebrows arching. "Excuse me?"

"Mr. Chandler's niece lives with him," Gaby explained. "She has more piercings than a soldier during the Napoleonic Wars, and tattoos that would grace a prison cell."

Madame looked toward the ceiling. "What perils are you placing yourself into?" She turned. "You should go back right now and tell that attorney the truth of why you went to see him."

"I will not," Gaby said softly. "It's a terrific opportunity."

"Lies come back to bite you, my sweet."

"These won't. It will be all right. Really."

Madame came forward and drew Gaby into a warm embrace while the delicate fragrance of Nina Ricci's *L'Air du Temps* wafted into her nostrils. It was the only scent Madame ever wore. "If you say so, my darling." She drew back and touched Gaby's soft hair. "You must not put yourself in any more danger than you already face."

"I'm not in danger." She pointed to Tanner Everett. "Ask him."

He chuckled. "She isn't in any danger," he parroted in his faint Texas accent. "I give you my word."

"Well, that is something, at least. But you have to live in? I shall die of boredom here alone," Madame wailed.

"You could invite Clarisse to stay," she suggested. "She loves you, too."

"Clarisse." She made another gruff noise under her breath. "She and her fiancé drive me almost mad. I have found them making out in every room of this apartment. Even the bathroom!"

"They'll be married in two weeks and she'll settle down."

"Not in time. No Clarisse." She sighed. "Well, perhaps I can tolerate Sylvie for a few days."

Sylvie was her cousin, a sweet and gentle older woman who loved soap operas and swashbuckling movies.

"She'll drive you mad with old Errol Flynn movies," Gaby commented.

"Oh, I like pirate movies," Madame said absently. "I'll nap while she watches those vulgar soap operas, so that I don't offend her with commentary."

"Good idea," Gaby said.

Madame sighed. "When do you move in with him?"

"With them," she corrected and smiled. "Monday morning, so I must go back to my own apartment and decide what to take with me." She moved forward, embraced her grandmother and brushed a kiss against the beautiful skin on her cheek. She drew back with a sigh. "You know, you have the most perfect complexion I've ever seen, even at your age."

Madame beamed. She touched Gaby's face. "Which you have inherited, *ma chèrie*," she replied, her voice as soft as the fingers that brushed over Gaby's face.

"I have only your skin, not your beauty," Gaby said, and without rancor. She glanced at the youthful portrait of Madame Melissandra Lafitte Dupont over the mantel.

She had been debutante of the year in her class, wooed by princes and comtes, but she chose instead a fast-talking salesman of a business executive with grand ideas and no money. As people said, there was no accounting for taste.

"You were so beautiful," Gaby remarked, staring at the portrait.

"The artist was blind," the elderly woman chuckled.

"He was not. He captured the very essence of you," Gaby argued as she moved closer to the portrait, so that the pale gray eyes were large enough to divine that they were alive with humor and love of life. "Grandfather never deserved you," she added in a cold, angry tone.

There was a sigh behind her. "We live and learn, do we not?" was the sad reply. "He could have been anything he liked. But he was greedy, and you paid for his greed, my baby." She hugged Gaby close. "I would give anything if you could have been spared that."

Gaby hugged her back. "I had you," she said softly. "So many people have less. I was lucky."

"Lucky." Madame made a curse of the word. She drew back. "I cannot convince you to give up this mad scheme?"

Gaby shook her head, smiling.

"Ah, well. At least I can make sure that he is your shadow." She nodded toward Everett.

"I already am her shadow," he chuckled.

"True enough," Gaby returned. "Heavens, he can squeeze into the most incredible places. You never even notice him."

"Which is why I'm still alive," came the sardonic reply.

"So you are. Make certain that no harm comes to my granddaughter," Madame told him. "Or I will find the deepest dungeon in my estate outside Paris, and you will rot there." She even smiled when she said it.

"Did I ever mention that I always carry a nail file?" he replied, used to her threats, which he found more amusing than threatening. She knew he was good at his job.

Madame chuckled. She loved their repartee. "Very well. Good luck to both of you."

"You mustn't recognize me if you see me on the street," Gaby cautioned her.

Madame made a face. "And what about my birthday party next month?" she asked haughtily.

"In six weeks I'll either have what information we need, or I'll be hanging from a penthouse apartment by a stocking with a gavel in my mouth."

At which statement, everybody broke up.

HER SUITCASE PACKED with enough to keep her going for a week, Gaby took a cab to Mr. Chandler's apartment. Everett was behind it all the way, in a black sedan.

She rang the doorbell at precisely 8:00 a.m.

There were voices muffled behind the door. One was deep and loud, one was high-pitched and loud. Abruptly they ceased, and the door opened.

Mr. Chandler looked at his watch. "Well, Ms. Dupont, at least you're punctual."

"So she can read a watch," the Goth Girl said sarcastically. "But can she catalog books and answer the phone?"

"I have many talents, one of which is alligator wrestling," she said with a straight face and looked directly at Mr. Chandler's niece. He muffled a sound that could have been laughter. The girl glared at both of them and stomped off into her room.

CHAPTER TWO

CHANDLER LED THE way down the hall and showed Gaby to a room.

"It's next to Jackie's, but she doesn't usually make too much noise," he muttered as the occupant next door suddenly turned her stereo with a rap song up high enough that the walls shook.

"Turn that damned thing down!" he shouted.

There was an immediate response. Gaby hid a grin.

"She'll try you," he said.

She shrugged. "I got through four years of college. I'll cope. Besides," she murmured, "I brought a whole library of my favorite tunes."

"Which are...?"

"Drum and bagpipe solos," she said with a straight face.

He started to speak, thought better of it and laughed instead. "Put your stuff down and I'll show you what I want done today. I don't have long, if I'm going to make it to the office on time."

"You're the boss, though," she pointed out as she followed his long strides down the carpeted hallway to his study.

"I have to set an example. If I show up whenever I

please, the staff might follow suit." He glanced at her with twinkling eyes. "Chaos would ensue."

"I guess it would. Okay. What would you like done?"

He outlined several tasks that he wanted completed by the end of the day.

"And we employ a daily woman who also cooks for us," he added. "She comes in at nine. You'll like her. Tell her what you want for lunch and she'll fix it."

"Oh, I'll eat anything. I'm not picky."

"Don't tell Jackie that, or she'll have the cook make you fish stew. Trust me, you never want to eat it." He made a face. "I told Jackie she couldn't go out late dancing with her boyfriend one Saturday. Dinner that evening was forgettable. Really."

She laughed. It was nice to know that the Goth Girl had ways of getting even, so that Gaby could forestall her. She knew her way around the kitchen, too. She'd just get to the daily woman first. She had an idea that there would be no truce even from her first day on the job.

SHE WAS RIGHT, in fact. She went into the kitchen at eleven, just after the Goth Girl had gone out with an airy description of her destination and a secret smile.

"Can I ask what Jackie ordered for lunch?" she asked the older woman.

The matronly cook and housekeeper, Tilly by name, just grinned. "Fish stew...?"

"Do you like quiche?" Gaby asked.

"Oh, I love it, but I can't make it."

"I can. I need a few things," she added with a conspiratorial smile. The cook laughed and went to get them.

Gaby made an impressive quiche lorraine, complete with delicate crust. The cook, invited to share a slice, was enthralled with the result.

"You cook beautifully," Tilly said.

"Thanks. My grandmother had me sent to a senior chef and taught to cook. She never learned, so I had to." She didn't add that the reason her grandmother never learned to cook was that she was filthy rich and employed a chef—in fact, the same chef who taught Gaby how to cook.

"Well, this is delicious. Should we save some for Jackie?"

"Oh, yes, we must," Gaby said with impressive faked concern. "If she didn't get anything to eat while she was out, she'll be hungry."

"I agree. I'll make sure it's put up properly."

"Thanks."

It was after dark when Jackie came home. She went right to Gaby's room and opened the door without knocking. Gaby was sprawled across her bed in sweatpants and a T-shirt, with her long hair loose around her face, reading a book on her iPhone. She looked up, surprised.

"Well, I guess you've settled in," the girl said haughtily. "Did you have a nice lunch?" she added wickedly.

"Very nice." She got up and took Jackie by the arm. She pulled her to the door. "This—" she pointed to it "—is called a door. When you go to someone's personal room, you knock." She took Jackie outside and demonstrated. "Then the person inside can decide whether or not he or she wants you to come in." She gave the girl a blithe smile.

"We had quiche lorraine for lunch. There's some left, in case you didn't have time to eat."

"Quiche...? But Tilly can't make quiche," she faltered.

"I can." She smiled again, went back into her room, closed the door and locked it audibly.

Curses ensued from the other side of the door.

Gaby just laughed and went back to her book.

SUPPER THAT EVENING was a subdued affair. Jackie glared at Gaby and picked at her food, which was a macaroni-and-cheese casserole and asparagus, cooked by Tilly.

"How was school?" Chandler asked his niece.

"Boring. Tedious. I hate it!"

"Well, cheer up. When you're seventeen or you graduate, whichever comes first, you can leave."

Jackie glared at him, too. "I miss my old school!"

"You can always get on a plane and join your mother wherever she's living in Europe," he said, barely noticing her as he made notes on an iPad for court.

Jackie put her fork down and actually looked sick. "I'm full."

He looked up. "Then you're excused."

"She's not eating, either," Jackie muttered, noting Gaby's apparent lack of appetite.

"Oh, I'm still full from lunch," Gaby said with a big grin.

"Were you here for lunch?" Chandler asked Jackie suddenly, looking up from the screen with hostile brown eyes.

"No," Jackie said shortly.

Chandler looked at Gaby. "What did Tilly feed you?"

"She was going to make fish stew," Gaby said, with a wry glance at Jackie, "but I suggested quiche instead."

"Tilly can't make those fancy dishes," he began.

"I can," Gaby replied. "I made the quiche."

"You can cook?" he asked, startled.

"My grandmother had me professionally trained when I was about the age of the Goth Girl, here." She indicated Jackie, who fumed and stood up, angrily.

"I am not a Goth Girl!" she almost screamed.

Gaby and Chandler both stared at her. She was wearing black pants and a black camisole. She had tattoos on both arms and pierced jewelry from her ears to her nose. She was wearing black nail polish and black lipstick.

"I can call you a Beatnik instead, if you like," Gaby said pleasantly. "They wore black and hung around coffee shops playing bongo drums and reciting poetry. In fact, I know of such a club, right downtown."

"That's the Snapshot, right?" Chandler asked.

Gaby chuckled. "Yes, it is. The owner said that everybody snaps instead of claps and they drink shots of espresso, so the name just seemed right."

"It actually does."

"I do not play bongo drums," Jackie growled. Not for worlds would she admit that she knew the place and loved to go there.

Gaby looked at her. "The original beatniks didn't wear tattoos," she remarked. "Did you know that they have actual tattooed human skin in one of the larger museums in the city?" she added.

Jackie made a horrible face. "I'm going to bed."

"It's just eight o'clock," her uncle said.

"TV. I'll go watch TV," she muttered.

"There's a new series about women in prison," Gaby called after her. "It might give you some pointers."

There were horrible curses, followed by a slamming door.

Gaby burst out laughing. "Sorry," she told her boss contritely. "Couldn't resist it."

He shook his head. "You've got her standing on her ear. I haven't been able to get so much as two words out of her since she's been here."

"She's hurting," Gaby said suddenly.

He scowled. "Excuse me?"

"Something or somebody has hurt her badly," Gaby said simply. "Have you asked her why her mother wanted her to stay with you?"

He hesitated. "It wasn't her mother. Jackie asked to come."

"That must have taken a lot of guts, at her age," was the soft reply. "I imagine her mother was insulted by it."

His firm, chiseled lips opened on a breath. "She was. How did you know?"

"We all have tragedies in our pasts," she said simply. "At a guess, her mother's boyfriend did or said something inappropriate, or she'd still be with her mother. Tilly said she loved her mom."

"She does. Not the new boyfriend, however. Frankly, I think he's the worst kind of layabout, and he's got a roving eye. I don't know what the hell my sister sees in him."

"Who can understand the leanings of a hungry heart?" She sighed and smiled.

"Have you ever felt them, Miss Dupont?" he asked pointedly.

She grimaced. She couldn't tell him about the trauma that had kept her chaste for so many years. "I was too busy being educated to hang out with wild crowds. My grandmother paid for my education, but insisted that I not go to any, as she referred to them, party schools. So I ended up in one known for its academic excellence and I never went to a beer party or even dated much."

He just stared at her, incredulous. "How old are you again?"

"Almost twenty-five," she replied.

"And you don't date?"

She cocked her head and stared at him. "Frankly, I find most men lacking."

"Lacking what?"

"Manners, decorum, intellect, compassion, that sort of thing." She smiled at him.

He let out a breath and shook his head. "At least you won't be after me."

"Mr. Chandler, I do not stalk fifty-year-old men!" she exclaimed haughtily.

He burst out laughing, recalling their first meeting, because she certainly knew he wasn't yet out of his thirties.

"Just as well," he commented after a minute. He sipped coffee. "You wouldn't know what to do with me, anyway."

"You can put a rose on top of that," she agreed. "I've never indulged, so I don't know what I'm missing. That's my macro for my lifestyle. You'd be amazed how often I have to use it in the modern world."

"Modern." He made a face. "I was raised by traditionalists."

"Me, too. It makes it hard to fit in. Even harder, because I don't own or watch television."

"You reactionary," he accused.

"Guilty as charged."

He finished his coffee. "I have briefs to work on." He stood up. "If you want to watch any of the new movies, we have most of them on Prime video," he said. "Feel free."

She shook her head as she, too, stood up. "I read in my spare time."

"Read what?" he wanted to know.

"Right now it's Arrian."

"Arrian?"

"And Quintus Curtius Rufus," she added.

"Alexander. You like to read about Alexander the Third, called the Great," he replied.

She nodded. "It truly fascinates me, that you can read something written almost two thousand years ago and feel what the author felt when he was writing it." She paused. "It's almost like having them speak to you, across the years."

He nodded slowly. "That's how I've always felt about it. I read the classic authors, as well."

She smiled. "I wish more people did. They might have less pessimism about the future."

He smiled back. "Yes. They might. How's the cataloging coming?"

"Slowly," she said. "But I'm getting them in some sort of order so that I can start. You have an impressive library."

"It was more impressive before Jackie pitched a temper tantrum and overturned two bookcases," he mused.

"We all have our issues. Perhaps a course in anger management…?"

"Please don't suggest that where she can hear you," he said with mock horror.

She grinned. "I'll try. Good evening."

He nodded. "Good evening to you, too."

GABY WENT BACK to her room, pleasantly surprised by her boss's laid-back attitude. But once she closed the door, through the walls came the loudest, most vulgar rap song Gaby had ever heard.

She reached in her closet for her recently purchased CD player, extricated a CD from its case and inserted it, placed it against the wall that adjoined Jackie's, and maxed the volume. The exquisite strains of "Scotland the Brave," played by a magnificent bagpipe band, almost shook the walls.

Within two minutes the rap music was abruptly turned down. Gaby turned off her boom box. She waited, poised over it, but the rap didn't reoccur. So Gaby got into her silk gown, crawled into bed with her iPhone, turned off the light and read herself to sleep.

THE NEXT MORNING the boss was missing from the breakfast table.

"Had to go in early to meet some important client," Tilly sighed as she put delicately scrambled eggs, bacon, sausage and biscuits on the table. That was followed with jars of preserves, all homemade.

"Tilly, this is wonderful," Gaby told the cook, smiling.

Tilly glared at Jackie, who was picking at her food. "Nice to know that somebody appreciates my efforts," she said and went back into the kitchen.

Gaby took another bite of her eggs and sipped black coffee. "What happened?" she asked the girl.

Jackie glared at her. "I beg your pardon?"

"What happened to you, with your mother's boy-friend?" Gaby persisted.

Jackie was so flustered that she dropped her fork. "Why...why would you think...?"

"Oh, give me a break," Gaby muttered, staring at the girl. "You might as well be wearing a sign. Come on. Talk about it."

Jackie's whole face tautened. "He backed me into a wall and I couldn't get away," she said gruffly.

"Did he...hurt you?"

"No. But he tried. I told my mother." Her eyes lowered. "She said I was lying, that he'd never do anything like that."

. "How did you get away from him?" Gaby asked.

She drew in a long breath. "I watched this movie. It's about a female FBI agent, and she taught this lesson about SING, about how and where you can hit a man for the best effect. I did the groin pull. Oh, boy, did he let me go. I ran into my room and locked it, and he cussed for five minutes straight. Then Mama came home and I told her. And she didn't believe me."

Gaby felt her anguish. "Something similar happened to me," she said tautly, not going into details. She didn't add that it was her own grandfather who'd sold her to the foreign man, or the details. That would have been much too personal at the moment.

"It sucks, the way some men are," Jackie said.

"It does," Gaby agreed. She looked up. "Your mother will come to her senses one day and she'll apologize."

"Yeah? Well, it doesn't help much right now, does it?" she muttered.

"No. It doesn't." She studied the younger woman and saw beneath the flashy black makeup and the piercings to a basically shy and introverted person who had a sensitivity that she carefully hid.

Jackie drew in a long breath. "I've been a horror. My uncle Nick has the patience of a saint, but he should have thrown me out."

"You're his niece," she said. "He'd never do that."

She looked up. Her dark eyes were full of pain and bad memories. "It wasn't the first time," she said and averted her gaze. "I just didn't tell her about the first one. She was getting over my dad dying, and I figured she was trying to hide her grief in a new romance."

"Your father died?" she asked gently.

Jackie nodded. "He drowned one summer when we were at a resort on an island in the Caribbean. There was a red flag warning about riptides, but he ignored them. He was depressed about his job. He was about to lose it, and it hurt his pride that my mother had all the money on her side of the family. She said he did it on purpose. I miss him…"

"My father and mother died together," Gaby told her. "They were on a dig, in Africa. Their jeep overturned."

Jackie grimaced. "How old were you?"

"Thirteen," she said. "I went to live with my grandmother. She's the kindest person I've ever known." She cocked her head. "How old were you, when you lost your father?"

"Ten." Jackie looked at her with sad eyes. "My uncle is nice. I just don't want to be here," she said harshly. "I want to be with my mother, and I can't. She said she loves me, but she didn't believe me, and I was telling the truth!" She bit her lower lip and tears welled up in her eyes.

Gaby got out of her chair, pulled Jackie up and hugged her, rocked her, while she cried.

"We all have storms," she said to the weeping girl. "They pass. Life can be sweet. You have to learn to sip it. Not gulp it down. You live one day at a time and live it as if it was the last day you had. I find that it works very well, as a philosophy."

"I guess it's not such a bad way," Jackie said after a minute. She pulled away and looked embarrassed. "Thanks," she added huskily.

Gaby just smiled. "Sometimes all you need to get a new perspective is a hug," she teased.

Jackie laughed. She wiped her eyes, smearing her makeup down her cheeks. "Mom isn't the sort to hug people. Neither is my uncle. When my daddy died, Mom went off with a new boyfriend. I felt lost. I still do."

"Your uncle loves you," Gaby said. "Even if he doesn't go around hugging you. But you have to meet him half-way."

Jackie made a face. "I guess so."

Gaby cocked her head and looked at the young girl.

"You know, you really do have a unique look. It's not at all bad."

Jackie flushed. "You really think so? I mean, most boys think I'm weird."

"I'm weird, too. I don't care what people think."

Jackie laughed for the first time since Gaby had arrived on the scene. "I noticed. Bagpipes?" she asked, eyes very wide.

"My forebears on my mother's side were Highland Scots who migrated to America. You might say that bagpipes are my ethnic music."

Jackie replied, "Well, to each his own." She looked up. "I really hate bagpipes."

"I really hate rap. So we're even," she teased.

Jackie smiled. "I suppose so." She turned away and then turned back. "Thanks. For listening. Nobody else ever did."

She went down the hall to her room before Gaby could say another word.

NICHOLAS CHANDLER CAME home late and in a temper. Jackie had long since gone to her room, and Gaby was in hers. She heard the boss muttering curses in the living room.

She put on a robe, her long hair trailing down her back over it, and padded barefoot into the living room.

"Good heavens, what bit you?" she asked.

He turned. "What the hell are you doing up?" he shot at her, and he looked fierce, with his dark eyes blazing.

"It's hard to sleep with people turning the air blue. The walls aren't that thick."

He glared at her.

She held up both hands. "I didn't do whatever it is that you're raging about."

He put down his briefcase, hard. "My firm is representing a millionaire whose wife attempted to kill for his inheritance." His lips made a thin line. "So tonight she came to his front door all in tears, begging for forgiveness, and he let her in."

She let out a breath. "So which hospital did they take him to?"

He glared at her.

She lifted her hands and let them fall. "Simple deduction. Was he raised by morons?"

"No. By a saintly woman who taught him that anything can be forgiven."

"And most everything can, but some things shouldn't," she replied. "I guess she didn't tell him that."

"He's on life support," he said thinly. "There were no witnesses, and she says he had a horrible fall, all by himself, from the second-story balcony."

"Did they look for fingerprints on his back?"

"This is not funny!" he bit off.

She lifted both eyebrows. "No, but it's predictable. Will he live, do they think?"

"He was doing well until someone disconnected his oxygen."

"Let me guess. She was the only person in the room."

"Her and three hospital personnel. Just not all at the same time." He ran a hand through his thick black hair. "I should have been a vacuum cleaner salesman."

She burst out laughing.

Her twinkling eyes drained some of the fury out of him. He shook his head. "You think reasonable people will act reasonably," he said. "They never do."

"You should hire him a bodyguard."

"I just did," he replied. "She's going to spend every night and day in his room until he dies or gets released."

"You hired a female bodyguard?"

"Men are too easy to get around," he pointed out.

She laughed. "I'm so glad you said that instead of me."

"It's sadly true." He went to the bar and poured himself a scotch, with one cube of ice from the small fridge that flanked it. "It's been a hell of a night."

"Who called you?" she asked. "Not the ex-wife, I assume?"

"No. The police detective assigned to the case. He's a distant cousin. We keep in touch."

"Probably saved his life," she guessed.

"No doubt." He sat down, one big hand going to loosen his tie and the top buttons of his spotless white shirt.

"I don't suppose they could arrest the ex-wife on suspicion?"

"She's not an ex," he pointed out. "And not without probable cause. It's a he-said, she-said situation."

"I'm truly happy that nobody has tried to kill me yet," she murmured, hands in the pockets of her thick, very concealing bathrobe.

"Why would they want to?" he asked and seemed really curious. "You're obviously not rich or you wouldn't be working for me."

Appearances could be deceiving, she almost said, but

then she smiled instead. "Right on," she told him. "I guess money brings its own issues."

"It does. I avoid parties like the plague unless I'm required to go to one. I'm on several spinster most-wanted lists around town."

"Obviously because of your intensely seductive and pleasant manner," she murmured.

He glared at her. "You're not my type," he said at once.

Her eyes opened wide. "I'm not? Thank you! I was really worried!"

The glare got worse.

"Well, if you're quite through turning the air blue, I'm going back to bed."

"You might as well," he returned with a surly glance. "Unless you think Prince Charming might ring the doorbell looking for you."

"Princes are a figment," she pointed out. "Besides that, they live this regimented, routine life that shackles them to public appearances and charity causes. I'd never be able to adjust to that sort of imprisonment."

He wondered how she knew about the lives of princes, but then he realized that the internet was a great source of information and he dismissed it from his mind.

"You don't want to be a princess and have servants and a Ferrari and your very own couture house of design to dress you?"

"I'm quite happy in old blue jeans, taking care of myself," she pointed out. "People who marry for money, earn it."

"Wise, and so young," he chuckled.

"I'm not that young," she returned. "I hope your bodyguard sleeps light. The victim's wife sounds like a deter-mined assassin."

"The room is wired like dynamite," he said with a faintly smug glance. "If she tries anything, she'll be doing some very hard time, whether he lives or not. And I got a warrant, to make sure it would hold up in court."

"Good for you. People who kill for money are even worse than people who marry for it," she said solemnly, and she knew more about that than he might realize. She'd been sold for money by her own grandfather, who would do anything for money, like the cousin who was after her inherited stocks and bonds. "Money is of so little con-sequence in the scheme of things," she said absently. "I never understood the obsession some people have with it."

"You'd have fit right in with those beatniks you were telling Jackie about," he pointed out.

She laughed. "I actually prefer coffeehouses to res-taurants. There is the matter of radical politicism that the beatniks were famous for. I don't want to blow up things."

"I wish the world at large shared that sentiment. We've had far too many people who think violence is the answer to any problem."

"Too much television," she said, standing erect. "Fie on video games and wrestling matches and other provokers of radicalism!"

"Go the hell to bed," he muttered.

"Just quoting the pundits," she said defensively, and with a grin.

"Like they know anything," he scoffed. "Opinions are like—"

"Yes, I know," she interrupted, "and everybody's got one." She chuckled.

"Aren't your feet cold?" he asked, frowning at her bare feet under the long concealing gown and robe.

She wiggled her toes. "A little, but I love shag carpet," she said. "It feels so good to walk on."

He laughed. "I'll bet you stand outside in thunderstorms."

"How did you know?"

"It takes one to know one," he said simply. "I was driving from Jax to St. Augustine, my mind on a case, and I didn't realize that the only vehicles I was meeting were cable and phone trucks and emergency personnel. It wasn't until I parked at the courthouse in St. Augustine that I realized why. There were gale-force winds."

She laughed. "I've done that, too," she said. "Stood on the beach and felt the wind whipping through my hair while the waves slammed against the shore, whitecaps foaming. I loved it."

He cocked his head, studying her. "What beach?"

She had to think fast. It had actually been on the Riviera. "Biloxi," she fished up.

"That's not how you pronounce it," he pointed out, and now he looked suspicious. "It's pronounced 'bi-lux-ie' by the natives."

"Well, I'm not a native and I can pronounce it how I like," she said with a grin.

"I guess."

"Anyway, I liked the beach at Panama City best. Such a shame how much those cities on the Gulf of Mexico have changed after all the devastating hurricanes."

"Everything changes," he pointed out. "It's the only real constant in life."

"I like change."

His dark eyebrows rose.

"Quarters best, but I'm partial to dimes also."

He glared at her.

She held up both hands. "Right. Bed. Please, no more nonstop cursing. And I hope your client survives, if for no other reason than to see his wife being shredded by the prosecuting attorney."

He chuckled. "Our DA would have her for lunch, without ketchup."

"I expect he's a friend of yours," she said. "You know, sharks congregating together...? Going away now!" she added quickly, turned and made a beeline back into her room.

He waited until the door closed before he started laughing.

Don't miss Notorious *by Diana Palmer, available now wherever Harlequin books and ebooks are sold.*

www.Harlequin.com

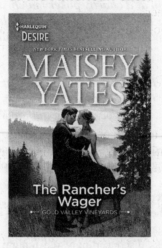

Cricket Maxfield had a hell of a hand. And her confidence made that clear. Poor little thing didn't think she needed a poker face if she had a hand that could win.

But he knew better.

She was sitting there with his hat, oversize and over her eyes, on her head and an unlit cigar in her mouth.

A mouth that was disconcertingly red tonight, as she had clearly conceded to allowing her sister Emerson to make her up for the occasion. That bulky, fringed leather jacket should have looked ridiculous, but over that red dress, cut scandalously low, giving a tantalizing wedge of scarlet along with pale, creamy cleavage, she was looking not ridiculous at all.

And right now, she was looking like far too much of a winner.

Lucky for him, around the time he'd escalated the betting, he'd been sure she would win.

He'd wanted her to win.

"I guess that makes you my ranch hand," she said. "Don't worry. I'm a very good boss."

Now, Jackson did not want a boss. Not at his job, and not in his bedroom. But her words sent a streak of fire through his blood. Not because he wanted her in charge. But because he wanted to show her what a boss looked like.

Cricket was…

A nuisance. If anything.

That he had any awareness of her at all was problematic enough. Much less that he had any awareness of her as a woman. But that was just because of what she was wearing. The truth of the matter was, Cricket would turn back into the little pumpkin she usually was once this evening was over and he could forget all about the fact that he had ever been tempted to look down her dress during a game of cards.

"Oh, I'm sure you are, sugar."

"I'm your boss. Not your sugar."

"I wasn't aware that you winning me in a game of cards gave you the right to tell me how to talk."

"If I'm your boss, then I definitely have the right to tell you how to talk."

"Seems like a gray area to me." He waited for a moment, let the word roll around on his tongue, savoring it so he could really, really give himself all the anticipation he was due. "Sugar."

"We're going to have to work on your attitude. You're insubordinate."

"Again," he said, offering her a smile, "I don't recall promising a specific attitude."

There was activity going on around him. The small crowd watching the game was cheering, enjoying the way this rivalry was playing out in front of them. He couldn't blame them. If the situation wasn't at his expense, then he would have probably been smirking and enjoying himself along with the rest of the audience, watching the idiot who had lost to the little girl with the cigar.

He might have lost the hand, but he had a feeling he'd win the game.

Don't miss what happens next in…
The Rancher's Wager
by New York Times *bestselling author Maisey Yates!*

Available January 2021 wherever
Harlequin Desire books and ebooks are sold.

Harlequin.com

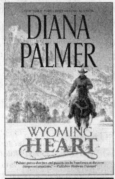 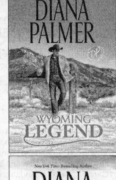
 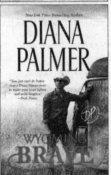

Get 4 FREE REWARDS!

We'll send you 2 FREE Books plus 2 FREE Mystery Gifts.

FREE
Value Over
$20

Both the **Romance** and **Suspense** collections feature compelling novels written by many of today's bestselling authors.

YES! Please send me 2 FREE novels from the Essential Romance or Essential Suspense Collection and my 2 FREE gifts (gifts are worth about $10 retail). After receiving them, if I don't wish to receive any more books, I can return the shipping statement marked "cancel." If I don't cancel, I will receive 4 brand-new novels every month and be billed just $7.24 each in the U.S. or $7.49 each in Canada. That's a savings of up to 28% off the cover price. It's quite a bargain! Shipping and handling is just 50¢ per book in the U.S. and $1.25 per book in Canada.* I understand that accepting the 2 free books and gifts places me under no obligation to buy anything. I can always return a shipment and cancel at any time. The free books and gifts are mine to keep no matter what I decide.

Choose one: ☐ **Essential Romance**
(194/394 MDN GQ6M)

☐ **Essential Suspense**
(191/391 MDN GQ6M)

Name (please print)

Address   Apt. #

City   State/Province   Zip/Postal Code

Email: Please check this box ☐ if you would like to receive newsletters and promotional emails from Harlequin Enterprises ULC and its affiliates. You can unsubscribe anytime.

Mail to the **Reader Service:**
IN U.S.A.: P.O. Box 1341, Buffalo, NY 14240-8531
IN CANADA: P.O. Box 603, Fort Erie, Ontario L2A 5X3

Want to try 2 free books from another series? Call 1-800-873-8635 or visit www.ReaderService.com.

*Terms and prices subject to change without notice. Prices do not include sales taxes, which will be charged (if applicable) based on your state or country of residence. Canadian residents will be charged applicable taxes. Offer not valid in Quebec. This offer is limited to one order per household. Books received may not be as shown. Not valid for current subscribers to the Essential Romance or Essential Suspense Collection. All orders subject to approval. Credit or debit balances in a customer's account(s) may be offset by any other outstanding balance owed by or to the customer. Please allow 4 to 6 weeks for delivery. Offer available while quantities last.

Your Privacy—Your information is being collected by Harlequin Enterprises ULC, operating as Reader Service. For a complete summary of the information we collect, how we use this information and to whom it is disclosed, please visit our privacy notice located at corporate.harlequin.com/privacy-notice. From time to time we may also exchange your personal information with reputable third parties. If you wish to opt out of this sharing of your personal information, please visit readerservice.com/consumerchoice or call 1-800-873-8635. **Notice to California Residents**—Under California law, you have specific rights to control and access your data. For more information on these rights and how to exercise them, visit corporate.harlequin.com/california-privacy.

STRS20MAX